From *The Bl*

I was dead tired, but I could not sleep. My mind was uncomfortably active and it would not let my body rest. I found myself thinking of Tony—and the more I tried to put him aside, the more I thought of him. I decided to get Mother and Father to take me to Australia as soon as possible

Then the Drucker dog started to howl, and the sound seemed to parade all the horrors I'd ever known before my eyes.

The room began to get gray, and I saw that the dawn was breaking. I was still wide awake, and the house seemed to weigh down on me—and I suddenly decided to dress and go out into the garden. It was rapidly getting lighter, and most of the shadows had disappeared.

I put on a few clothes and went quietly downstairs. I saw no sign of Froby or Moley, and I let myself out the back door.

The air was cooler and fresher in the garden, and I took several deep breaths and was glad that I had come. Cato had stopped howling and was giving voice to an occasional injured whine—which sounded not unlike Wilbur, Jr., when things had annoyed him.

I walked slowly among the flower beds and came at last to the wooded section. I thought of the gloves at once   and it seemed an ideal opportunity for an uninterrupted search. I plunged in and set to work.

To my surprise, I caught sight of one of the gloves almost at once. It seemed to have caught on the bark of a tree and was apparently hanging there, some distance from the ground. The light was poor and I could not see it very well—and as I got closer, there seemed to be something peculiar about it.

I had actually reached out and touched it before I realized that the glove had a hand in it.

Books by Constance & Gwenyth Little

The Grey Mist Murders (1938)
The Black Headed Pins (1938)
The Black Gloves (1939)
Black Corridors (1940)
The Black Paw (1941)
The Black Shrouds (1941)
The Black Thumb (1942)
The Black Rustle (1943)
The Black Honeymoon (1944)
The Great Black Kanba (1944)
The Black Eye (1945)
The Black Stocking (1946)
The Black Goatee (1947)
The Black Coat (1948)
The Black Piano (1948)
The Black Smith (1950)
The Black House (1950)
The Blackout (1951)
The Black Dream (1952)
The Black Curl (1953)
The Black Iris (1953)

The Black Gloves

By Constance & Gwenyth Little

With an Introduction
By Tom & Enid Schantz

The Rue Morgue Press
Boulder, Colorado
1998

The Rue Morgue Press
P. O. Box 4119
Boulder, Colorado 80306

PRINTED IN THE UNITED STATES OF AMERICA

Introduction
Meet Constance & Gwenyth Little

ALL BUT ONE of their books had "black" in the title, but the 21 mysteries of Constance (1899-1980) and Gwenyth (1903-1985) Little were far from somber affairs. The Littles were much more interested in coaxing chuckles than in inducing chills from their readers.

Set in large old country estates, big-city boarding houses, or private hotels or hospitals, the books were usually told from the point of view of a young woman with only her own caustic wit standing between her and matrimony. Pick out the one eligible bachelor in the book able to trade barbs with the heroine and you can immediately knock one person off your list of suspects.

That list is probably going to be pretty long. The Littles loved to fill the bedrooms of those houses with an enormous cast of eccentric characters who seemed to have temporarily escaped from a Kaufman-Hart play. In their books, you'll find little old ladies who while away an afternoon idly playing Russian roulette or a murderer who can't resist a game of solitaire. There are always strange noises emanating from the attic or cellar and you can never count on a dead body or an important clue staying put.

Their privileged and slightly spoiled young heroines are products of Prohibition. Bright, independent-minded, and cheerful, they learned to drink and smoke and party during the 13 years of that so-called noble experiment.

Lissa Herridge, *nee* Vickers, in *The Black Gloves* is a typical Little heroine. She married once when very young, had her parents buy her a nice Reno divorce, and then had them take her traveling for a few years to recover from the mean brute. Mean, in this case, probably indicates that he expected her to pick up after herself. Gainful employment certainly isn't a high priority for a Little heroine, as long as a father is around to provide (usually quite handsomely). Getting a new husband isn't either, although Lissa expects to have no trouble finding one when she's ready. Imagine the Claudette Colbert character—but with a more acid tongue—from *It Happened One Night* or Tracy Lord from *The Philadelphia Story* and you've got Lissa.

Like other Little heroines, she's very close to her parents, especially her father. She may constantly trade insults with him but they obviously adore each other. It's a pattern that runs through many of the Littles' other books and appears to mirror the authors' own lives.

"We were a very close family," explained Iris Little Heitner, the youngest of the Little sisters, who herself published two mystery novels (*Board Stiff*, 1951, and *Death Wears Pink Shoes*, 1952) under the pseudonym Robert James with her sisters' publisher, the Doubleday Crime Club. Four of the five Little children were born in Sydney, Australia, where their father worked as an actuary. They later moved to western Australia before their father decided to pull up stakes, almost on a whim, and move to England.

"In those days you didn't need a passport," Iris said, "so they just took off. He didn't even have a job lined up." Their childhood travels took them to London, Mexico City, and New York before they finally settled in East Orange, New Jersey, the setting for many of their books, including *The Black Gloves*. All the Littles loved to travel, as do the characters in their books, and before they wrote their first novel, Constance and Gwenyth made three trips around the world. They attended art school in England where they were "paying guests" in private homes.

After they married (Constance to a clothing company executive and Gwenyth to an insurance executive), the two settled down to a life as suburban matrons when the bug to write mysteries hit them. Their parents were pleased, although Gwenyth told Ellen Nehr in an interview shortly before she died that "our mother said she would like them better if we didn't have such horrible murders in them."

Constance, whose real loves were tennis, golf, bridge and the theater, cooked up the plots and provided bits of dialog while Gwenyth, who had longed to write since childhood, did the final drafts. It didn't always go smoothly. Although both were living in New Jersey when they started writing, Constance eventually moved to Boston. In the midst of one book, Constance called Gwenyth to complain: "You've had the murderer sitting in the living room while the crime was being committed in the upstairs hall."

Mysteries from this period were mostly free of strong language, especially those published by the Doubleday, Doran Crime Club, but the characters in the Little novels made as much use of the acceptable swear words of the time as possible and hinted at frequent use of unacceptable ones. "We did get some complaints about the language we used," Gwenyth said. "In those days 'damn it' must have been shocking to some people, but now no one even blinks."

Unlike many writers of the period, the Littles didn't go in for continuing characters, although their publisher insisted that each of their books (after their first, *The Grey Mist Murders* in 1938) have the word "black" in the title. The sisters obliged but joked about coming up with a plot that had a green horse or a chartreuse coffin to see what their editors might do.

Their books were immensely popular, especially with patrons of rental libraries, who read them to tatters, and today their books are extremely difficult to come by, in any condition, on the antiquarian market. In our nearly thirty years specializing in mystery fiction, we've constantly searched, usually futilely, for their books. We've had otherwise proper lady customers resort to the kind of language that would have been taboo in mysteries of that era when told that we had already sold that copy of *The Grey Mist Murders*.

Between 1938 and 1953, the Littles produced 21 novels. In her 1984 interview with Ellen Nehr, Gwenyth said the two stopped writing after their husbands took ill and died. But their sister Iris tells it differently. While Gwenyth's husband did die from cancer in the 1950s, Constance's husband remained healthy and actually outlived her. Iris said they stopped writing simply because the books didn't sell as well in the 1950s as they had in the 1930s and 1940s.

Similar fates befell other cozy mystery writers from the same period. Charlotte Murray Russell also gave up writing mysteries (after 20 books) in 1953 because either she or her publisher (again the Crime Club) were disappointed by decreasing sales. Many other cozy writers, like Frances Crane, also experienced a dwindling readership and though Crane herself held on for a few years more, her last books could not find a U.S. publisher and came out only in England.

There are several possible reasons for this decline in sales. Television may well have been the major culprit. When TV antennas went up on roofs, sales of pulp magazines, for example, went down and within a very short time, these colorful publications vanished from the newsstands. At about the same time, rental libraries—where people borrowed books for a small daily fee—began to fail.

And it was a different era. The world had experienced a dreadful war and perhaps those cozy mysteries seemed somehow out of place. Certainly, the 1950s saw an explosion in the number of hardboiled novels. Mickey Spillane's gun was quick and his sales were even faster. The Macdonalds, John D. and Ross, got their start in this period as did scores of other tough-guy writers. The cozy mystery would not return again in great numbers until the 1980s.

When it did, there was perhaps less emphasis on plot. Writers like the Littles began their careers in the late Golden Age when readers still demanded complicated—and hopefully fair-play—puzzles. A lot of seemingly zany things happen in a Little novel but in the end they're all explained. There's a reason why that body was moved, why the coal was shoveled in the night, why someone played the nine of spades on the red ten. Readers today seem content with fewer plot twists if they are provided with other distractions, such as an attractive setting or an interesting occupation.

The period between the end of the Depression and the beginning of World War II seems very distant to the readers of today. Books set then seem like historical mysteries, but with one very important difference—writers like the Littles are describing their own times while living though them. W. Somerset Maugham, the English author of *The Razor's Edge*, said that readers in the 21st century would turn to the detective novels of the 1930s to find out how people actually lived and talked in that era.

You may be amused, perhaps even put off, by some of the attitudes and antics of the characters in *The Black Gloves* (particularly the constant smoking and drinking), but there's no doubt that this is how people in Constance and Gwenyth Little's time lived and thought. That's part of the charm of their books and one of the reasons why they'll continue to be read by each new generation of readers.

That, and because their books are just so much fun.

Tom & Enid Schantz
Boulder, Colorado
April 1998

The editors are indebted to the late Ellen Nehr and Iris Little Heitner for much of the information in this introduction.

The Black Gloves

CHAPTER 1

IT WAS MY FATHER who persuaded us to go back to the old homestead for the summer. Father's name is Hammond Vickers, but that doesn't mean that he isn't bright. He talked up the suburban life to us, and how we'd enjoy the space and relaxation and peace, after five years of traveling and hanging around in hotels, until Mother and I could hardly wait to get out there.

I realize now, of course, that Father had it figured that after five years of practicing golf all over the world he'd be able to beat all his friends at home—only he forgot that they'd had time to practice, too.

The house is in New Jersey—suburban to New York— and Father is sentimental about it, because it has been in his family for nearly sixty years.

We took a trip out to the place late in May, to see what had to be done to it, and to hire a couple of servants, and Father was all excitement and happy anticipation.

I don't suppose the lack of any zoning laws in the district had ever bothered him—if he knew anything about it —so that, when the station taxi turned into our street, he nearly had apoplexy.

The Bakers, who had always owned the house next to ours, had had it pulled down, had a street put through the middle of their property and were in the process of erecting a double row of small houses. Five of them were already completed, their backs facing the side of our house and their tiny yards bordering our side garden.

"The place is ruined!" Father yelled. "Utterly ruined! I can't sell it—I couldn't even rent it with those dirty little cottages and their back yards spilling all over the place. Tom Baker did that on purpose."

11

"You can always do the same with our house, Father," I suggested, "and get even with Harry Barnes on the other side."

"Mops!" he groaned, almost in tears. "And garbage cans. Clothes lines!"

"Pay the taxi," said Mother. "Mr. Baker probably needed the money."

Mother is practical, and it's just as well. There should always be one practical person in a family.

The house was in fairly good shape, and Mother walked around contentedly, jotting down the things we'd need in a small notebook. I got bored with it after a while, and sat down in the hall and smoked a cigarette.

I glanced up at the fine old staircase, and remembered myself, on a day six years earlier, slowly descending in my bridal finery.

I was eighteen at the time. My veil had been worn by Father's mother and my dress had cost a pretty penny. The bridesmaids had worn flowerpot hats, and they were all envious. It had been a lot of fun, then, but sitting in the hall there, thinking it over, I came to the conclusion that it was entirely too much fuss to make over a marriage that had lasted for only a year. Because, at the end of that time, I decided that my husband was a mean brute, and I put this view before Father. He and Mother hurried me off to Reno—and that was that.

They took me traveling afterwards, and we'd been roaming about for five years.

I crushed out my cigarette and realized that Father, with his head in the hall closet, had been talking to me for some time. "And then," he was saying triumphantly, "we won't be able to see those beastly hovels at all."

I supposed he was planning some sort of a screen, so I said, "Good idea, Father—that ought to fix it."

He pulled his head out of the closet, shut the door and dusted off his hands. "Then I'll get in touch with the gardener. He's kept the grounds up pretty well—you could play on the tennis court just as it is."

I wandered through into the dining room and looked out of the rear window. There was no doubt about the tennis court's being ready for play—it had been freshly marked out and the net was in place. I realized at once, if Father did not, that the gardener would not have gone to that trouble every day for five summers, on the off chance that we might show up. Some trespassers were obviously using our court and probably giving the gardener a handout to keep it in condition.

Mother called me, and I went to help her interview a couple of maids who had been sent up by the local agency.

We wrangled for an hour, and in the end Mother and I were worsted on a couple of points. They refused to launder our silk underthings and they insisted on Thursdays and Sunday afternoons for their time off. Mother painted up Tuesdays and Wednesdays as being perfectly lovely days to have time off, because she did not want both of them going together, but they merely shook their heads and tightened their lips. We gave up, in the end, and decided to have dinner out on Thursdays and Sundays.

I wandered outside for a bit of fresh air and walked about admiring the various blossoms that were prettying up the garden. I could not put a name to any one of them, and I thought idly of my ex-husband, who had always been pat with the right name for anything that grew out of the ground.

"Always did know too damn' much about everything," I thought comfortably, and rounded the house to the back.

Unexpectedly, I heard voices, and I walked quietly up to the tennis court and peered out from behind a bush. The trespassers were there, all right. A girl and a man, playing, and an older woman sitting on the bench, watching.

I advanced slowly to the edge of the court and stood staring at them. The players ignored me, but the woman on the bench turned her head and gave me a dirty look. I returned it leisurely and decided that she had a thoroughly disagreeable face. She was small and plump, and her grayish hair was arranged in fussy waves and curls. Her dress was a frivolous pink cotton, over-ornamented with costume jewelry, but her mouth was tight and thin-lipped.

The young people were unattractive. The man was slight and inclined to be short, with brown hair receding from his forehead, buck teeth and a long nose. The girl was tall and thin, and her mouse-colored hair had been permanently waved and arranged over her head like a corrugated-iron bowl.

I turned back toward the house, and reminded myself not to be so critical of other people and to look in the mirror once in a while, and pick out my own faults. It was time to powder my nose anyway, so I did just that—but so far from being reduced to a state of humility I found myself thinking that if the girl with the corrugated hair would take a few pointers from me she'd improve herself no end.

I met Father in the living room and he was in a towering rage again.

"Who are those people playing on our court?" he shouted. "Why didn't you turn them off? I won't have those cottagers trespassing on my property—I'm going to tell them!"

I caught him by the arm and said soothingly, "Let them alone, Father. They're having a good time, and they're not really doing any harm. When we come out here to stay, we can take steps to keep them off."

"Well—I'd go and see them off if we had time," he said reluctantly, "but it's nearly six o'clock. Mother's finished with the house and I think we ought to go."

"Have you looked up the trains?"

"No," he said airily. "I thought we'd just go down to the station—sure to be a train along—pretty good service, you know."

"I don't know," I said coldly, "and I'm not going to sit on that station for an hour. You go on inside, and I'll go over to one of those little houses and telephone."

He stood his ground and defied me. "You'll do nothing of the sort—I want no truck with those wretched little eyesores."

"So how do you propose to get to the station?" I demanded. "Walk? Mother will love that. Go on, Father—I'm going to telephone, and I'll get a taxi in time for the next train."

He went off, grumbling, and I made my way to the first of the five little houses. There was no answer to my ring, so I went on to the next. The door was opened promptly this time by a peroxide blonde, with a small, grubby child hanging on to her dress. The kid was whining, and continued to whine throughout. I longed to box its ears, although I have always thought, and said, that I loved children.

The blonde graciously led me to the telephone, and while I was trying to find out about the trains she explained that her name was Mrs. Drucker—Edith Drucker. The kid was Willie—Wilbur, Junior. She wanted to know if we were back for good—was I married—who were the other members of my family—did I really think I'd like the suburbs—and when could she come and call on me.

I answered as best I could, but I had to cut it a bit short, because there was a train leaving in ten minutes and Mother and Father had still to be rounded up.

I hurried back and got them together, and just as the taxi came up the drive I started off on a last, hasty round of the lower floor, to make certain that all the windows were closed.

Everything seemed to be in order, and I worked my way back to the front hall, where I stopped—puzzled by a curious, muffled sort of sound, which seemed to come from below me. After listening intently for a moment, I could have sworn that someone was shoveling coal in the cellar.

CHAPTER 2

THE TAXI'S HORN began to blow wildly, and I realized that we had only a few minutes in which to catch the train. I ran out and slammed the door behind me, and Mother and Father pulled me frantically into the car as though we were on the point of missing a boat to Europe. The driver gave me a look of reproach, and we shot down the drive and skidded out onto the road.

"We really ought to go back," I said uneasily. "I think someone was shoveling coal."

"What do you mean?" Mother asked.

"I thought I heard someone shoveling coal in the cellar— just before I came out."

Father said, very loudly, "Oh no—nonsense. You imagined it. Must have been something else—mouse, perhaps." He was afraid that Mother would insist on going back to investigate.

But she merely flicked him a scornful glance, and said, "Lissa is neither imbecile nor deficient of hearing, Hammond—she could hardly confuse a mouse and a—a shoveler of coal. Is there any coal in the cellar?"

Father grunted.

"Hammond!"

"Well, yes." Father admitted reluctantly. "I stocked up, just before we left, that summer—got a good price, and of course I didn't know we'd be gone so long. I suppose it's still there."

Much to his relief Mother let it go, and we made the train. But when we came out to the house to stay, a week later, we had no more than got inside the door when Mother remembered about it and told Father to go straight down to the cellar and look around.

"All right, Janice," he said cheerfully. "Just let me get some of these things out of the way."

He was clattering around with his golf clubs at the time, and of course he promptly forgot all about it, and so did Mother and I—until later.

We were busy most of the day, getting the place settled. Father disappeared completely after lunch, but we didn't worry about him, because we knew he'd sneaked off to the country club to snatch a bit of golf and date up some of his old boy friends.

At five o'clock Mother and I sat down to tea in the drawing room and wearily congratulated each other on our handiwork. The place looked comfortable and attractive, and the two maids, Dora and Grace, seemed to be working out pretty well.

We had cleaned up the sandwiches and were relaxing over cigarettes when we heard voices raised in talk and laughter. We got up and went to one of the back windows, and saw that there was quite a social gathering on the tennis court. I recognized Edith Drucker and the unattractive couple who had been playing a week earlier; and there were two other men, and another girl.

"They must know we're in residence," Mother said, putting on the dog. "You'd think they'd have the common courtesy to ask, before using our court."

"I believe they're going to," I said, peering over her shoulder.

They were standing in a group, but two of them had broken away and were moving toward the house.

We returned to the drawing room, and Mother sat elegantly on a brocade chair and tapped her foot impatiently. "I'll tell them they must find another court—we can't have them overrunning the place."

"I suppose you're right," I said slowly. "If I have anyone out for the week end, and we want to play, it would be pretty silly to have to wait our turn."

"It would be absurd," Mother said firmly. "I shall tell them that they must not use it."

The doorbell rang, and Dora let herself out of the kitchen, and presently admitted a surprisingly handsome couple. The girl was tall, a natural blonde, with a superb figure and delphinium-blue eyes. The man was about six feet, and well built. He was unusually good-looking, with dark hair and eyes and a small mustache.

They introduced themselves as Miss Catherine Reed and John Rickey—though it subsequently turned out that the fascinating Rickey was known to all and sundry simply as Rick.

Mother waved a languid hand in my direction, and murmured,

"My daughter Lissa," and Mr. Rickey gave me a little bow.

I realized, suddenly, that I wanted to know him, and that I'd have to think fast to keep Mother from putting him out of my life forever. She had suffered them to sit down, but she was looking distinctly cold and formal.

Mr. Rickey said, politely, that he was afraid they had been trespassing. All last summer they had paid the gardener to keep the court up, and had played on it. "I hope you don't mind," he said pleasantly. "The house was closed—and we brought our own net and equipment."

He paused, obviously to give us a chance to say that it was all right, but Mother, with slightly elevated brows and eyes full of cold query, remained silent.

I swallowed, and said brightly, "Oh, that was quite all right."

Mother stirred, turned her head slowly, and looked full at me. I could almost see a huge question mark hanging above her. Mother can be obtuse at times—Father, for all his foolishness, would have known at once.

I raised my voice slightly and said, "Did you hear, Mother? They used the court last year, but they brought their own equipment. Naturally, we don't mind, do we, dear?"

She caught on, then, but she was not in sympathy. She continued to look at me for a space with narrowed eyes, and then she washed the visitors with a frosty stare. "No," she said, in a faraway voice. "Quite all right."

"And there's no reason why the tennis club should not continue, is there?" I pursued relentlessly.

"None whatever," she snapped, and appeared to be talking to the ceiling.

Miss Reed and Mr. Rickey thanked us prettily, and we all stood up.

"There's only one condition," I said, smiling, "and that is, that I may play with you occasionally."

Rick said warmly, "We'd be very glad." And Catherine Reed, with a charming mixture of shyness and cordiality, suggested that I come out with them and meet the others now.

"I'd love to," I said, not looking at Mother, and trying not to giggle when she drew a sharp, vexed sigh, which could be heard all over the room.

I led them to the rear of the house, and we went out the french doors that opened onto the terrace from the dining room.

The group on the tennis court turned their heads as we approached, and Rick hailed them triumphantly. "It's all right—and here is Miss Vickers, herself, with a personal O.K. for the tennis club."

It seemed odd to be called Miss Vickers again, after six years of being known as Mrs. Herridge—but I did not bother to correct him as I felt that it wasn't of any consequence.

The unattractive pair were introduced as Gertrude Potter and Ben Amherst. The other man, who immediately sidled over to Catherine and unobtrusively kissed her left ear, was Charlie Carr. I liked Charlie—he was good-looking, and seemed very pleasant. Edith Drucker—minus Willie, Jr., who was nowhere to be seen—recalled herself to me. I smiled at them, one after the other, and by the time I had met them all I felt that my face was ready to crack.

"Oh, but we saw you last week, didn't we, Ben?" Gertrude said brightly. "Only, we didn't know you belonged here, then. We thought you were just passing by."

I smiled again, and swallowed down a yawn. I was beginning faintly to regret my impulse. I had merely wanted to play around with the handsome Rick, and I was not quite prepared to become one of the gang.

However, Catherine and Charlie and Gertrude and Ben presently went off to play doubles, and Rick, Edith Drucker and I retired to the bench to watch.

I was idly wishing that the Drucker pest had died young, when I realized, with a certain amount of amusement, that she was wishing the same thing of me.

She put her rather heavy, over-rouged lips into a pout and said, "Rick—cigarette, please."

He reached into his pocket rather absently, lit a cigarette and handed it to her, and almost at the same time he turned to me. "Nice-looking couple, aren't they?" he said, indicating Catherine Reed and Charlie Carr.

I agreed—sincerely.

"They're engaged, you know."

I declared, heartily, and perhaps a trifle too enthusiastically, that that was just fine. What I actually meant was, that with Catherine safely tied up I had only Edith Drucker to contend with, where Rick was concerned—and it would be merely a matter of taking candy from a baby.

I had made up my mind to have Rick dangling at my elbow all the summer—because there's no doubt that a woman looks effective with a handsome and attractive man dangling at her elbow.

Edith evidently thought so, too, because she kept up a continuous line of chatter sprinkled with high-pitched giggling—and all directed at Rick. I remained silent—with the result that he tried, several times, to talk to me through the noise.

I got a bit bored with it, though, and almost made up my mind to look up my old friends and see what they had to offer—and not bother with Rick.

The others finished their game just then and came over to the bench, and Rick went to play singles with Ben Amherst.

Gertrude pushed the stiff waves of hair off her forehead, and said, "When do you leave, Charlie?"

"Tonight." He glanced at Catherine, and added, laughing a little, "I'm taking a train from Newark—Cathy's going to drive me down."

"No, I'm not. You can take a taxi—or walk."

"Please," he said, laughing at her and touching her flushed cheek with his finger tips.

She moved her head away and appealed to me. "I wanted him to save all of his vacation for our honeymoon in the fall, but he insists on taking a week of it, now, to go to a gathering of his fraternity at Washington. And then he calmly asks me to drive him to the station."

"Wait and see what I'm going to bring you back from Washington."

"It had better be good," Catherine said sternly.

Dora appeared just then, to say that dinner was ready, so I made my adieus, and left them.

At dinner Mother and Father had plenty to say about the tennis club—but I've always been more than a match for them. I told them that a new era was dawning, when all men were brothers.

Mother said to let her know when it had actually dawned and she'd swallow a little poison and leave them to it.

We spent the evening quietly. I played the piano for a while, twice wandered to the telephone with the idea of calling up one or two of my old friends and decided against it each time.

I got hold of a book, at last, that interested me, and I hardly noticed when Mother and Father went up to bed.

It was nearly half past one when I finished the book, and I went to the kitchen to get a glass of milk before going to bed.

I took the bottle from the ice chest and started to pour the milk into a glass—and went right on pouring, so that it spread over the table and began to drip onto the floor.

Someone was shoveling coal in the cellar.

CHAPTER 3

I KNEW I was not mistaken this time. Coal was being shoveled, and dropped again almost immediately—and even through my scare that struck me as being curious. If someone was going to the trouble of shoveling coal at all—why not take it somewhere?

I set the bottle of milk down with a bang and flew upstairs to my parents' room.

I rapped nervously on the door, and Mother answered almost immediately.

"What is it?" she called sharply.

"It's that coal-shoveling business again," I replied, and felt a bit silly.

"Come in, Lissa—and for heaven's sake explain what you mean."

I opened the door, and Mother switched on the lamp between their beds. I gave a fleeting thought to the fact that she always looked immaculate—even when you woke her from a sound sleep. Her hair was kept in place with a net, her satin nightgown looked smooth and unwrinkled, and the only thing that marred her was her double-chin reducer.

Father heaved himself over, grunted and suddenly opened his eyes. "Whassa matter?" he shouted. "Who is it? What's going on here?"

"I am trying to find out," said Mother. "Lissa, do explain yourself."

"I've been telling you. There is positively someone shoveling coal in the cellar."

"Oh nonsense!" said Father loudly. "She's always saying that. It's ridiculous."

But Mother was not to be put off. She said, quietly and firmly, "You had better go and see."

Father looked pained, and I asked, "You haven't got the furnace on, have you?"

He glared at me. "Why in hell would I have the damn' stinking furnace on, with the temperature at eighty?"

"Hammond!" Mother never swore, herself, and could not understand why Father and I had to do so much of it.

He flung out of bed, pulled on his dressing gown and stalked to the door, muttering under his breath. I followed him, and heard Mother nervously tapping a cigarette as we went out.

On our way through the living room I picked up a poker from the fireplace and clutched at it firmly.

When we reached the kitchen, Father slowed down, and we both listened—but there was no sound whatever.

He switched on the cellar light, hesitated at the head of the stairs, threw out his chest and started bravely down. I followed close behind with the poker.

But, as far as we could see, there was no one down there. We had no flashlight, and so did not investigate the darker corners; but everything was quiet, and the place seemed in order.

The coalbin was filled to the brim, and there was another huge pile in a square space beside the bin. Two shovels were propped against the wall near by.

"Why on earth did you buy all that coal?" I asked.

"Well—I had a chance to get it at a bargain price—and we're bound to use it up sometime. But you'd better get your ears examined, because that coal is exactly where it was, right after they delivered it. I know, because I came down here and bawled hell out of them for putting the extra load on this side of the bin instead of the other side."

We went back upstairs, and Father carefully locked the cellar door. "Just in case we overlooked a couple of second-story men down there," he explained.

Mother was waiting for us at the head of the stairs, and we answered all her questions truthfully, until she asked us if we had searched the cellar thoroughly. We lied heartily, and together, then, because we knew that otherwise she'd make us go straight down again and do it.

I went to bed, and slept badly. It did not seem possible that I could have been mistaken twice about a thing like that. And what other combination of noises could sound like coal being shoveled?

We had two callers the next day. One was the woman I had seen watching Gertrude and Ben on the tennis court, on our first trip out, and who turned out to be Gertrude's mother, and the other was a tall, dark, rather handsome woman, who was Catherine's mother.

They said they had come to thank Mother for allowing the tennis club to go on, and Mother received them with cold formality and some afternoon tea.

Gertrude's mother, Mrs. Potter, was a great talker, and she told us all about the occupants of the five little houses. She said that they were having some trouble selling the houses—Mother brightened visibly at that—and that three of them had been rented. The first one in the row was rented to a bachelor of whom they saw very little—but he was good-looking, and drove an expensive car.

Next in line were the Druckers, who had bought their house. They were up to their ears in debt, though, and Mrs. Potter was afraid that they were going to lose the property. She went on to say, with a faint touch of malice, that Edith Drucker was not satisfied with her nice husband, but was always chasing after Ben and Rick, and even Charlie. And she had her eyes on the bachelor, next door.

I thought of Gertrude, unattractive and ineffectual, and knew that Mrs. Potter was fretted because she was afraid that Edith was spoiling Gertrude's possible chances.

Mrs. Reed smiled, and said tolerantly, "Edith is only playing around, Martha. The boys don't take her seriously."

"Charlie doesn't, perhaps," Martha conceded, with a worried frown. "But I don't know about the others."

She shook her head, as though to brush away the troublesome thought, and went on with her story.

Rick, Charlie and Ben lived in the house that was next in line. They rented it, and furnished it with their various possessions, and hired a dayworker. They were all fine men, and the right kind.

Martha Potter took a long breath, and Mother sniffed.

The Reed home came next. Catherine and her mother lived there, on an annuity, and they had bought the place. The Potters rented the last house, and it developed that Gertrude had a position as secretary and was her mother's main support.

"It means more work for you, though," Helene Reed suggested. "When Catherine and Charlie are married, I shall give them the house for a wedding present, and go to live in a hotel—which means no more housework, as far as I am concerned."

She laughed a little, and Martha shook her head. "I don't see why you couldn't live with them. You'll be lonely, by yourself."

"Oh no—I couldn't do that. I'm too anxious to remain friends with them."

Mother stirred and murmured, "Very sensible of you."

Martha backed down, and said indecisively, "Well—I suppose so." She sipped at her tea, and then asked brightly, "Did Charlie get off all right last night?"

Helene Reed set her cup down.

"I suppose so. I guess he took a taxi. Catherine was so mad that she wouldn't drive him down."

"Was she really mad?" Martha asked, obviously eager for gossip.

"Oh well—not really. Catherine's so good-natured—she was only joking."

Martha sighed. "You must be glad to get Catherine so nicely settled. Charlie is such a fine boy, and doing so well."

She spoke without rancor, and I felt faintly sorry for her. It was so obvious that she longed to have Gertrude nicely settled, too.

Helene Reed said pleasantly, "I'm glad to see Catherine so happy, but I often think that a girl like Gertrude, with a good position, and complete independence, is as well situated as most married women."

I decided that she was trying to be consoling. Martha Potter smiled brightly, murmured, "Well—maybe so," and stood up.

The two made their farewells and went off, and Mother turned on me immediately.

"Lissa, I simply don't understand you. If you want to play around with that theatrical-looking man, surely you can manage it so that I don't have to sit and listen while those two pests discuss their daughters and their daughters' beaux—or lack of beaux. I might just as well have been taking my nap while they were here—they wouldn't have known the difference. Why should they come to my house to do their gossiping?"

I giggled. "Never mind, darling," I said, kissing her ear. "It's time for the club to meet, right now, and I'll go out and enjoy myself grimly—so that all your sacrifice shall not have been in vain."

"Take a sweater," she said shortly, "and don't forget to put it on when you finish playing."

I dressed carefully, and made a mental note to go into town the next day and buy some more tennis costumes and a decent racket.

The club was assembled on the court, and I noticed that only Catherine and Charlie were missing. They gave me a rousing welcome, and we started with a doubles—Gertrude and Ben against Rick and myself.

Ben explained that I had better play with Rick until they could get an idea of my game. If I were better than Gertrude, they'd change us, as Rick was stronger than Ben.

I decided not to be better than Gertrude, for the present at least. I could improve later—but I had no desire to play beside Ben, with his buck teeth hanging out.

We played along for a while, and when we were at five-five, I decided to win at seven-five.

I was waiting for Ben's serve, and I had a vague feeling that some-one had come up behind me and was watching. Ben had already raised his racket, so that I could not turn around, and an instant later he put over his most Sunday serve. I was conscious of a flash of annoyance, because I wanted to finish the set and have a rest—but I could not possibly take the serve without giving myself away, so I made a wild lunge, and sent the ball straight up in the air.

There was a peal of hateful, familiar laughter directly behind me, and I whirled around to look straight into the mocking green eyes of my former husband, Tony Herridge. Tall, redhaired, and well dressed, he stood there, grinning at me.

The others began to drift toward us, and Tony said, in a clear, carrying voice, "Pretty bum shot for a girl who's played at Wimbledon and Forest Hills."

I could feel my face burning, and for a moment I was too furious to speak.

Tony went on, "Really, Rick, I must apologize for my wife, but I suppose she's putting on this act because she wanted to play part-ners with you. She always was a sucker for a good-looking man."

My arm twitched with a desire to slap his wide, grinning mouth, but I controlled it, and said coldly, "Hello, Tony. What are you doing around these parts?"

He looked me up and down. "I live here. The mellow associa-tions, you know."

Rick broke in. "Good God, Tony! Are you two married?"

"We were," Tony said indifferently. "But I ought to warn you, Rick, if you have any sentimental ideas that include her—she's a spoiled brat. And as for the money angle, they actually have much less than they appear to. I know I thought I'd be on Easy Street after I married her—but no. The old man coldly informed me that I could continue to arise at the crack of dawn and slave all day."

Gertrude and Ben had joined us, and Gertrude looked decid-edly popeyed. "What is this?" she asked.

Rick was enjoying it all immensely. "We have a divorced couple in the club," he explained.

Gertrude murmured "Oh," rather feebly, and she and Ben fell back a couple of paces. They both looked acutely embarrassed.

I felt that I was losing my poise, too. I flashed a look of scorn at Tony. "If this redheaded monkey belongs to the club, then I resign," I said, and walked swiftly away—being careful not to trip.

I spent a boring evening. Somehow, I could not tell Mother and Father about Tony, and yet it nagged at my mind.

I called up one of my old friends, but all I could get out of her was a detailed account of the life histories of her two children.

I wandered around the house aimlessly, trying to decide on an assortment of people to have out from New York for the week end.

I finally drifted to one of the side windows, and saw that the first of the little houses was lit up like a Christmas tree. It was the one that Mrs. Potter had said belonged to the bachelor—obviously Tony. I peered more intently, and could distinctly see parts of the kitchen and the dinette through the back windows. There seemed to be a great deal of drink-mixing going on, and I supposed that Tony was throwing a party. I caught occasional glimpses of him slopping about with ice and soda.

It made me feel lonely, and I began to wish that I had not been so smart about walking off in a huff. I made up my mind, then and there, that I was not going to withdraw from the group, just because Tony was one of them. After all, I could treat Tony as I would Ben.

I went up to my bedroom, and was glad that it was on the other side of the house, as I did not want to hear the noise of their party.

I undressed, and as I opened the window, I was surprised to see a stream of light lying across the grass below.

"Oh damn!" I muttered. "Must have left the dining-room light on."

I could not be bothered going down again, so I got into bed, and decided to forget about it.

I was just drowsing off when I remembered, suddenly, and very clearly, that I had turned the dining-room light off.

CHAPTER 4

I HAD stretched my hand to the bedside lamp when it occurred to me that Father had probably gone down to get something to eat and left the light on. He was always leaving lights on, and Mother was always turning them off after him.

I turned over restlessly, and reflected that it was a good thing the dining room was on the opposite side of the house from our new neighbors. Otherwise, Tony's party would have thrown Father into a fresh fury.

The next day was very warm. A group of my old girl friends came around and took me under their wings—and I did not get home until two in the morning. I yawned my way upstairs, reflecting cattily that some of their husbands were frights—and the rest merely passable by comparison.

I noticed, just before I got into bed, that Father had left the dining-room light on again, and I decided that hereafter I had better make the rounds before going upstairs. After all, we were not millionaires.

The following day was warmer still, and Father asked me to play a round of golf with him.

"Where are all your boy friends?" I asked. "Did they throw you over for bragging too much?"

"They are all at work," he explained coldly. "If you're coming, say so. I can't wait all day."

As we left the house, Mother said, quite without humorous intent, "Keep your hat on, Hammond. The sun is very hot, and your hair has got positively threadbare lately."

Father threw his clubs into the taxi with such violence that they all came out of the bag.

It was very hot on the course, and I started out very badly. Father was in difficulties, too, and it wasn't ten minutes before we were both in a thoroughly bad temper. It gave me a certain amount of relief to ask Father, irritably, what he thought he was doing by leaving the dining-room light on night after night.

He turned on me belligerently. "I haven't been near the damn' dining room, except for meals, since we got here. What with your mother hounding at me about my blasted figure, I don't get a chance at the icebox." He pulled out his handkerchief, mopped at his face and gloomed, while my caddy teed up my ball. "Nothing but dog biscuits for lunch," he muttered.

"You shouldn't leave the dining-room light on all night, no matter why you go there," I said crossly.

"I tell you I haven't *been* in the God-damn' dining room," he shouted. "You must have left the light on yourself."

"Sorry to intrude on a private row," said a voice behind us, "but do you mind if I go through? Then you can finish your fight, and I can finish my game, in peace and comfort."

It was Tony Herridge—and I saw Father's face grow purple as he recognized him.

"You!" he spluttered. "What are you doing here, you young skunk? Get out of here—get off the course! I'll have you run out of town!" He went on to give a colorful display of profanity which made even me blush. Tony calmly teed his ball, hit a good drive and walked off grinning hatefully.

"Never would have brought you back here if I'd known the fellow was still about," Father puffed.

We finished our game, and did a bit better, toward the end, so that by the time we got home, we were both in a good humor again.

Mother was sitting on the porch. "Hammond," she said, as soon as we appeared, "Grace tells me there is quite an odor in the cellar. I wish you would go down and see what's causing it."

Father went off, and was back again almost immediately. "Can't smell a thing," he said cheerfuly. "Janice, that fellow Tony Herridge is hanging around here. Saw him on the golf course."

"Well, that's all right," Mother said calmly. "We don't own the town. I hope you were dignified enough not to be rude to him."

"Oh, absolutely," Father replied heartily. "Wouldn't bother with him on a bet. It's a free country—even for snakes."

I went out to the tennis court again that evening. Catherine and Rick were there alone, and they were deep in what appeared to be a serious conversation.

"Charlie had better watch his step," I thought, as I approached.

They did not notice me as I came up, and I heard Catherine say, "I don't care, Rick, Charlie always sent me a post card—even before we were engaged."

I called out hastily, "I'm here in person. Don't let me eavesdrop."

They sprang up, and greeted me cordially. "I thought you'd resigned," Rick smiled.

"Oh no," I said airily. "I was busy yesterday, but just because there are sharks in the ocean, it doesn't mean that I can't go bathing."

"Is it true that you've played at Wimbledon and Forest Hills?" Catherine asked curiously.

"Tony's a liar," I said hastily. "I've played in a few minor tournaments, and once I actually got to the semifinals."

Rick said sternly, "Come on and play me a singles, and I'll find out how good you really are. But no fooling, mind!"

"Oh no," I assured him. At that, absentmindedly, I almost beat him, but I caught myself in time, and lost out at seven-five.

I shook my head, clicked my tongue and was about to walk off the court when Rick motioned me back. "Wait a minute. Tony just turned up, and he wants to play you."

Tony came bounding up from nowhere and waved his racket at me. "One short set, Lizzie," he called cheerfully. "Maybe I can beat you—I've been doing a lot of practicing."

I looked him over with loathing—torn between a desire to stalk away with my nose in the air, and a longing to stay and lick the pants off him.

I decided to stay—and in ten minutes I had mopped up the court with him. I don't believe he got one point.

He came loping over, looking innocently crestfallen. "Well, I did think I'd be able to give you some sort of a game, Liz. It's very odd, isn't it? Rick beats you—you take me over at six-love—and yet I can beat Rick."

I told myself that I might have known the thing was some sort of a trap—and of course I'd walked straight into it. And to add insult to injury, if there was one thing I hated more than another, it was being called Lizzie.

I colored, and glanced at Rick, who was looking at me oddly. "Do you have trouble with Tony's game?" I asked mildly. "I can't understand it—his strokes are quite easy. You must be taking them the wrong way."

He smiled in a way that did not tell me whether I had put it over or not, and took my arm. "Come on—let's sit down under the tree, and you can tell me how to take him while you cool off."

We walked away, and I looked back over my shoulder and made a face at Tony—who winked at me by way of return.

I sat down with Rick, and we chatted aimlessly until Dora called me for dinner. He made a date with me, then, for the evening.

I found Mother and Father washed, brushed and generally dressed up, and it developed that they had been invited out for bridge.

"Which means," I told them, "that you will return between two and four in the morning, argue about the hands all the way upstairs and into your room, and continue arguing until you fall asleep— with Mother saying, every time she loses a point, 'Hush! You'll wake the child.'"

"There wouldn't be any need to argue," Father said, "if your mother would listen to me, and take a few lessons." He guffawed loudly, but Mother wasn't amused.

I dressed carefully, that night, and Rick looked pretty spick-and-span, too. We had quite a good time. Rick turned out to be a better dancer than conversationalist, which suited me, because I like to do the talking, myself. And he made a nice, sympathetic listener.

We came back fairly early, because I can take just so much dancing, and no more.

We noticed that Edith Drucker's house was lit up, and people seemed to be milling around inside.

"Let's go and join the party," Rick suggested, all enthusiasm.

"Well—but she isn't expecting us."

He laughed. "It won't make any difference to Edith—she probably wasn't expecting any of them. Come on—she'll be glad to have us."

I agreed, then, because I knew she'd be glad to have Rick, at any rate.

We climbed the steps to the porch, and rang the bell, but it was Catherine who opened the door for us. She said, "For heaven's sake— where have you two been?"

"Shaking a gay leg at Jersey's most popular palais de danse," I told her casually. I walked through into the living room, and looked about me.

Several people were getting stewed comfortably and together. I did not know any of them, and they ignored me. I turned to say something to Rick, and discovered that he had remained in the hall, with Catherine, and they were engaged in a low-voiced conversation.

I felt a bit annoyed with Rick for not dancing attendance on me, and with Catherine for not being satisfied with her intended.

I drifted on into the tiny dinette, where I found Gertrude, Ben Amherst and another man. Gertrude and Ben took me to their bosoms and introduced me to the other man, who turned out to be Wilbur Drucker, Senior. The three of them were more or less deadwood, so I said something pretty, and plowed on to the kitchen, from where I could hear peals of drunken laughter.

I found that the laughing was being done entirely by Edith, and she and my ex, Tony, had the kitchen to themselves. She had one arm draped around Tony's neck and the other hand clutched a high-ball, which was slopping onto the floor at intervals. Tony was mixing drinks as well as he could, with his encumbrance.

I held my nose and started to back out again—and then thought better of it. After all, what was there for me, in the rest of the house? And my handsome Rick was paying attention to Catherine in the hall. I decided to flirt a bit with Tony, and see if I could make Rick jealous. I never would have made such a resolution if I had been myself—but I always find, when I go out dancing, that there is nothing much to do, in between times, but drink—and so I was slightly fuzzy.

I went over to Edith, who was more than fuzzy, and untwined her from Tony's neck. I steered her to a chair, put her in it and said firmly, "Stay there."

She blinked at me, and her face twisted up as though she were going to cry. "I was having such a good time," she whimpered. "Why did you have to spoil everything?"

"Be a good girl," I said, "and put your face back on—it's all smeared. You can have him back after a while—and then, when you're through with him, you can give him to the garbage man."

Tony looked up when he heard my voice, and I gave him a brilliant smile. "Hello, Stupid," I said brightly. "Will you flirt with me, so as to make my beau jealous?"

He bowed to the ground. "I'm a bit out of practice, lady—but anything I can do to help "

He straightened up suddenly, threw his arms around me and kissed me.

"Wait a minute," I gasped, shaking him off. "Why waste all that where he can't see us ?"

"Rehearsal," said Tony, with an evil grin.

"Why don't you rehearse with me, Tony?" Edith mumbled, and took a sloppy gulp at her highball.

Tony took my arm companionable.

"We'll go and find your beau, and do some blatant flirting right in his face."

As we left the kitchen, Edith called after me, "Who are you, anyway? I don't believe I ever saw you before."

We went through the dinette, where Gertrude, Ben and Wilbur

Drucker had started some kind of a card game, and on to the living room. People were still milling around and drinking there, and one of them called to Tony, "Hey! Where are those drinks you promised us?"

He said, "In the kitchen. And don't bother me—I'm busy flirting."

We found that Catherine and Rick had disappeared from the hall, and Tony went over and opened the door of the closet. He stuck his head inside, and withdrew it immediately. "They're not here," he informed me. "Nothing but umbrellas, rubbers and Wilbur's winter coat."

"It should have been put away in camphor a couple of months ago," I said absently. "Maybe they went out for a walk."

"We'll trail them," he decided promptly. "Come on. And if we don't find them, we can sit under a tree and spoon. No sense wasting an evening like this."

"You can get Edith or Gertrude," I said, yawning. "I'm pretty well fed up with the evening, and I'm going to bed."

But we ran across Catherine and Rick not far from the tennis court. They were standing under a tree, and were locked in each other's arms.

CHAPTER 5

TONY gripped my arm sharply and pulled me behind a bush. We heard them murmuring, after a while, and then they moved off somewhere.

Tony muttered, "It's a damned shame. Charlie's such a decent fellow." I felt, in some indefinable way, that the gaiety had gone out of him, and I wondered vaguely whether he was upset entirely on Charlie's account.

I yawned again, and said, "I'm going to bed."

He walked with me to the front door, which we usually left open, because Mother had the only key. I went in, and Tony followed me into the hall. He left the door ajar, but almost it once it slammed violently.

"Wind blowing up," he said briefly. "Storm coming, I suppose."

We listened for a moment, and it sounded like a young hurricane.

Tony stirred, and said abstractedly, "Well—good night. I'll be getting home before your old man catches me here."

He went off, and I thought him over for a while. I came to the conclusion that he must be sweet on Catherine, himself. I could not believe that his sudden dejection was all concern for Charlie.

I shrugged, and turned toward the kitchen, with the idea of making some coffee to take the taste of the liquor out of my mouth.

I was stopped short at the door by a highly unpleasant odor that seemed to blow straight into my face. I backed away, and decided that I would not be able to stand the smell long enough to make coffee. "Father will simply have to see to that tomorrow," I thought grimly.

I left one light in the hall, for Father and Mother, and made sure that all the others were turned off, and then I went upstairs.

The smell seemed to follow me up, and I stopped in the upstairs hall and sniffed violently. It was still there, but considerably fainter. The wind was blowing gustily, and a shutter had worked loose somewhere at the back of the house and was banging at intervals.

I went into my room and closed the door firmly. I opened the back window, and then went to the side window, which was already open, and peered out. The patch of light streamed out across the grass as brightly as ever!

I straightened up, shook my head to try to clear it, and decided that I must be drunk. But I did not feel drunk at all—and I was certain that I had turned the dining-room light off.

It occurred to me, suddenly, that Mother and Father must have come home, and in another minute I was running down the stairs. I called out, "Hello," but there was no answer. And the dining room was in darkness.

I suffered a moment of panic, which drove me out the front door and on to the lawn. "Someone must be in the house," I thought shakily, "turning the dining-room light on and off—and it's been going on for several days."

I wandered around in the darkness of the front lawn for a while, and considered putting in a call for the police. The wind had died down abruptly, and a light rain began to fall.

I had to go in. I was tired, and I was getting wet—and Father and Mother might not turn up for hours.

I sternly dismissed my feeling of panic, and went back inside. The dining-room light was still off, and I went up to my room and walked straight to the side window. The patch of light was still there.

I wanted to call up Rick, or even Tony, and say that the dining-room light was always on when I was upstairs, and always off when I was downstairs, but I knew that Tony, at least, would tell me to put a wet cloth on my head, go to bed, and take a Bromo-Seltzer in the morning.

I clenched my fists, and stamped downstairs again. The dining-room light was off, of course, and I stood in the doorway for a moment, and then plunged into the room and looked out one of the side windows. The patch of light lay across the grass, directly below me.

I was suddenly weak with relief. The light came from the cellar, of course. Grace or Dora had probably turned a light on down there at some time, and had forgotten it. I'd have to go down and turn it off.

I went to the kitchen, and turned the light on. The wind had died away completely, and the shutter had stopped banging. I noticed that the bad smell was much fainter.

I made some strong coffee, and drank it black, and after that, I felt considerably better.

I opened the door to the cellar, and looked down into blackness unrelieved by a single glimmer of light anywhere. The bad smell drifted up more strongly against my face.

I turned back to the kitchen, and poured myself another cup of coffee. "Damn it," I whispered. "There should be some sort of a faint glow from somewhere."

I walked out, and into the darkened dining room, with the cup of coffee still in my hand, and peered out the side window. The light was still there. I raced back to the kitchen, and looked down the cellar steps again—no faintest sign of light anywhere.

I put the cup of coffee onto the kitchen table with a clatter, went directly to my father's liquor cabinet and poured myself a long, straight scotch, which I swallowed in one gulp. It was the first time I had ever had straight scotch, and it took me a minute or two to recover, but after the spluttering was over, I went bravely to the cellar stairs, switched on the light and started down.

The cellar looked as it always had, but the smell was stronger there. I thought it might be a dead rat, and I looked about a bit, but I could not see any rats, dead or otherwise—nor were there any lights but the main one, which I had switched on at the head of the stairs.

I walked over, and sat down on the steps to think it over. I looked at that portion of the cellar which lay under the dining room, and after I had wrinkled my forehead in vain for a while it hit me suddenly. There was a room there. It had been unused for many years, and was built by a former chauffeur of ours. We had had two maids at the time, and since the chauffeur was not married to either of them, Father would not let him sleep on the third floor with them.

I remembered that he had asked permission to build a room of beaverboard in the cellar, as he did not want to pay rent anywhere. The door was of beaverboard, too, so that when the handle fell off, sometime after the chauffeur left, it was hard to pick it out from the rest of the partition. You had to look for the cracks.

I walked over and looked around. One of the beaverboard walls was serving as part of the temporary coalbin, and it was there that I finally located the door. I could see the cracks quite clearly, but the coal was piled up against it and I could not get to it.

I went back to the steps, and sat there, looking at it.

That smell—and somebody shoveling the coal—shoveling it away from the door of that long-unused room, so that they could go in there, and then come out again, leaving the light on. And the coal must have been shoveled back across the door again. But why? I shook my muddled head, and could only come to the conclusion that somebody was using the room for something that had gone bad.

I blame Father's scotch for what followed. If I had stuck to coffee, I should simply have gone upstairs and waited for my parents to come home. As it was, I got up suddenly, and taking one of the shovels, I set to work to try to clear a space in front of the door, so that I could open it.

It wasn't easy. Every time I got some of the coal shoveled away, a small avalanche would come pouring from the top of the heap to take its place. It was very exasperating, and I found myself getting hot and cross.

Once, I thought I heard my parents come in, and I went to the foot of the stairs and called, but everything was silent, and there was no answer.

I went back to the coal, and after a while, rather to my surprise, I made a space large enough to permit the opening of the door.

It would not open easily—I had to put my fingernails in the crack and ease it gently for some time. It gave, at last, and as it swung toward me, a blast of the foul smell hit me in the face. Light streamed out from the room. I put my handkerchief against my nose, and walked in.

An armchair faced the small high window—its back to me. And there was a man sitting in the armchair.

I stood there for an instant, staring at the back of his head, while a rising tide of terror and panic throbbed at my temples. Then, quite as though some outside force were moving me, and somehow, against my conscious will, I tiptoed around to the front of the chair.

The man had no face—there was only a dark, putrefying mass where it should have been.

I screamed sharply, and flung myself at the door, but my voice was drowned out as an avalanche of coal came pouring down outside. I battered wildly with my fists, but it was too late. The door would not budge, and I realized, with dull horror, that I was shut in with the thing.

CHAPTER 6

I PUSHED and strained and banged on the door, and called wildly for Mother and Father, but the door held fast, and there was no answer to my cries. I gave up at last, and leaned against the wall, panting, and trying to avoid with my eyes the armchair and the still figure in it. I noticed the window—small, and set high in the concrete wall, and I flew to it, and wrenched it open, but there was no hope of climbing out of it, for it was barred.

I looked at the bars blankly for a moment, and then I filled my lungs to their fullest capacity. It was no time to be self-conscious—I let out a series of shrieks that must have been heard for miles.

I stopped for breath, and thought I saw someone standing in the shadow of a tree. The figure was nothing more than a dark blur, but I made an anguished appeal to it. "Oh, please," I yelled, "come and let me out."

The thing seemed to move back behind the tree, and disappeared entirely—but the next instant I heard voices and footsteps.

"I'm here!" I cried wildly. "Here! In the cellar!"

Catherine and Rick stumbled into the patch of light, on the grass outside, their faces white and their eyes dark with excitement.

I explained to them, hysterically, how to move the coal and free me, but I insisted that Catherine sit on the grass, directly outside the window, and let Rick go alone.

I felt as though I were waiting for hours, while he forced an entrance into the house, but at last I heard his step on the cellar stairs, and a minute later he was fumbling with the coal shovel.

I felt such a wave of relief and returning confidence that I was able to turn around and look at that ghastly thing in the chair—although I still avoided the head.

The body was clothed in an ordinary, dark blue business suit and dark brown shoes. It was while I was looking at the shoes that I noticed a small blue flower lying on the floor not far from the chair. I picked it up, without thinking, and turned it over in my fingers curiously. It was a dandelion—there was no doubt about that—and it was blue. A blue dandelion. I did not think of it as being particularly strange at the time—I wanted only to be released from that terrible place.

Rick pulled the door open, finally, and came in. He took one look at the figure in the chair, and said hoarsely, "My God! It's poor Charlie!"

There was a gasp from the window, and Catherine called shrilly, "Oh, Rick, what do you mean? What is it?"

We both looked up, and Rick said sharply, "Go to the front door, Cathie, and we'll let you in."

I heard her crying as she went off, and Rick took my arm firmly and led me upstairs. I went to the door to let Catherine in while he telephoned for the police.

Mother and Father poured in behind Catherine, and for a few minutes the confusion was hopeless. Catherine sobbed hysterically, Rick patted her hand and murmured, while Father loudly demanded explanations and would not stop talking long enough to listen to any. Mother took off her wrap, looked at all of us in turn and then stepped to the telephone and called Mrs. Reed. She asked her to come over at once.

"And now," she said, sitting down in our midst, "tell me what has happened, Lissa."

I went over the whole thing for them, and just as I had finished, Mrs. Reed arrived, and I had to do it again. I felt dazed and sick, and I was exhausted from spasm after spasm of trembling that shook me from head to foot.

Father was inclined to be indignant about everything, but Mother told him to be quiet. He kept patting my shoulder, and telling me not to worry.

Mrs. Reed, her arm around Catherine, listened to my story with wet, frightened eyes. Catherine, her head on her mother's shoulder, continued to cry helplessly. I felt sorry for her. I could imagine her self-reproach, when she thought of Charlie lying there, while she mooned around with Rick.

The police arrived, and the confusion started all over again. There was a tall, bony individual with sparse blond hair, who wore plain clothes, and there were some bluecoats. The bony man had a measuring tape, and he went around, with a great deal of energy, measuring almost everything. He even measured my feet once. "They're a bit too long," I admitted, "but I don't see why you need to put it on record."

"My dear young lady," he said, in a high, precise voice, "I must know the length of your feet, so that I can distinguish them from the other footprints in that room."

Mother raised her eyebrows and said coldly, "This house is kept scrupulously clean."

The man flashed her a glance. "I beg to differ, madam." He reached up an incredibly long, lean arm and ran his finger across the ledge over the door. He then pointed the finger, unquestionably soiled, at Mother. "You see?"

Mother saw, and looked as though she'd like to bite the finger off. It was promptly withdrawn, however, and its owner set to work to do some more measuring.

One of the bluecoats stepped forward and murmured pacifically something about "He will have his little joke." Mother said "Really?" and started to tap her foot on the floor.

Father was nearly purple in the face by this time. Rick was walking back and forth across the room, smoking innumerable cigarettes, and Catherine leaned against her mother, and looked as though she were on the verge of collapse.

The bony individual presently put his tape measure away and crawled out from under the piano, and there followed a question bee that I began to think would last until dawn.

The arrival of the medical examiner and the ambulance finally delivered us, and during the respite Mrs. Reed suggested that she get Catherine home.

The bony wonder would not hear of it.

"I don't think you have any right to keep us here," Mrs. Reed said resentfully. "What is your name, anyway?"

The man said promptly, "Timothy Frobisher—and if you wish to report me to my superior, I can save you trouble by giving you the telephone number."

"Impertinence," said Mother, still tapping her foot.

Mrs. Reed stood up, and helped Catherine to her feet. "My daughter is in obvious need of attention," she said curtly. "We are going."

They went—and Timothy Frobisher put his hands on his hips, shook his head and said, "Tch, tch."

Mother, Father, Rick and I still remained, however, and he gave us a sweeping look, told us to remain exactly where we were and went off to join the activity in the cellar.

Father glared after him, and stood up immediately. "So far from being a schoolboy," he said loudly, "I am a taxpayer—which means that I help to pay his salary. And it's too high—even if he's a dollar-a-year man."

Mother said "Hammond" automatically, and yawned behind her handkerchief.

Father glanced at the remaining bluecoat, and then at Rick, cleared his throat and suddenly offered them both a drink.

The bluecoat refused with obvious reluctance, but Rick accepted cheerfully.

He and Father joined forces companionably, and as they walked out of the room Father asked, "Who are you, anyhow?"

I heard Rick say, "Confidentially, Adolf Hitler, but I'm incog. Just call me Rick."

The bluecoat looked after them uneasily, and took a step toward Mother. She looked so formidably Park Avenue and Newport that he took time out to mention, politely, that his name was Moley. Mother received this graciously, so he ventured to inquire if the gentlemen were coming back.

"I don't know, I'm sure," Mother said innocently. "If I were you, I'd follow them."

"Right," said Moley, looking relieved. "I know you ladies will stay put." He went off in a bit of a hurry.

Mother got up immediately. "I'm going upstairs. I was simply determined not to ask permission of a policeman to go up to my own bedroom."

I laughed, and watched her disappear up the staircase. As soon as she had gone I found myself shaking and trembling again. I could not stop, so I got up and sneaked to the head of the cellar stairs, and strained my ears toward the voices down below.

Frobisher's precise, mincing tones came floating up to me. "You say, then, that he was shot directly in the face?"

"Yes," someone answered him briefly. "Been dead for some days—condition of the body—I'm taking him off now."

Timothy said something about photographs.

"All done," said the other voice. "Let you know later—more details—the bullets—"

I silently cursed Father, who was talking loudly in the dining room, and making it hard for me to hear all that was said.

Timothy presently piped, "All right," and I heard him making for the stairs, so I raced back to the library, and sat down. He appeared, a moment later, and was distinctly put out to find that I was the lone survivor.

"Where are they?" he asked.

"Moley is tailing two of them," I said meekly, "but the third one made a clean getaway."

He tch-tchd again, and decided to concentrate on me.

"Now," he said, "I want you to think carefully. Are you sure that you did not touch anything when you were in that room?"

"Quite sure," I told him, with a clear conscience. "All I wanted was to get out of the place."

"Yes, of course, I quite understand. But, even in your excitement, you might have picked up something—or disarranged something."

"No," I said definitely. "All I did was yell for help."

Father and Rick came back just then, and Moley shuffled along behind them, looking distinctly uncomfortable.

Mother never did show up again, and although Frobisher made some caustic remarks about her absence, it did him no good.

He questioned Father and Rick for a while, but his heart was not in it, and he presently left in a bit of a huff. He first cautioned us to be at home in the morning, and added, with squeaky menace, that this time he meant it.

Moley stayed with us all night, and I believe he slept on Mother's Sunday couch in the drawing room.

Rick said good night and went off, and Father and I went upstairs to talk things over with Mother. She was smoking a cigarette in bed, and she asked us, with a touch of malice, if Frobisher had put handcuffs on the guilty party yet.

Father sat on the end of his bed, and said gloomily, "I knew those damned cottages would do us no good."

"Do you suppose the poor boy could have killed himself?" Mother asked thoughtfully.

"No," said Father importantly. "I gave Moley a drink, and he told us they looked for a gun, first thing—and there wasn't any. I think Frobisher was a bit suspicious that Lissa, or that fella, Hitler, had taken it off."

"Hitler?" Mother and I chorused.

"Fella with the bit of fluff on his lip. Said his name was Andrew Hitler, or something."

Mother and I looked at each other sadly, and Mother said, "Run along to bed, Lissa—you look half dead. I'll untangle Mr. Rickey and Andrew Hitler for Father while he's getting undressed."

I got up and kissed them both, and as I left, I heard Father say, "We'll have to leave at once—can't stay here after this." And I agreed with him thoroughly.

When I got to my bedroom, I locked the door carefully behind me. Even though Moley was snoring in the drawing room, I did not intend to take any chances.

As I took off my dress, my handkerchief fell out of the pocket. I stooped to pick it up, and saw that the little blue flower had dropped out with it.

I felt absolutely criminal. I had withheld evidence, and to make matters worse, I had lied about it. But I had done it in good faith— I had simply forgotten the dandelion. Only, I was very much afraid that Timothy Frobisher would never believe that now.

I shrugged, and told myself that it was probably of no consequence. I put the withered little flower into a small box on my dressing table, and finished my preparations for bed.

I did not sleep much that night. The Drucker dog howled until dawn—and every time I drowsed off, I dreamed that I was in that terrible little room in the cellar again.

CHAPTER 7

I WOKE up quite early the next morning, and lay for some time thinking not so much of poor Charlie Carr as of the blue dandelion. I felt that I could not face Timothy Frobisher's scolding, if I told him about it now, and I made up my mind to say nothing. It probably did not matter, anyway. I rolled over onto my back, but could not enjoy the sunshine and late spring warmth that was pouring in at the window. I found my mind returning to that silly blue flower. Why should it be blue, anyway? I remembered that it was flecked with yellow—but the general effect was certainly blue. I decided to ask Tony if dandelions came in any color but yellow, and lazily pulled myself out of bed.

When I got downstairs, I found that Timothy Frobisher was interviewing the maids in the kitchen, and was making such a thorough job of it, that I had to make my own breakfast.

I went out to the lawn afterward, in search of a dandelion, but there was not one to be seen, and it took me about five minutes to connect this with the fact that the grass had just been cut.

I went around to the side garden, and made a tour of the row of small back yards. There were some dandelions in Tony's yard, and some behind the Potter house. I decided to pick one of the Potter blooms, but I had no sooner wriggled through the hedge than Mrs. Potter came flying out of the back door.

"Oh, Miss Vickers!" she shrilled. "Is it really true—this awful thing about Charlie Carr?"

"I guess it was Charlie," I said. "Rick said it was."

"Oh yes—it was Charlie. He's been positively identified—by his teeth, you know."

I said "Oh," rather flatly, and wondered where she'd heard that—and why I hadn't.

"Yes indeed. It seems he's been dead since last Tuesday or Wednesday—you know, he was due back today from Washington. And only to think that he never went there at all—that he never got any farther than your cellar!"

I stooped down, casually, and picked a dandelion. "It's a terrible thing. I can't see why anyone would want to kill him."

"Well, but are they sure it wasn't suicide?" she asked, her small eyes blinking nervously in the sun.

I began to edge away. "They say not."

"I happen to know that he had his troubles," she said significantly.

I stopped edging away and eyed her. "What sort of troubles?" I asked curiously. "I thought he seemed very happy. He was obviously in love with Catherine—and they were going to be married soon. I shouldn't have thought he had any troubles."

She hesitated, and then lowered her voice. "You wouldn't know about it—but, you see, Catherine liked Rick, too—and we all know that if he'd asked her first, she would have accepted him. Charlie knew it, too. And then, this trip of his—she was seriously against it."

"You mean she was on the point of breaking the engagement?" I asked bluntly.

She backed down a bit, and said hastily, "Oh no—no, no, of course not. The marriage was all arranged, and I'm sure Catherine had no idea of breaking it up." She paused, and added innocently, "Besides, how could she be sure that Rick would ask her, if she put Charlie off?"

I tried not to laugh, because she seemed to take it all very seriously, and at that moment Mrs. Reed appeared at her kitchen window and asked us for the latest developments.

We had nothing to tell her, but she asked us to come in and join her in a cup of coffee. Mrs. Potter accepted graciously, and I followed along, although I particularly dislike coffee in the middle of the morning.

We all sat down in the tiny dinette, which overlooked the back yard, and Helene Reed poured three cups.

We sipped daintily, and after a while the Potter woman asked after Catherine.

Mrs. Reed said she was prostrated with grief.

Five minutes later Catherine appeared, to give her the lie. She was sober, and her face was pale, but she was quite composed, and very far from being prostrated.

She was clearly annoyed at finding us all in the dinette, and refusing, rather curtly, her mother's offer to prepare her breakfast, she went on into the kitchen, and began to prepare it herself. I judged by the assortment of smells that it was a fairly substantial one.

"Feeling better, Cathie?" Mrs. Potter called, too sweetly.

Catherine grunted, and banged a lid.

I began to find the heat of the dinette and the coffee too much for me, so I moved a few yards away into a rocking chair—which put me into the living room.

Rocking and smoking, I felt more comfortable, and I listened idly while the two mammas tried to persuade Catherine to bring her breakfast into the dinette. She refused shortly, and apparently sat down to eat it in the kitchen.

Mrs. Potter started a long detailed story about a rich aunt of hers, and my attention wandered.

I gazed around the living room, and automatically, in my mind, improved its arrangement, and threw out certain things that offended me.

A maple secretary, open, and cater-cornered, stood at the other side of the room. I mentally shifted it around, so that it was flat against the wall, and decided that it could stay. But the bottle of ink that stood on the blotter should be concealed.

I suddenly abandoned interior decorating, and my eyes remained fastened on the ink. If you dipped an ordinary dandelion into a bottle of ink, would it come out blue?

I simply had to know at once. Mrs. Potter was still deep in her yarn, so I got up quietly and went over to the secretary.

The dandelion I had picked in the Potter yard hung limply in my buttonhole. I pulled it out, uncorked the ink and dipped it in.

When I pulled it out again, I had to grab for a piece of blotting paper in a hurry. And the experiment was disappointing. My dandelion, much bedraggled, looked like a dandelion dipped in ink, and nothing more. It was mottled untidily, with most of the yellow still showing. I dipped it again, and twirled it around, and then I left it to soak for a while.

Mrs. Potter finished her story just then, and Mrs. Reed laughed, and called to ask me if I had heard it.

I laughed falsely, and said "Very amusing"—and pulled my dandelion out of the ink. I put it on the blotter, and realized guiltily that Mrs. Reed must be wondering what on earth I was doing out of her sight, and quiet, for so long.

I picked up the blotter carefully, went out the front door, and after a hasty glance around, I put it under some tulips that were growing beside the porch.

I hurried back inside, and reached the dinette a little out of breath.

The two women eyed me with obvious inquiry.

I could not think of an explanation off hand, and to give myself time, I asked for another cup of the foul coffee. My first impulse—to tell them I had had to spit—I put sternly aside. Father would have enjoyed it, but Mrs. Potter, what with her rich aunt, and all, would certainly condemn it as coarse.

I took a sip of coffee—and then it came to me. "I just saw the loveliest bird," I said shyly. "I went outside to get a better look—but it flew away."

They both showed a flattering interest, and asked after the color.
I took another sip of coffee. "Pink," I said, coming up for air.

"Pink!" they repeated incredulously.

"Or rose. Ashes of roses, really."

They stared at me. "I've never seen anything like that around
here," Mrs. Reed declared. "I'll have to look it up."

"I'll write to the Bird Lovers' Society," Mrs. Potter decided.

"Oh, don't bother," I said modestly.

"But of course I shall. They want people to write in reports about
unusual birds."

"They'll think you've been drinking," I said faintly.

But they didn't hear me. They moved toward the secretary, intent on getting the letter off without delay.

I said good-by, and slipped out the front door. I retrieved the
blotter and dandelion from the tulips, and made swiftly for home.

I did not meet anyone until I was halfway up the stairs, and then
I ran into Father.

He said, "Hello—where have you been? I've looked high and
low for you." He caught sight of the dandelion and its blotting paper then, and gasped. "What the devil have you got there?" he demanded excitedly.

I brushed past him impatiently. "It's nothing. Only an experiment."

I went on to my bedroom, and tried to shut him out, but he put
his foot in the door, pushed it open and followed me in.

"Now, look here, Lissa," he said crossly, "if you try to hide things
from me, I'll go straight to Timothy Frobisher and tell him what I
saw you carrying."

"Well, shut the door, then," I snapped, "and stop shouting. And
if you tell anyone about this, I'll tell Mother on you."

"What have I done?" he demanded belligerently.

"I don't know—but there's bound to be something."

"I'm not going to tell anyone," he said impatiently. "What are
you doing?"

I realized that I'd have to explain it to him, so I tried to do it in a
few terse words—which was a mistake. Father never has, or never
will, understand a terse explanation, and in the end I had to draw a
map, as usual.

He did not seem much interested, either, after all my trouble.
He merely said, "Hmm. Well, there's a lot of rubbish in that cellar.

What do you want to go running around putting bits of it under a microscope for? Pretty silly, I think."

I said patiently, "Father, will you please go and play with your paper dolls? I'm busy."

"You'll be busier when Frobisher catches up with you," he said significantly.

"Why?"

"He wants to know why you said there was a light in that room in the cellar. He said there wasn't any light when he got there, and not only that—there aren't even any light fixtures."

CHAPTER 8

I STARED at Father with my mouth open. "What are you talking about?" I asked at last. "Start all over again."

"Well, listen then, can't you?" he said impatiently. "I'm telling you that Frobisher couldn't find any way of getting a light in that room where they found the young fella—and, what's more, Frobisher is of the opinion that there wasn't any light. He's been after you to find out about it."

"Then I wish he'd hurry and catch up with me," I said hotly. "I'll tell him a thing or two. Not only was there a light in the room, but it had been on for three days—maybe longer." I dropped onto the bed, and felt tears suddenly stinging at my eyes. "Oh, Father! It's so awful."

He murmured a few comforting words, and patted my shoulder. Mother called to him just then, so he went off—probably to murmur comforting words to her, and pat her shoulder.

I dabbed at my wet eyes with my handkerchief, pulled myself off the bed and went to look at my dandelion.

It was not blue. Where the ink had stayed on, it was a blackish color. I compared it with the original, and although there was some similarity, the color was quite different. The inked one was fresher, of course, too.

I considered going to Timothy Frobisher and telling him all, but finally decided against it. After all, it was only a dead dandelion— and what connection could it have with anything?

After I had salved my conscience, I got a piece of tissue paper, tore it in half and wrapped the two dandelions separately. I labeled the first one "original," and the other "Mrs. Reed," and put them carefully away in my jewel-case. I hoped that Frobisher would not come snooping around and find them—but I didn't put it past him.

I sat down then and tried to figure how I could go about finding out how dandelion number one had been made blue. I had some sort of vague idea that if I could settle that point I'd have the murderer backed into a corner.

I was convinced that someone in the locality had killed Charlie, and had planned it in advance. I had heard the coal being shoveled a week before the thing had happened, and then I had heard it again—presumably when the coal was being replaced against the door. And whoever had done it knew our house pretty well. I shivered, and was filled with sudden determination to solve the thing.

For a start, I decided to dip a lot of dandelions in a lot of local ink, and if I got a blue to match the original, I could go on from there. My wrist watch showed that there was still a few minutes before lunch, so I powdered my nose and started downstairs, intent on dipping more dandelions.

I ran straight into Timothy Frobisher in the lower hall.

"Oh, Mrs. Herridge," he said, absently settling his tie. "I would like a word with you."

I eyed him coldly.

"It's about that light—in the cellar room." He cleared his throat. "Are you sure there was such a light?"

"I'm certain of it," I said frostily. "It had been on for some days."

"Well, yes—so you said. Will you please come down and show me just where it was located?"

I accompanied him silently. The coal had been cleared away from the door, and Timothy held it open for me while I walked in.

I really looked at the room this time. It was quite small, with a cot in one corner and a battered chest of drawers beside the cot. There was a table against the opposite wall, and near it the armchair in which Charlie had been found.

There did not seem to be anything else. The walls were quite bare, and so was the ceiling, and the only breaks in the expanse of beaverboard and concrete were the door and the small barred window. Very definitely, there were no light fixtures.

Frobisher was looking at me. "Can you remember where the light was?" he asked, elaborately avoiding sarcasm.

I couldn't. I had not the remotest idea where the light had come from. "When you walk into a lighted room," I said defensively, "you don't bother about locating the source of the light. I don't know where it came from—but I tell you that there was a light."

He let me go, then, but it was a few minutes past one o'clock, and I had to postpone my experiments until after lunch.

Mother and Father spent the time during lunch in making plans for leaving the house as soon as possible. Mother said she never wanted to live there again, and Father declared that it made no difference to him, because the cottages had spoiled the place anyway. But Timothy Frobisher had asked that we stick around until the thing was cleared up, and Father said that, of course, it was the only thing for us to do. As a matter of fact wild horses couldn't have dragged him away—he was having the time of his life. He said with faint regret, "I think they expect to clear it up this afternoon. Now, let's see—this is Saturday—we ought to get away by Monday. Can you girls be packed?"

I laughed at him. "I'm not going to pack a solitary article until they have the handcuffs on somebody. The thing will probably drag out all summer."

After lunch I went up to my room and got an old leather purse, which I carefully lined with blotting paper. I put it under my arm and then sauntered downstairs and out the back door.

As soon as the screen had banged behind me, I made a beeline for the Potters' back yard. I picked a bouquet of the nicest dandelions I could find, and was putting them carefully in the purse when I heard someone move behind me.

I whirled around guiltily, and came face to face with Tony.

"Gathering posies?" he asked, staring at the purse. "Dinner party tonight? And you haven't invited me."

I snapped the purse shut and put it behind me. "You can't do one thing around here," I said bitterly, "without someone snooping after you."

He raised his eyebrows, put his hands in the pockets of his blazer and leaned against a clothes pole. He was smiling lazily, but his green eyes were chilly and unfriendly. "I've been indiscreet, Lizzie—I'm sorry. But, really things have come to a pretty pass when your old man, after going through his money, sinks so low as to send his daughter out to catch dandelions for dinner."

"Oh, dry up, will you?" I said fretfully. "You always talk so much without saying anything. Go away, for heaven's sake. Father would be furious if he saw me talking to you."

"I'm probably more welcome in the Potters' back yard than ever you will be," he said mildly. "By the way, why didn't you scream a bit louder last night? I slept through the whole thing."

"What do you know about it?" I asked shortly.

"Detective Sergeant Timothy Frobisher is a personal friend of mine—I saw him this morning. I'd rather have been on the scene, though."

"You should learn not to nose into things that don't concern you," I said, and began to walk away. I did not want him to find out anything about my dandelions.

He did not move, but he called after me, "You can't fool me, Lizz. You're up to something, with that purse full of weeds, and I'm going to find out what it is."

I stopped, and turned around. "If you're out of a job again we can let you have yesterday's paper. Grace used some of it to line the garbage can—but I think she left the classified ads out. Even if she didn't, I guess you can take the thing out of the garbage can—we had a pretty dry breakfast."

"I'm not wasting my time," he said equably. "I married you once, and lived on the old man's bounty—why couldn't I do it again?"

I hurried out of earshot, because it's hard to worst Tony with the tongue.

I went on home, and hid the purseful of dandelions in my bed-room.

I found Mother in the living room, sitting stiffly upright, and looking as though someone had forgotten himself and told her a dirty joke.

I dropped into a chair, and said, "Relax, Mom. Whatever it is, it won't matter in a hundred years."

"But it matters now," she declared, sensibly enough. "I have been turned completely inside out, and—and shaken. There isn't a thing they haven't found out, from the moment I drew my first breath until lunch time today."

"'They'?" I said. "Frobisher, and who else?"

"I haven't seen Frobisher. It was two men from the prosecutor's office. They came this morning."

"To give our Timothy a hand?"

"To put him in his place," Mother said grimly, "and humiliate him—or so it seems. Their names are Albert Hahn and Mack Brewster, and they appear to be in charge of the thing. They've done

Father and myself, and Dora and Grace, and they're champing at the bit to do you."

"I'll go and hide," I said promptly.

"It's a good idea," said Mother, and stood up. "Let's go to your bedroom and plan where to travel when this thing is cleared up. I don't see how we can stay on here after what's happened."

"No," I agreed absently. "I suppose not."

We opened the door of the living room cautiously and peered out. The hall seemed to be deserted, so we slipped out and began to tiptoe across to the stairs.

We had not gone more than halfway across, however, when suddenly, and quite quietly, I was captured and led back to the drawing room by a couple of strange men. Mother and Timothy Frobisher trailed along behind us.

Before they could start anything, Mother suggested, with a certain amount of firmness, that we would all be more cozy in the library, so we all shifted over there. I knew that she did not want three men sprawled all over her delicate drawingroom furniture, but I heard one of the strangers mutter something about "Who wants to be cozy in this heat?"

They questioned me at great length, and every time Timothy Frobisher ventured to put in his two cents' worth, they either glared at him scornfully or interrupted him.

The two of them pounded at me about the light that I insisted had been on in the cellar room. They said that it could not have been there, and they became rather offensive about it.

I lost my temper, and was about to snap at them, when Mother got in ahead of me.

"Mr. Hahn," she said coldly, "I strongly resent your obvious implication that my daughter is trifling with the truth."

I don't think they knew what she was talking about. In any case, they merely sent her out of the room, and continued to pound at me.

"I don't care what you say," I told them stubbornly, "there was an electric light in that room when I went in. And not only that, but it had been on for several days. Maybe it was some sort of an extension that was removed later."

"The cellar's been searched thoroughly," Mack Brewster said, keeping his cold little eyes on me, "and there's nothing of the kind down there. Now, why would anyone take a thing like that away?"

"You'd better find out," I said nastily. "Why ask me to do the job you're paid for?"

Timothy cleared his throat, and thrust his high, squeaky voice into the fray.

"Mrs. Herridge, when you first had the room built, it must have been supplied with a light of some sort. I understand it was built for the use of a former chauffeur?"

Albert Hahn and Mack Brewster gave him a couple of dirty looks. "We were just coming to that," said Brewster.

Frobisher bravely sent them a glance of defiance.

"The chauffeur built it for himself," I explained. "There must have been some sort of a light, of course—but I've no idea what it was, or how he arranged it."

"We'll have to search the house," Hahn decided. "And if you've no objection, we'll begin now."

"Go right ahead," I said airily. "And if it isn't too much trouble, will you keep your eyes open for a red pot-holder while you're about it? The cook mislaid it, and she's dying to get it back."

I left them and went straight upstairs, and told Mother, who was furious. I couldn't find Father, so I went along to my room and got my purse full of dandelions. I added the two tissue-wrapped specimens to it and then went quietly down the stairs.

I left the house by the side door which was an entrance to both the attic and the cellar stairs, and faced another door that opened into the back hall of the ground floor.

I had not gone two steps before I came face to face with Timothy Frobisher—and I had an instant conviction that he had been waiting for me.

"May I see what you have in the purse?" he asked nasally.

CHAPTER 9

I FELT that I had to do some quick thinking in order to save the lives of my dandelions.

I laughed nervously, opened the bag and contrived to push the two tissue-wrapped blooms to the bottom. "Just dandelions," I said foolishly.

He stretched his neck and glanced into the bag. The tissue paper was entirely concealed and all he saw was a mass of wilting yellow.

He transferred his gaze to my face and asked simply, "Why?"

Why, indeed? I swallowed, and shook my head helplessly. He made it a bit clearer for me. "Why are you carrying around a bag full of crushed flowers?"

I gave a laugh that came out high and false. "Oh—you mean these? They're for my class. My—botany class."

"What botany class?" said the demon.

I felt that I had lost my poise completely. I waved a feeble hand, and jabbered, "Mr. Herridge, you know—Tony. They—they gave him the custody of the garden, and he knows all about those things. He's giving me lessons—botany lessons."

Detective Sergeant Frobisher said, "Oh," and continued to stare at me.

I tried a change of subject. "Did you find out about the light in the cellar?"

"No."

I clicked my tongue. "And that room was in absolute darkness when you arrived last night?"

"Absolute darkness," said Timothy gravely. "We had to use flashlights."

"Very mysterious," I murmured, and began to edge off.

He let me go, but I could feel his eyes boring into my back, and I had a silly fear that I was going to trip over something and go sprawling. I concentrated my mind on the sort of clothes I would affect while I was waiting for Father's lawyers to get me out of jail.

I went over to the Drucker place, and Edith welcomed me with open arms. All I wanted from her was a sample of her ink, but since I couldn't tell her that, she sat me down in the tiny living room, and talked long and gustily about poor Charlie.

I spotted her ink almost immediately. It was in a glass inkstand, on the open secretary, and matched a fancy tooled-leather desk set, "a present," I thought, "from Edith to Wilbur, at Christmas."

I realized that I'd have to stick around until four o'clock, or after, in order to get Edith out of the room. She would eventually be forced to ask me if I would like afternoon tea, or a cold drink—I would admit thirst or hunger, but would fear that it was too much trouble, which would corner her into saying "Not at all," and departing for the kitchen. And then I could dip my dandelion.

I came out of a brown study to find her looking at me interrogatively. Obviously, she expected some sort of response—and I had not taken in a word she'd said for the last five minutes.

I nodded my head gravely, with various expressions appearing in succession on my face, and hoped that that would fill the bill.

She seemed satisfied. "I thought you'd agree with me," she said smugly. "I'm afraid there are a lot of women like that."

"Isn't it the truth?" I said mournfully.

"And, anyway, as far as Rick is concerned, he certainly never paid any attention to Catherine until after she became engaged to Charlie—and then he started to give her a rush. I know for a fact that she wanted to break the engagement when she saw how the wind was blowing, but Rick wouldn't hear of it. Talked a lot of noble stuff about how he wouldn't hurt his best friend like that—you know the line. So Catherine postponed the marriage until fall." She took a long breath, which she badly needed, and summed up: "Aren't men conceited? And aren't women fools?"

"Terrible!" I murmured. "But, Edith, tell me, do you know why three men like Charlie, Rick and Ben were living in a small suburban house? It's a bit out of the ordinary."

Edith shifted her gum and nodded. "Charlie rented the house because he wanted to be near Catherine—he was crazy about her. He and Ben worked in the same office, and Ben offered to come out for the summer and share expenses, and Charlie agreed. That was last year, in the spring, and Rick came at the same time. He was a friend of Charlie's, and he wanted to cut down his expenses or something. He and Ben were just going to stay for the summer, but I guess they found it comfortable, and cheap, too, and when winter came they stayed right on instead of going back to town, and they've been there ever since. They have an old colored woman, you know, who comes by the day, and does the housework, and cooks their meals. I guess they live the life of Riley, there."

"When did Catherine become engaged to Charlie?" I asked.

"In April. And honestly, Charlie was more unhappy after it happened than he ever was before."

"Oh well—that's understandable," I said, "if Catherine immediately started fooling around with Rick. Charlie would be bound to notice."

We chatted on for a while, and at last Edith suggested iced tea, and clicked out to the kitchen on her high heels to make it.

I went swiftly to the secretary, opened the inkstand and dipped one of my dandelions. I let it soak as long as I dared, and then hauled it out, and dropped it into the purse against the blotting-paper lining. I snapped the purse shut, fanned my hot face with my handkerchief a couple of times and relaxed.

I turned around—and stopped short. The round shoebutton eyes of Wilbur, Junior, were fixed gravely and intently upon me.

I looked him over, came to the conclusion that he was about four years old and decided that it did not matter what he had seen.

"Hello, there," I said cheerfully. "How's the little man?"

"I'm Willie," said the little man, reproving me coldly. He pointed to the ink. "I wanna do that, too."

I controlled a desire to drop him out the window. "No, dear," I murmured, through clenched teeth, "that's messy. Let's play something else."

He transferred his gaze to the ink, and moved a step nearer. "The other lady let me."

"What other lady?" I asked sharply.

He backed away defensively, under my change of tone, and at that moment Edith appeared with a loaded tray.

"Go on outside, Willie," she said impatiently. "I don't want you in the house. Here—you can have a cookie."

She handed him one, and the kid snatched it and went out—after first giving me a fearful look.

I could have kicked myself for not having taken more trouble with him. I'd have to start all over again, now, to try and win his confidence, and find out who the other lady was, and what she had let him do with the ink.

Probably there was nothing in it, and the kid did not know what he was talking about. But I knew I'd never rest until I found out.

After we had finished with the iced tea and cookies, Edith said briskly, "Just help me with these dishes, and then we can go out to the tennis court. I guess everybody's there, by now."

I cursed inwardly, and followed her to the kitchen. "It's too early for the club, isn't it?" I asked. "The men won't be home from work."

"It's Saturday," she reminded me. "We won't want to play much tennis, but I know everybody will want to talk it over—about Charlie."

When we got to the court, everyone was there, except Tony. Mrs. Reed and Mrs. Potter sat on the bench, and the others were sprawled around on the grass.

They greeted us gloomily, and we added ourselves to the group.

I immediately began to consider excuses for leaving them, again. Their houses were invitingly empty, and I'd be able to get my dipping over in short order, if I were free to go through them when nobody was about.

I was not listening to the conversation, but I did notice that Catherine, who sat like a stone, and never spoke a word, had Rick on one side, and Ben on the other—and that Ben was paying her a certain amount of clumsy attention.

Gertrude sat on the other side of Rick, and I felt sure that she was quite undisturbed by Ben's behavior. I supposed that Ben took a flutter, like that, whenever he got a chance—and his chances had been pretty meager, previously. Catherine's time had been taken up by Charlie and Rick—and Ben had fallen back on Gertrude's company. It seemed all wrong, to me. Ben was so utterly unattractive that he should have been more than satisfied with a girl like Gertrude. But, no—he had to want Catherine, like all the others—and of course his chances were just simply nil.

I heard Father calling me from the house, and I excused myself and left them. They hardly noticed my going. They had Charlie on a platter in their midst, and were looking at him from every angle.

By the time I got to the house, Father had forgotten what he wanted, so I told him to sit down in a deck chair, and stay absolutely quiet until it came to him.

I sneaked off, then, and went to the Potter house.

I did not know anything about jimmying windows, so I tried the back door, first—which saved me a lot of trouble, because it was open.

I went to the living room, and found the usual secretary—but this one was closed, although fortunately, it was not locked. I had to burrow for the ink, but I found it eventually, dipped my dandelion, labeled it, and returned it to my purse.

I left the house with a buoyant feeling that sleuthing was easy.

I went to Charlie's place, next. The door was open there, too, and when I got to the living room, I found that there were two desks, neither of which seemed to have any ink.

I made a rather panicky search, and was distinctly nervous and out of breath when I finally tracked the ink down in the pantry, beside the sugar canister.

I made a hurried job of my dipping, and flew out the back door—practically into Father's arms.

He tried looking stern, and said, "What are you doing, Lissa? I saw you sneaking into that other house, and this one, too—and they're all over on the tennis court. There's such a thing as trespass, you know."

I took his arm, and steered him toward home. "And suppose they sent me to their houses on a couple of errands?" I suggested.

"I wouldn't suppose anything so damn' silly. Ever since I've known you," he said bitterly, "you've had people running your errands— but it's never been the other way around."

"Harsh words, Papa," I said cheerfully.

He suddenly turned to me, a new idea obviously dawning on him.

"Was it—you know—the dandelions?" he asked, in the tone of a conspirator.

I nodded.

"Get anything to match?"

"I don't know, yet."

"Hmm." He walked on for a while in silence. "Oh," he said abruptly, after a while, "I remember, now, what I wanted you for. That ass, Frobisher, wants to know which one of the maids plays solitaire. He says there's a pack of cards up in their room in the attic, and every day it's laid out for solitaire. Seems to me the poor twirp has asked all the sensible questions he can think of—and now he's just asking anything that comes into his head, to keep his hand in."

"But, wait a minute," I said slowly. "That's not so senseless, Father. The maids use that small room and lavatory next to the kitchen. They never use that room upstairs—and they go home every night!"

CHAPTER 10

FATHER SAID, "Hmm. Let's go up to the attic now, and investigate."

We went in the side door and started up the back stairs. "Is the search over?" I whispered.

He nodded. "Went through the blasted house like a cyclone — and never found a thing. Because there probably isn't anything to find."

On the second-floor landing I made him stop and wait while I opened the door into the main hall and went swiftly along to my bedroom. I hid the bagful of dandelions under the pillow on my bed, and flew back again.

The attic had been finished and divided into five rooms and a bathroom. There were three small storage rooms, a small bedroom and a rather large bedroom. This last—the only one that was furnished—was quite a pleasant room, with windows on two sides, full-sized twin beds, two bureaus, two easy chairs, two straight chairs and two plain tables of a fair size. We found that one of these tables had a pack of cards on it, laid out in a game of solitaire. I walked over for a closer look, and noticed that there was a move to be made in the game.

"It's obvious," I said to Father, feeling rather clever, "that the person who was playing this game was interrupted suddenly."

Father was unimpressed. "Interrupted, anyway," he conceded.

"No," I insisted, "interrupted suddenly. Something put the game right out of his mind. Otherwise, I'm sure he'd have put that nine of spades on the red ten before he got up and left the game. The nine of spades was taken from the top of the pack—it's the next card to be played, and there's an obvious place for it. And yet it was just dropped onto the table—and not onto the discard, mind you."

Father looked at me and said jealously, "Don't strain your brain, Lissa—it always was the weakest part of your anatomy. Grace and Dora probably don't speak to each other, and one of them comes up here to rest. She's playing cards, and suddenly hears your mother calling—in that certain voice of hers—so she drops everything, and runs."

"Suppose you leave the surmising to me, Father," I said kindly. "You see, I observe things before making silly guesses about them. In the first place, Dora and Grace are as thick as thieves, and talk together all the time. In the second place, you couldn't bribe either one of them to come near the attic. The size of the house, and the fact that it's old, insures the attic being haunted—to their minds. They won't even do any cleaning up here. But the thing that really throws your whole idea on the dust heap is that no living maid will jump up to answer you in a hurry when you call. I believe the union says wait five minutes by the clock before answering."

I could see that Father had lost the thread after my first few words, so he merely said irritably, "I wish you wouldn't talk so much. If you have another idea, let's hear it—and for God's sake keep it down to words of one syllable."

"All right, listen then." I began to feel a bit like Timothy Frobisher, and I believe, in the enthusiasm of the moment, I even raised my voice a little higher. "These cards have been in this position for some time, because they're dusty."

"Your mother'll get somebody for that."

"Don't interrupt," I said impatiently. "Mother and I cleaned this room the day we got here—because neither Dora nor Grace would. We haven't been up here since, and I'm sure the maids haven't, either. And I remember those cards. They were in the drawer of the table, and I took them out when I dusted the drawer. I forgot to put them back again, and I noticed them lying on the table when we left the room, but I was too tired to go back and put them in the drawer again."

"Maybe *you* left them laid out like that," he suggested brightly.

"There's no doubt," I said, in exasperation, "about which side of the house my weak brain came from."

I started on a slow inspection of the room, and felt vaguely sorry that I didn't have a magnifying glass with me. Father sat on the end of one of the beds and tried to look scornful instead of jealous.

"Why don't you open up the old suitcase?" he said presently. "Might find a hand in it, or a couple of ears or something, and then you could have a swell time telling me that they'd been cut off a tall ex-paperhanger, with a decided limp, who was in the habit of beating his wife."

"What suitcase?"

"The one in the corner."

It was a man's case, well worn and nondescript, and I looked at it with sharply rising interest.

"Father—that's not one of ours!" He got up off the bed in a hurry, and we hauled the thing into the middle of the room.

We tried long and earnestly to open it, but the lock would not give, and before we could form any other plans we heard the dinner gong.

"We'll have to go," Father said regretfully. "Dinner is one meal your mother won't have held up. Of course we ought to turn this bag straight over to the police—but, as a matter of fact, I have a bunch of old keys downstairs, and if we get a chance, after dinner, we can slip up here again and see if one of them will fit. We can let the police have their whack after we're through with it."

We went downstairs together, secure in perfectly understood, but unspoken, agreement that Mother was not to be told anything. We knew quite well that Mother would never countenance withholding evidence from the police.

She wanted to know what we had been doing in the attic, and Father explained, too carelessly, that he was trying to track down a leak in the roof in one of the storage rooms.

Mother asked, rather acidly, how he could tell, when there had been no rain.

"An ounce of prevention," Father told her airily, "is worth a pound of care."

She gave up, then, and started to talk bridge. They promptly got into an argument that lasted through dinner and coffee in the library.

Father was so excited that I knew he had forgotten all about the suitcase, and I had to nudge him three times before he turned on me and bellowed, "What the devil are you prodding at me for?"

I tried to kill him with a look, and said sweetly, "Mother's quite right about that hand, so why argue? Anyway, I want you to get that bunch of keys you have and see if you can open a suitcase for me—it's jammed." I felt very clever about that.

I was able to tell the truth without rousing Mother's suspicions.

Father rounded up all his stray keys, and we crept up to the attic again.

He began to fumble with the lock of the suitcase, and after I had watched him for a while I was struck by a sudden thought.

"Father!"

He grunted, and tried another key.

"Father, listen. We've put our fingerprints all over that bag, and we'll have to wipe them off so that we won't get into trouble—and maybe we'll be wiping off fingerprints that are vitally important to the investigation."

Father's crimes never weighed very heavily on him. "They had the run of the house," he said, shrugging. "If they overlooked important fingerprints, they don't deserve to get them."

He began to get very impatient with the lock, which still refused to budge, and after he had tried the last key he threw the bunch down in a fury. "Not a damn' one of them fits the blasted lock."

"Here," I said, taking the keys, "let me try."

The second key I put into the lock worked easily, and the bag fell open. Father and I bumped heads as we both tried to look in at the same time.

It was very disappointing, though—merely a neatly packed assortment of men's haberdashery. Four shirts, three sets of underwear, six pairs of socks, a white silk scarf and a pair of gloves—and that was all.

We both felt distinctly let down. I don't know exactly what we had expected to find—but after Father's talk of human ears, and things, the gents' furnishings seemed very tame and flat.

We closed the bag again, and wiped it carefully to get rid of the fingerprints. Then we gave one last look at the room, and went off in search of Timothy Frobisher. It appeared, however, that our favorite investigator had departed to have his dinner. Father and I were almost annoyed about it. We were so used to Timothy that he was getting to be like a familiar piece of furniture.

"That's the trouble with these fellas," Father complained. "Always underfoot when you don't want them. Raise holy hell if you pass a red light, but just can't be annoyed with a piece of vital evidence in a murder case."

"The man needs nourishment, like anyone else," I said mildly. "Listen—let's try and get a sample of Tony's ink—I have all the others. Only I don't quite know how we're going to do it."

Father cheered up at once. "If he's out, we can take over a bunch of keys and try them on the back door."

"He's in," I said. "Look."

Tony was clearly visible in his dinette. He was reading the paper, and there was a meal of what appeared to be sardines and a bottle of beer on the table in front of him.

Father studied the situation, and then asked in a businesslike voice. "Is there any sort of a servant in the place?"

"I guess not. Edith Drucker says he has a maid who comes in the morning and cleans up. He probably cooks everything himself—he never liked anybody's cooking but his own."

"Well, of course," said Father, with heavy sarcasm, "it's important to have the right cook for canned sardines and beer."

I giggled, and he went on importantly, "I have an idea. We'll sneak over and try the front and back doors. If one of 'em is open, you stay there and I'll go around to the other and knock. When Tony comes, I'll get into an argument with him while you dash in and test the ink."

"That's brilliant," I said admiringly. I went and got a dandelion and a piece of blotting paper and we set out.

Tony's back door was open, so I stayed there while Father went around to the front. He presently gave three long peals on the doorbell, and I heard Tony push his chair back and walk through to the front of the house.

I slipped through the door, and as I made for the living room, I heard Father say loudly, "Tony, come out here on the lawn for a minute, will you? I want to show you something."

Tony went out, and I began a frantic search of the living room, but there simply wasn't any ink there.

I flew around the entire lower floor, without result, and at last I raced up the stairs. I could hear Father bellowing outside, and I had a fleeting, uneasy thought that he was carrying the thing too far.

I did not dare to put any lights on on the second floor, but after a bit of groping I found that Tony's bedroom was the only room that was furnished, and it was there, on a bureau, that I found the ink. It was too dark to see properly, but I managed to dip the dandelion, and taking care not to let it drip onto the floor, I wrapped it in the blotting paper and felt my way to the stairs.

I hurried down, but when I was only two steps from the bottom, I was caught, fairly and squarely. The front door opened, and Tony walked in.

He stood in the hall and stared at me, and I remained frozen to the second bottom step.

I saw his eyes drop to the blotting paper in my hand, and I looked down at it hastily. The beastly dandelion was sticking out beyond the edge of the blotter, oozing inky tears.

I looked at Tony, and was surprised to see that he was suddenly in a towering rage.

He said nastily, "So you're going to try the blue dandelion gag."

CHAPTER 11

MY EYES WIDENED, and I drew a quick, sharp breath. "Tony, what do you mean? What do you know about the blue dandelion?"

He was not even listening. He caught my arm in a viselike grip, pulled me down the last two steps and propelled me to the door.

"Have you any interest in the world beyond your own personal affairs?" he asked, still in a cold fury. "Anyone would suppose that a murder in your own house would have given you something else to think about—but with you, it's yourself in the headlines, always."

I thought he'd release me on his doorstep, or throw me out into the night, but without relaxing his hold he started to walk me home.

I noticed, with acute embarrassment, that there were a group of people sitting in deck chairs, on the Drucker front lawn.

"Tony, please—"

"What I can't make out," he interrupted rudely, "is why you should think I have the means of making a dandelion blue. Silly, stupid sort of reasoning—it would be too inconvenient at my house."

I tried to pull my arm away, but I might as well have struggled with an ape. Tony was strong—and when he got mad, he got mad.

"Really," I said, with as much dignity as I could muster, while being run across the garden, "you've been doing a lot of talking, but it might as well be Chinese. I wish you'd tell me what you know about the dandelion. It's—it's *important*."

"Not to me," Tony said in an ugly voice. He pushed me up the steps to our veranda, and rang the bell.

"We leave it open," I said meekly. "You needn't ring."

He rang again—twice.

Mother opened the door, and as soon as I saw her face I knew that she was angry—although a casual observer would not have known. You had to know Mother well to read her emotions.

As soon as she saw Tony, her eyebrows moved up and her eyes frosted over.

"Mrs. Vickers," Tony said formally, "will you be kind enough to keep your daughter out of my house, and off my premises entirely?"

"You appear to me to be quite capable of dealing with your ex-wives yourself," Mother snapped, and shut the door in our faces with a firm click.

It was too much for me. I burst into hysterical laughter.

Tony released his grip on my arm, and I rubbed it to bring back the circulation. "Thanks," I said. "I thought you were going to hang on to it until you broke it."

He moved back a step and looked me over, coldly, from head to foot.

"Your mother," he said distinctly, "is the only member of your family who is not cracked." He turned away, and walked rapidly off into the darkness.

I called after him anxiously, for I was desperate to find out what he knew, but he would not answer.

I sighed, and laid my hand on the doorknob just as Father emerged quietly from a clump of bushes.

"He was mad, eh?"

"He was furious," I said. "What on earth did you say to him?"

"Well—I hadn't planned an argument in advance, and when I got him outside, my mind seemed to go blank."

"Normal condition," I said impatiently. "Go on—what happened?"

"I had to think quickly, and the only thing that came to me was to pretend that I was drunk—so I did."

I had opened the front door, but I closed it quickly again. "What!" I whispered sharply.

"Certainly. Y'know, Lissa, the stage lost a great actor when my father pushed me into business. I don't think I'm showing prejudice when I say that that was a really outstanding bit of acting."

"It stood out all right," I agreed bitterly. "Do you realize that you've disgraced us in this neighborhood? There was a group of people watching you being drunk on Tony's front lawn—and the same group saw him run me out of his house. How do you think that looks ?"

"Those miserable cottagers," said Father, cheerfully snapping his fingers, "can hardly expect to understand the actions of the gentry."

I couldn't help laughing, but I said, "If you had to put on a drunken act, you could at least have carried on until I got out of the house."

"I did. The fella simply turned tail, suddenly, and said he was going to telephone Mrs. Vickers. And I don't mind telling you that I was damn' glad you were still there to turn his mind to something else."

The front door opened suddenly, and Mother stood there, with the light from the hall behind her, and her eyes glittering dangerously. "Come in at once, both of you," she said briefly.

We obeyed instantly. Mother, in that mood, is always to be obeyed quickly and quietly, for the best interest of all concerned.

She closed the door behind us and then faced us in the hall. "Now listen. I don't know where you two have been, or what you've been doing—except that Lissa has been teasing Tony Herridge. But I want you to understand this—that you're going to stay here and behave yourselves. We're in a decidedly unpleasant position, and I've been bothered all day with reporters and policemen and questions. And every time they wanted to question either one of you, you were mysteriously absent. Now I insist that you stay here and conduct yourselves quietly—or you may end up in jail."

Father and I nodded solemnly, and the three of us were suddenly diverted by a slight, dry cough.

We turned around, and saw that Detective Sergeant Frobisher was standing just inside the drawing room, apparently admiring a portrait of Father's grandfather.

Mother clicked her tongue in annoyance, and said under her breath, "He's been listening, of course. Anyway, he wants to question you both—you'd better go and see about it."

Father and I went into the drawing room, and Timothy started to question us automatically. But the first three or four questions were ones we'd heard before, so we stopped him, and told him about the suitcase.

He seemed pleased and excited. "I thought it belonged to one of the maids," he said, making for the attic stairs, while Father and I trotted along behind. "I tried to open it, but it was locked, and it seemed so light that I supposed it was empty."

"No clue, however seemingly trivial, should be overlooked in a case like this," Father said. "As a matter of fact, there isn't much in it—"

I kicked him sharply, and looked fearfully ahead at Timothy, who, luckily, seemed not to have heard.

We switched on the light in the attic room, and Frobisher bent over the suitcase. He could not open it, of course, and Father said casually, "I have a bunch of keys around somewhere—maybe one of them will fit. I'll go and get them."

I knew quite well that the keys were still in his pocket, and to my horror I heard him pretend to walk down the stairs. I inwardly cursed his native laziness, and the silly idea he's always had that he can do any sort of acting, and raised my voice loudly to Frobisher, to drawn out the artificial sounds coming from the landing outside.

I held forth on my ideas concerning the game of solitaire, and pointed out the dust on the cards.

In a little area of quiet, that was supposed to represent Father's arrival on the floor below and his search for the keys, Timothy said that he had observed the dust and the position of the nine of spades. He made some further remark, which was drowned out by Father's presentation of a man coming up the stairs. He put his soul and all his art into it, and by the time he was supposed to have reached the top, he was stamping so loudly that I feared for the ceiling below.

Frobisher gave him an odd look as he pounded into the room, but Father didn't notice. He was beaming with pleasure at his cleverness. "Found them," he said, handing over the keys. "Maybe you'd better let Lissa try it—she's clever with keys."

Frobisher took the bunch and opened the case promptly, while I scowled at Father over his bent head. He turned the contents over thoughtfully, and then straightened up and stood looking at them, while Father and I peered over his shoulders.

"I presume," he said at last, "that these are the clothes belonging to Mr. Carr. It looks as though he had been playing solitaire up here and was interrupted—probably by his murderer—who proceeded to entice him down to the cellar and shoot him."

Father and I made no comment, and he stood musing for a while longer.

"But it's curious," Frobisher said presently. "The contents of that case—"

He gave himself a little shake, and went into action. The care that he took, to wrap a handkerchief around the handle, and to avoid touching any part of the bag, seemed downright pathetic to me. He carried the thing off and muttered as he went, "Must get the clothes identified."

Father and I looked at each other. "What did he mean by saying the contents were most curious?" I asked.

Father yawned. "Let's hit the hay. We can figure it out in the morning."

We went down to the second floor, and found Mother in the hall. "You two had better go to bed," she said curtly. "At least I'll know where you are for a few hours. They're all gone now, anyway."

I kissed them both, and went along to my bedroom, after promising to lock the door.

I was half undressed when I remembered the dandelion I had dipped in Tony's ink. The fact was that I had lost it. I could not remember where I had put it down—or whether I had put it down at all. I was furious at my carelessness, for, though the dandelion had looked as hopeless as all the others, I had still a faint hope that it would turn a bright blue.

I pulled the purse out from under my pillow and arranged the other dandelions, complete with labels, on my desk. I stood and looked at them admiringly for a while, but I felt that I simply had to have Tony's specimen to make it complete.

It occurred to me that I might have dropped it downstairs some-where. I distinctly remembered having it when I came in, and I de-cided to go down and look for it before the maids swept it away in the morning.

I pulled on a negligee, kicked into a pair of slippers and went out into the hall. It was faintly illuminated by the night light that Mother always had burning there, and I went on down the stairs with nothing on my mind but the missing dandelion.

The lower hall was in complete darkness, and I hesitated, look-ing over my shoulder uneasily, and suddenly conscious of the still-ness and space, and of the fact that my parents were sleeping behind a locked door some distance away. There was no one else in the house, either—no one who had any business there.

I gripped the newel post in a mild panic, and silently cursed the false courage that had taken me out of my room when I should be safely in bed, with the door locked. I had no right to be interfering with the police.

Withholding evidence was what it amounted to. I made up my mind to tell Timothy everything in the morning and just hope that he would not put me in jail.

My eyes had become more accustomed to the darkness, and I recognized the dim height of the old grandfather clock and the low sweep of the console with the round mirror above it. My panic died away, and I decided to return to my room and let Timothy worry about the dandelion.

In the instant before I turned around, I glanced across to the drawing room—and froze into terrified immobility.

I distinctly saw a dark form bending over one of the chairs.

CHAPTER 12

I WAS afraid to move. I wanted to go flying up the stairs to my par-ents, but I had a vague idea that the thing had not heard me come down, and that if I made any sort of move it would look up and come after me so swiftly that I would not be able to get away.

I huddled against the newel post and watched it straighten up and move soundlessly in the direction of the library, where it be-came lost in the shadows.

I had a sudden wild fear that it knew all about me, and was qui-etly working its way around to me in the darkness.

I opened my mouth and yelled—and began to stumble madly up the stairs.

By the time I got to the top, Mother and Father had come out of their room, and they both clutched at me and started talking together.

"Phone the police!" I babbled. "There's something down there— some awful thing."

Mother led me back into her room and made me sit down, but when she had heard the whole story she decided against getting the police.

"You were obviously in a highly nervous state when you got downstairs, and it's very easy to imagine anything as vague as a dark shape in that condition. You don't even know whether it was a man or a woman, you see. I think you'd better go to bed and take a couple of aspirins. I warned you about conducting yourself quietly and leaving everything to the police—and you see how much better it would have been if you had listened to me."

"Quite right, Janice," Father said virtuously. "Think I'd better take a look around downstairs?"

"Yes," Mother decided. "Turn on the lights, and just make sure there's no one there."

I went with him, of course—he would have been scared to death to go alone—and we searched the lower floor. There was no one there, and nothing seemed to be out of place, but we carefully locked the cellar door. We both knew that nothing would have induced us to extend our search to the cellar, but we did not put it into words.

Just as we were ready to go upstairs again we discovered that the side door was slightly ajar. It had an ordinary spring lock, and had only to be closed firmly for the lock to catch. Father closed it, and we assured each other comfortably that one of the maids had neglected to pull it to after her.

We reported everything in order to Mother, and I went off to bed for the second time.

I did not go to sleep at once, though. I tossed around for a while, fretting over the fact that I had not investigated that chair in the drawing room, over which the thing had been bending. I drowsed off at last, soothed by a determination to see to it early in the morning, and secure in the knowledge that my door was locked.

I felt much more cheerful, and a good deal braver, the next morning—so much so, that I changed my mind again, and determined once more not to tell Detective Sergeant Frobisher about the dandelions.

I got up early, and made a hurried search for the one I had lost, but I could not find it anywhere, so I gave it up, and went to the chair in the drawing room.

I drew a blank there, too. The space around the cushion yielded two pencils and a match folder containing three matches, and though I wrapped them carefully in a handkerchief, I could not feel that they really meant anything.

Special Prosecutor Albert Hahn came to question me about the previous night's alarm at that point, so I kindly showed him the pencils and the match folder. He cut them dead, and concentrated on me, so I folded them in the handkerchief again. When he had finished with me, I took them upstairs and put them with my dandelions. I felt that they had probably been lying in that chair for at least five years—but I did not want to overlook anything.

After breakfast Father took me aside and whispered to me that poor Charlie had been shot five times, directly in the face, with a .22-caliber revolver.

"They've searched high and low for the weapon, but they can't find it. They've been through those cottages, and I think they're starting on the grounds now."

"But five times!" I said, and shivered. "Why five times? And how is it we didn't hear the shots ?"

"I think we did," Father said thoughtfully, "or, I did. Remember we went to bed early, and you were reading downstairs. I was still awake, and I thought I heard a car backfire several times. Mother woke up, and wanted to know what the noise was, and I told her it was a car. But you were downstairs—didn't you hear anything?"

I shook my head. "I was deep in a book, and sounds don't register much with me when I'm really absorbed. Probably my mind automatically filed those shots away as a car backfiring. What time was it, when you heard it?"

"Quite some time after we had come upstairs—it must have been after midnight, because I had only just dozed off when you came up and told us about the coal being shoveled in the cellar."

I asked him if he had seen my dandelion anywhere, and he got into quite a temper about my losing it. "All that ruckus last night for nothing," he said peevishly. "Why the devil can't you hang on to your things?"

I soothed him by promising to get another sample without de-lay. "And this time you won't have to be drunk on the front lawn. I'll make sure that Tony is out before I go."

"Maybe he's out now," Father suggested, cheering up. "Let's go and see."

We went on out, and as we were crossing through the garden, we saw Mrs. Potter mounting the steps to our veranda.

"Just in time," I whispered. "She'll be Mother's cross now."

We slid our way behind some shrubbery, and skulked to the Herridge back yard.

"All this is probably wasted time," I told Father. "Tony seems to know all about the blue-dandelion business—and, from the way he talked, I don't believe he has anything to do with it."

"No clue, however small—"

"All right," I said hastily.

The doors of the garage were standing open, and we went over and found that Tony's car was not there.

"Golfing at the club," Father decided. "Now's your chance."

I picked a healthy-looking dandelion from the grass, and we sidled up to the back door and found that it was open.

"You wait out here," I whispered, "and if you see him coming, whistle. And make it loud."

He nodded and walked off unconcernedly around the house. In fact, his unconcern was so obvious that I thought he looked highly suspicious.

As I opened the door, I caught a glimpse of Edith Drucker peer-ing through her dinette window at me. I waved nonchalantly, and she snapped back the curtain and disappeared.

I slipped inside the door and closed it after me, feeling rather clever.

It was unfortunate that Edith should have seen me walking into the house of my divorced husband, alone and unaccompanied—but I was sure that it would have made things worse if I had pre-tended not to see her. My friendly and unembarrassed salute would at least have her puzzled.

I shook her from my mind, and started to search the lower floor. It had occurred to me that Tony might have more than one bottle of ink, and if he did, I meant to find it.

It did not take me long to finish up downstairs—there was not much furniture, and no ink at all.

I went upstairs, glanced into the two empty bedrooms and the bathroom, and then prepared to concentrate on Tony's room. The bottle of ink was still standing on the bureau, but I could not give up the idea that there might be another bottle concealed somewhere, and I started to go through the bureau drawers. I had almost finished when a voice behind me sent my heart crashing against my ribs.

"You didn't do the drawer above very thoroughly."

I whirled around, gasping, to face Tony, who was sitting up in bed, with the pages of the Sunday paper spread around him. The bed was to the right of the door, its head partly concealed when the door was open, and I had walked straight to the bureau without looking around.

I stared at him with suddenly rising irritation. "Who's got your car?" I snapped.

"One thing at a time," he replied coolly. "I say you made a poor and inefficient search of the second bottom drawer."

"And I insist that I did it thoroughly," I said, trying to match his tone, while my heart pounded uncomfortably. "There isn't much in the drawer, anyway. You need new underwear—and I'd suggest white this time. Those gaudy colors are vulgar."

He suddenly heaved himself out of bed, shut and locked the door, dropped the key into his pajama pocket and got into bed again.

I laughed, and hoped it sounded more amused than I felt. I took a cigarette from a pack on his bedside table and broke two matches trying to light it while Tony watched me with his eyes like green ice. I muttered "damn" and he laughed nastily as I lit it with the third match and proceeded to burn my finger.

I inhaled deeply, moved over to an armchair by the window and asked almost steadily, "Am I to be kept here until Papa pays your mortgage or something?"

He ignored that, and said, "I designed these houses myself, you know—but they don't seem to be going very well. I'm living here to keep the occupancy list up."

I laughed almost naturally. "Serves you right—it's a fitting punishment. I always suspected that you were a punk architect—and these little eyesores prove it." I laughed again—heartily.

"You're the only one who doesn't like them," he said nastily, "so, of course, you must be right. As a matter of fact, they're too far from the station for such small houses."

I flicked ash onto the carpet. "Don't make excuses for them—it's a waste of breath. What I don't understand is how you manage to run such a handsome car, if this is the sort of piffle you produce."

"That's the second time you've brought my car into it," he said, diverted. "What's your interest?"

"Nothing—excepting that's how I knew you were out."

He looked me over, and said oddly, "So that's how you knew I was out."

"Well, I mean, I thought you were out, naturally, since your car wasn't in the garage. If it had been there, I wouldn't have come in, because I'd have known you were here."

"Very clever reasoning," he murmured, and whitewashed it with sarcasm. "Just a little too clever."

I sent a quick, restless look at the door, and asked, with as much ease as I could assume, "Do you always lock your visitors in—so that they'll stay more than two minutes?"

He gave me a long stare. "Most of my friendships are entirely pleasant—but I do have a certain amount of trouble in keeping the Vickers clan out of my house and off my front lawn. Trespassers irritate me, and I'm getting tired of it. And incidentally, Liz, it's time you grew up. A young and pretty girl can get away with the spoiled-baby—but it's downright ghastly in a woman of thirty-five. That gives you ten or eleven years to mend your ways—and God knows you'll need every day of it."

I was so furious that I could not trust myself to speak. In the silence I heard Father tramping around the house, and part of my anger was deflected to him. I found myself mentally calling him a goat for making so much noise.

I heard Tony lift the telephone and dial a number, and in another minute I was standing over him, sweating and horrified, as he said calmly, "That you, Tim? Will you come over here at once? I have bagged Lissa Vickers Herridge, alone, and single-handed."

CHAPTER 13

"TONY!" I CRIED. "You can't do that. Don't be such a lemon."

"Just be nonchalant," he said, and disappeared behind the rotogravure section of the newspaper.

"I'm going," I said wildly, and looked around for an exit—but it was quite hopeless. There was not even a drainpipe outside the two windows, and my dignity rejected a tussle with Tony for the key.

"Close the back door after you," he said, from behind the newspaper.

I returned to my chair in silence and concentrated furiously on ways of extricating myself from the mess.

About five minutes passed before the doorbell rang stridently. Tony dropped his newspaper, heaved himself out of bed and stuck his head out of the front window. "Come in the back door, Froby," he called. "It seems to be open, and come right upstairs."

I listened painfully to Timothy's mincing steps on the walk outside, and after a short space I could hear him in the room below. When he reached the stairs, my heart seemed to stop and turn over, for the sounds indicated, beyond any doubt, that he was not alone.

I knew it was Father, and I felt something like despair. I might have eeled out of the thing if left to myself—but with Father around, throwing spanners into the works with unerring aim—

Tony opened the door, and Frobisher and Father stepped into the room.

I brushed past Father and waved my dandelion in Timothy's face. "I'm so glad you've come," I said, putting a catch into my voice. "I came for my botany lesson—as usual, you know—and Tony—well, I think he must be feeling the heat. He dragged me up here, locked the door and telephoned to you."

"You can dispense with the botany lesson, Mrs. Herridge," said the detective sergeant briefly. "Sit down."

"I'll get a lawyer," Father announced belligerently.

"Be quiet, or leave the premises," Timothy directed, in a voice of ominous calm.

"I will not be quiet!" Father roared. "My daughter has told you that she has been brutally handled by this ape and damnably insulted—and you want me to be quiet!"

"I insist upon it," said Timothy, "or we shall have to put you out."

To my relief, Father subsided. There is nothing he dislikes more than being put out when a row appears to be blowing up.

"Now, Tony," Frobisher said quietly, "what's on your mind?"

Tony lit a cigarette, glanced at me carelessly, and said, "This girl had been doing a good deal of snooping on her own hook."

"I know that," said Timothy.

My eyes flew around to him, and I swallowed convulsively.

"Last night I thought she was merely grinding her own ax," Tony continued, "but this second unwarrantable intrusion into my house convinces me that she is doing her own investigating—aided and abetted by her father, who ought to know better—and probably withholding valuable information and evidence from the police."

I gave Father an automatic kick to keep him from exploding, and was utterly stunned to hear Timothy say unemotionally, "She is. She has in her possession a blue dandelion that she picked up at the foot of the murdered man."

I was so completely taken by surprise that my wits were plunged into confusion.

Father cleared his throat, rattled the change in his pockets and stared at his shoes, and I knew he was nearly as confounded as I was.

From the haphazard whirl of ideas in my mind one presently became a bit more clear than the others, and I found myself thinking, "Try flattery."

I took a step toward Timothy, and breathed, "How perfectly marvelous that you could have reasoned all that out. It's—why, it's like things you read. It's almost incredible!"

"Oh, stow it, Lissa, and dry up," said Tony irritably.

But I could see that I was making headway. A slight thaw had set in on Frobisher, and I took a long breath and continued, "I wanted to tell you about that dandelion—but you see, I forgot about it when you first asked me, and after that I simply did not have the courage. I—I guess I'm a little afraid of you. You know, I even went out and picked a bunch of dandelions to give you, to experiment with—"

"And you went out and experimented yourself, instead," Timothy put in.

"I know—I'm so terribly sorry. I've been such a coward about it all. But after I had told you I hadn't touched anything, I was frightened and ashamed when the blue dandelion fell out of my pocket that night, and I remembered about it. I should have confessed at once—I know that—but you seemed so—so cold, and stern."

Tony said, "Oh, for God's sake turn it off. You're overdoing it."

He turned to Timothy. "Don't let her take you in, Froby. She's tough."

Froby gave him a remote wintry stare and observed nasally, "It's quite clear that you're prejudiced, Tony. You're unduly bitter, just because you were once married to her."

I felt my heart ease off to a normal beat. Our detective was on my side—and I wouldn't get into trouble, after all.

Tony shook his head pityingly, and said in a voice of mild wonder, "It seemed like a thoroughly ham performance to me."

Timothy gave me a nice smile, and I smiled shyly back at him.

He dug out a blackened and withered dandelion from some inner compartment of his clothing, and showed it to me. "I found it on the floor, in your front hall. Can you explain it to me?"

"I think you're only testing me," I murmured, still shy. "I'll bet you have it all figured out. But I'll tell you every single thing."

He beamed at me, and then listened carefully, while I explained about the dandelions. He was particularly interested in Wilbur, Jr.'s remark about the other lady having let him dip dandelions in ink.

"We must find out who she is," he said thoughtfully. "I shall question the child.

"And now, Mrs. Herridge, I should like to see your collection of dandelions. I have seen them once, of course, but I want to go over them again."

He'd been prowling around my bedroom, then, and snooping into things. I swallowed my annoyance and gave him a bright smile.

Tony yawned. "You've been going through her bedroom while she's been going through mine. I wonder if anyone has been going through yours, Froby?"

"You'd better keep yourself out of this," said our detective sergeant frostily.

"I'd like nothing better," Tony said, in an injured voice, "but it seems to be impossible. My one modest wish, this morning, was to read the paper in peace—instead of which, all these people pour into my bedroom and stand around, ably proving to each other that they are still mentally in rompers."

"You ought to be up and out in the glorious sunshine," I said, enjoying myself. God knows, he had said the same thing to me often enough.

Frobisher touched my arm. "Suppose we go?"

I nodded, collected Father with a glance and we went chummily down the stairs together.

There were some rustic chairs and benches in Tony's back yard, and Timothy courteously seated Father and me on a bench and arranged his prominent bones in a chair beside us.

"Now," he said, "let us put all our cards on the table. I'll tell you what I know—and you tell me what you know."

It smelled slightly of fish to me. Why should he tell us anything?

And why should he display such a spirit of bonhomie to two people who had deliberately withheld evidence from him? I scented a trap, but there was nothing much that I could do about it, so I turned on the charm again. "Do tell me how you knew that I had found the blue dandelion at Charlie's feet."

"Well"—he shrugged self-consciously—"the floor was thick with dust, you know. Most of it had been walked on, and scuffed about, but there was a little area close to the armchair that had not been disturbed—except for a small spot close to the dead man's feet. It seemed to be the imprint of the tips of two fingers—looked very much as though someone had picked something up, in fact. You remember, I asked you carefully, if you had picked anything up."

I nodded, and clicked my tongue in shame.

"When I found the blue dandelion among your effects, I knew at once that it was what you had found in that room. When I saw you, later, with the bag of dandelions, I thought you were experimenting—and when I found the darkened one in the hall, I was sure of it."

"But I took those dandelions out with me when the search was going on," I said wonderingly.

Timothy gave a disdainful sniff. "That was the Hahn and Brewster search. I had done my own previously. And I shall continue to search until the case has been cleared up."

"But I've never seen you—you must do your searching very unobtrusively."

"Oh well—that's my business." He looked faintly embarrassed, and added, "I wouldn't have told you, except that I promised to lay my cards on the table. And now I want you to tell me *anything* and *everything* that you know."

"I guess there's only one thing I haven't told you," I said slowly. "It's about Tony. He said something to me about trying on the blue-dandelion gag—and I believe he knows just what that blue dandelion means."

He uncoiled himself from his chair with extraordinary rapidity, streaked across the lawn and disappeared into Tony's back door.

Almost at the same moment Tony, fully dressed, appeared from around the side of the house, and was followed by his car, which someone drove slowly into the garage. Tony waited until the engine was switched off, the door slammed, and a man in overalls came out, wiping his hands on a rag. "She's O.K. now, Mr. Herridge," he said.

Tony nodded to him, pocketed the keys and strolled over toward us. The man walked away.

I wanted to be on the scene when Frobisher questioned Tony about the dandelions, so I gave him a bright smile and said, "I never thought of that. The car was being repaired?"

"No," said Tony rudely, "he takes it out for me occasionally, to keep it from getting lonely. If you amateur sleuths would stop sometimes and consider all the possibilities, you wouldn't pull so many boners. My car and I don't invariably accompany each other when we go out."

"Come and sit down for a while, Tony," I suggested. I did not want him to go until Frobisher got back, but I was a little embarrassed at the two surprised stares I received from him and Father. I had to kick Father sharply.

"Why don't you two go on home and play in your own back yard?" Tony asked.

"Damn it, Lissa—" Father began explosively.

I nudged him, and at that moment, to my relief, Frobisher came tearing around the side of the house. He plunged straight through a small bush, without appearing to notice it, and pulled up in front of Tony.

"You might have told me," he panted.

"Told you what?"

"About the blue dandelion."

Tony glanced at me, and frowned.

"I don't believe it has any bearing on the matter."

"It's for me to judge. Tell me," Frobisher said eagerly.

Tony jammed his hands into his pockets and took a half turn about the garden. "I hate to do this," he muttered. "Keep it under your hat if you possibly can, Froby, will you?"

Timothy's face was bright pink. "Certainly, certainly," he cried, almost dancing up and down in his excitement.

"The blue dandelion was used by Catherine and Rick," Tony said reluctantly, "as a message of some sort. They would leave one in the tulip bed between their houses—one or other of them—and that night—unless I'm much mistaken—they would meet in the Vickers home."

CHAPTER 14

WE ALL stared at Tony, and then Father opened his mouth and roared, "Impossible! Utter rubbish! He's making it up!"

We transferred our stares to Father, and after a moment Frobisher asked mildly, "Why?"

"Eh?"

"Why is it utter rubbish?"

Father was clearly at a loss. I knew that he was merely incensed at the idea of any of the serfs using his house for a rendezvous.

He glared at the Drucker dog, who was sniffing at his trousers, and said finally, "The place was tightly locked up, and the police inspected it regularly." He looked hard at Frobisher. "At least they were supposed to."

Timothy shrugged. "According to your daughter's testimony, somebody must have entered the house at least three times."

Father frowned. "That was when we were there, ourselves. Somebody left a door open." He shoved at the dog who was still sniffing, and added irritably, "Confound the beast! Can't you call him off, Tony?"

"Cato!" Tony said sharply, and the dog abandoned Father's trousers reluctantly. He trotted over to Tony and slumped down onto the grass with his tongue hanging out.

Tony pulled his ears and said absently, "He's caught the local sleuthing fever."

"How do you know that Miss Reed and Mr. Rickey used the Vickers house for their rendezvous ?" Frobisher asked.

"I'm convinced of it, although I can't exactly prove it," Tony said slowly. "They'd come out of their homes, and start to stroll, casually, straight in that direction. I never actually saw them entering the place, because the rhododendrons blocked the view."

"Did you see them put a blue dandelion in the tulip bed at any time?"

Tony nodded. "When I was dressing in the morning, I could see them from my window. Time and again, either Catherine or Rick would walk casually to the flower bed, admire the flowers for a while and then drop something in among them. I got so curious about it, at last, that one morning, after Catherine had been there, I went over and had a look. It was at the end of May. The tulips were finished, and they'd put some pansies in the bed—and though it wasn't very obvious, I finally spotted the blue dandelion. And that night I noticed both Catherine and Rick making solo strolls toward the Vickers house. I didn't pay much attention after that—the whole thing seemed a bit unsavory. But I haven't noticed them at the flower bed, or making their casual strolls, since the Vickers opened up their house."

Frobisher suddenly stiffened, turned on his heel and streaked across the lawn. He crashed through a bush and disappeared around the side of the house. The dog, Cato, scrambled to his feet, and with a hysterical bark fled after him.

Tony swore under his breath and muttered, "First he injures my lilac and then damages the forsythia."

Mack Brewster appeared suddenly. "Any of you seen the detective sergeant?" he growled.

We advised him to follow the sounds of happy canine yelping that came from the front of the house, and he loped off. "He's avoiding me," I heard him say angrily. "I'll chop his flapping ears off when I get him."

I wanted to follow him, but I heard Mother calling from the house, "Hammond! Lissa!" and from the sound of her voice I figured we'd better go home.

Tony said "Ha! Are you two going to catch it for playing with the dirty little boys in the tenements."

"No," said Father, "she permits us a certain amount of social-service work," and chuckled all the way home at what he called his stinging wit.

We found that Mother had enticed us straight into an ambush of reporters, and we had to fight until Father was hoarse to get them out of the house. At that, we mislaid one and left him in. He had lunch with us.

He simply sat down at the table, and asked Dora to lay another place. We told him to leave, and he said he'd like to oblige us but he was terrible hungry, and as a matter of fact all he wanted to talk about was Mother's antique furniture.

Mother fell for it, and though Father and I made frantic signs to her not to be a sucker, she chatted amiably with him throughout the meal, and ignored us.

After lunch he tried to edge the conversation around to the murder—so Mother put him out at once.

Mother and Father were visiting friends for the afternoon and evening, and since it was the maids' afternoon off, they tried to persuade me to go with them. They said they did not want to leave me alone in the house.

I laughed at them. "Don't worry," I said. "What with the reporters, Froby, Brewster and Hahn—to say nothing of the cop, Moley— I can hardly be alone."

Mother fidgeted a bit, and asked, "What about your dinner?"

"I'm learning all the time," I told her equably. "I shall sniff at the various kitchen windows of the cottages, and when I find the smell I want, I'll simply walk in, sit down at the table and tell them I've come to discuss their lovely furniture."

Mother actually blushed. "The young man knew quite a lot about antiques," she said defensively. Father and I laughed at her.

They went off at three o'clock, and the reporters disappeared at about the same time. There was no sign of Brewster, Hahn or even my pal Frobisher—and it must have been Moley's day off, too.

The house and grounds seemed to be deserted, and I felt quite cheered. I changed my dress, prettied up a bit and sauntered out into the garden.

Rick joined me almost at once. He was carefully dressed in careless flannels, and was as handsome, amusing and fascinating as ever. He said he'd been hoping to find me alone for some time.

I thought perhaps he had some special information for me — but it wasn't that.

He declared he'd been wanting more of my company, and the way he put it would have made one suppose that his life was made possible only by the occasional glimpses he got of me. He did it well, too. I came to the conclusion that he'd had a quarrel with Catherine.

We hung around in the garden for quite a while, and I found that I was enjoying myself. Rick could be very amusing if he wanted to. Once I caught Catherine looking out of her kitchen window at us, and I felt quite guilty.

Ben Amherst wandered over after a while and smoked a cigarette with us. He didn't stay long. He kept glancing at the Reed house, and at last he stamped out his cigarette, said a brief farewell and made straight for the Reeds' back door.

He went in without knocking and Rick laughed. "Poor Ben— he's crazy about Catherine."

"Why the sympathy?" I asked. "Hasn't he a chance?"

Rick very nearly blushed. He snapped off a lilac leaf, crushed it in his fingers and said rather formally, "I don't really know."

He left soon afterward, saying he had an engagement to play bridge at his club. But he made a date with me for the following night.

I watched him idly as he disappeared inside his back door, and then wondered what I'd do with the rest of the day.

Gertrude Potter came out and dragged a lawn mower from their garage, and her mother presently appeared with a trowel and a pair of gardening gloves.

The Drucker two-door sedan rolled into the Drucker driveway, and Wilburs Sr. and Jr. and Edith unpacked themselves from it. The two big Druckers were bickering and the little one was whining.

I yawned, and turned back toward the house. I heard Mrs. Reed call a greeting to the Potters—and then, quite clearly, I heard Tony swearing. I knew it was Tony—I could recognize his oaths a mile off.

I altered my course and made for his yard. He was working on his car, and I reflected that it was just exactly like him. He would have his car repaired, pay for it, look it over and then decide to undo everything, and do it properly, himself.

I stood and watched him, but he didn't notice me, because he had his head right inside the thing. But when I presently lit a cigarette, he pulled his head out and turned on me.

"Put that cigarette out!" he yelled. "What do you think you're doing? Do you want to blow us both to hell?"

I threw the cigarette away, and told him not to exaggerate.

"What are you standing around for?" he demanded irritably.

I moved off, feeling a trifle embarrassed, and he went on with his swearing.

I walked back to the house, and went around to the side door. Mother had insisted on keeping the front and back doors locked since the murder, but we had the spring lock on the side door set so that it would not catch during the day. Mother, herself, saw to it that it was locked at night.

As I approached the door, something glinted on the ground beside the step and half under it. I stooped and picked up a nail file—large and strong, and a bit rusted.

I took it in and put it on the kitchen table, thinking that perhaps it belonged to one of the maids.

It was very quiet in the house, and I felt a fleeting regret that I had not gone with Mother and Father, after all. I was distinctly nervous, and I felt a bit foolish, as I went around closing and locking all the doors and windows on the lower floor. I tried to tell myself that it looked as though a storm were blowing up.

I picked up a book and tried to read, but the closed windows made it hot and stuffy, and after a while I went up to my bedroom, where the windows were still open. I stretched out on the bed, and felt vastly more comfortable, but I could not concentrate on my book. I kept thinking about the dandelions—and how different the grayish, inked ones were from the bright blue of the original.

Presently I noticed that a bank of black clouds had piled up in the sky—and suddenly it was raining furiously, with vivid flashes of lightning and an almost constant crashing of thunder. The rain was not coming in on my side of the house, so I left my windows open and flew across to the bedrooms on the other side. It was pouring in there, and for several minutes I worked frantically in an effort to get all the windows closed before Mother's curtains and rugs were drenched.

When I had yanked the last window down, I rested my forehead against the pane and stood for a while, admiring the violence of the storm. It had grown quite dark, and several lights had sprung up in the row of small houses. Rick's dinette was lighted, and I could see parts of him sprawled in a chair, so he hadn't gone to his club, after all. The thunder was getting fainter, and as I stood there the rain slackened off sharply and almost ceased.

The view into Rick's dinette became a bit clearer, and I discarded abruptly a half-formed idea of going over and joining him. Rick had a visitor. The person, whoever it was, must have been about to leave, because, though I could see nothing beyond the hands, they were busy donning a pair of gloves.

The hands, complete with gloves, presently disappeared. Rick continued to sprawl in his chair—and I wondered a little at his discourtesy. The hands might have belonged to Catherine, of course—and I was pretty sure he had quarreled with Catherine—but it did not seem a sufficient excuse for his rudeness. I began to think that he might be drunk. His usually immaculate hair was ruffled and one lock hung untidily over his forehead. I was conscious of a faint feeling of distaste for him.

I went back to my room, stretched out on the bed and promptly fell asleep.

It was quite dark when I woke up. I yawned, stretched and made a wry face over the cigarette taste in my mouth. I decided to brush my teeth, and I presently pulled myself off the bed and went out into the hall.

I stopped and listened, and in the complete silence I distinctly heard the side door close.

CHAPTER 15

I DREW in my breath sharply, and switched on the upstairs hall light.

There was no further sound, and after a moment I leaned over the banisters and called shrilly, "Who's there?"

There was no answer, of course, and after a minute or two of pulling my courage about me I marched downstairs and flooded the lower floor with light. I searched briefly, to no purpose, and at last I went right out to the side door. It was locked, as I had left it earlier in the afternoon.

The cellarway was in black darkness, and I closed the door and turned my back on it, and looked up the stairs that led to the top of the house. There seemed to be a faint glow somewhere up above, and I remained rigid, staring up until my neck ached.

I tried to believe that the glow was coming from under the door that gave onto the upstairs hall, since I had left the light on up there, but I could not convince myself. I stood there, wondering wildly who was up in the attic, and what they were doing there.

The silence was broken abruptly by a long, strident ring of the front doorbell.

The bell, itself, was situated on a wall in the kitchen and was quite close to where I stood, and the sound was so loud and unexpected that I was completely demoralized. I flew out the side door and slammed it behind me.

I stood on the path for a moment, until I had recovered myself, and then I walked along the side of the house on tiptoe and peered around cautiously at the front door.

I drew a great breath of relief, and felt an inexplicable desire to giggle. It was Tony.

"How's the car this evening?" I called. "Better, I hope?"

Tony jumped this time, and stared hard in my general direction. "Where are you?" he asked. "I can't see you."

I came out from behind a rhododendron and sauntered toward

him. "Have you come to register a complaint, or is it just a social call?"

"Simple curiosity," he said, looking me up and down. "There has been a light on in your attic for some time— then, suddenly, the entire lower floor is illuminated, and the second floor remains in darkness. Are you still sleuthing? And if so, what are you trying to find that could be only in the attic or on the first floor?"

The attic light! My heart began to race again, and in an effort to try to keep calm, I said to Tony with false flippancy, "Do you spend a lot of your time keeping track of your neighbors' activities?"

He lost his temper, as usual, and said stiffly, "Certainly—very amusing pastime," and marched off into the darkness.

I did not want to be left alone—I wanted him to stay, even if it was only to quarrel with me, and I called after him desperately, "Tony! Come back—please!"

He made no reply, and shortly afterward I heard his car start up.

I mentally cursed him, and wondered why he'd come over at all. I didn't believe it was just curiosity.

I backed away from the house and looked up—and there was certainly a light shining from the same attic room in which we had found the suitcase. The second floor was dark except for the faint glow of the hall light that I had left on. The lower floor looked as though we were giving a party.

I walked slowly back toward the front door, making up my mind on the way to telephone Froby, or somebody, and leave the door wide open while I was doing it.

And then I remembered that all the doors were locked. I had slammed the side door after me, and had carefully released the spring lock earlier in the afternoon when I was barricading the lower floor.

I realized, with complete exasperation, that I had no keys with me—I hadn't even a handkerchief or a cigarette.

There was a light rain falling, and I was beginning to get pretty damp. I looked over at the cottages, and saw that the Drucker and Reed houses were lighted, and so was Rick's dinette. Tony's house and the Potter place were in total darkness.

I decided to go and ask Rick to help me. I could not see him through the window, from where I stood on the ground, but I supposed that either he or Ben was hanging around, since the light was on.

I plodded over the wet lawn, through mud and puddles, and

paused under the dinette window. I called Rick's name a couple of times, but the windows were closed, and the rain was making a steady patter so I slipped along to the back door and tried it. It was open, and I went in.

The kitchen was in darkness except for the light that shone from the dinette. I took a step in that direction, and then came a halt. Someone was moving about in the living room.

It definitely was not Rick's heavy tread, nor was it Ben's clumsy shamble. It sounded to me like a woman—and I turned on my heel and fled soundlessly.

I pulled up in the back yard, to get my breath, and murmured, "Phew! Far be it from me to walk in on the love interest."

I was drenched through by then, so I glanced along at the other cottages leisurely. The Reed house was ablaze with light, so I decided to go in there.

I had made two squashy steps when I saw the glow of a cigarette almost beside me.

I caught my breath sharply, and quavered, "Who is it?"

"What in the name of God are you up to now?" asked Tony's voice irritably. "I'm utterly damned if I can make you out."

It was no time to quarrel with him, so I said meekly, "I can't get back into the house. I came to ask Rick to help me—but I guess he's entertaining. I—I thought you'd gone off in your car."

"Why can't you get into the house?"

"It's locked," I said helplessly.

"Where are the keys?"

"Mother and Father have some of them, and the rest are inside the house," I explained, and waited for him to swear.

But he merely observed, "Very typical," and dropped his cigarette into a puddle.

We were standing on the edge of the driveway that ran between the Reed house and Rick's, and looking down the narrow space, I could see part of the Reed porch and their front steps.

It was mere chance that I was looking in that direction when Catherine, clearly visible in the light from the living room windows, hurried up the steps and let herself in the front door.

"So it was Catherine, in there," I reflected. "She must have patched it up with Rick."

I peered at Tony through the darkness, and saw that he was staring in the same direction.

"Did you see Catherine?" I asked.

He said "yes" rather absently, and added, half to himself, "She ought to relax, and skip Rick."

"Is he cutting you out?"

"Listen," said Tony, "your wit slays me—but there's a time and place for everything. I'm getting wet. Come on."

He started back toward our house, and I squished along beside him, with my hair dripping down my neck.

He had a key ring, and he tried various keys first on the side door, then the back and then the front—but none would fit. He had a brief try at the windows, although I assured him that I had carefully locked every one.

"We could ring the front doorbell," I said dispiritedly.

He looked at me coldly, and said, "Not so funny."

"I mean it, though. Somebody must be in the house. The attic light is on—I didn't put it on—and I distinctly heard the side door close when I was upstairs."

He backed away from the house without a word, and stared upward; then he returned slowly and said, "Why in hell didn't you tell me before?"

"You're so impatient, you won't wait for anything," I said crossly. "I didn't get around to it."

He considered for a moment. "We ought to get Froby."

"Why not Mack Brewster?"

"Because Froby wants to solve the case single-handed, and make Brewster and Hahn look silly."

"Then he ought to stick to the job," I declared, trying to wring out my hair. "He shouldn't go off home on his half holidays."

"Make no mistake," said Tony; "he's not resting. He has his nose to the ground somewhere."

"Let's whistle for him," I said. "Maybe he'll come loping up."

Tony ignored me, and began to walk purposefully toward the back of the house. I trotted along beside him.

He ripped the screen from a small pantry window, broke the glass, and after only one cuss word got it unlocked, and raised the sash.

"You can get through there," he said briefly.

"Oh no," I said, hanging back. "You go through."

"Not me. It isn't my house."

"Do you mean you want to put me in there and then walk off?"

He admitted it carelessly, and added, "I see too much of you as it is."

"Think again," I said shortly. "If you're not coming in, I'm going over to the Reeds' and phone the police."

"Oh, all right," he said resignedly. "But I don't believe there's anyone in the attic now. Whoever was there left the light on—but they wouldn't have stayed there all this time."

"Just the same—"

"Get through the window," he interrupted rudely. "It's too small for me. You can open the back door for me."

I agreed reluctantly, as there seemed to be no help for it, and he hoisted me up. He nearly dropped me when I told him to stop tickling, and requested me, in a voice of outrage, to save my clowning until it was wanted.

I dropped onto the floor of the pantry and flew wildly to the back door in a panic.

Tony walked in and made straight for the back stairs.

"Wait a minute," I said. "Don't you think we ought to phone Froby, or somebody, first and let them look?"

"No," said Tony shortly. "I'm going to look myself."

He started up the stairs, and I followed him, because I was afraid to be left alone. Our footsteps seemed noisy out of all proportion in the still house, and I kept looking nervously over my shoulder. I had a sort of nightmarish idea that there was a third set of footsteps keeping time with ours so that they could not be distinguished.

Tony walked into the attic room and stood by the door looking around. I crept close up behind him and peered fearfully through the crook of his elbow.

The room appeared to be exactly as before except for the light's being on.

Tony walked over to the clothes closet, yanked the door open and looked in. I took a couple of steps after him and then glanced down at the table on which the game of solitaire was still spread out.

There was something different about it. I stared, and then gave a little gasp. The obvious move had been made. The nine of spades was now reposing on the red ten.

CHAPTER 16

I LOOKED at the dusty cards but did not touch them. Whoever had been in the room had probably moved the nine of spades—and I did not think that the police had done it. Father might have, of course—it would be just like him—but I could soon settle that by asking him. I wondered a little why Froby and the others had left the cards lying there like that.

Tony closed the door of the closet, and I asked him if he had found anything.

"No," he said. "Nothing there but an old electric-light extension."

I let out a shout, and while he stared at me I pushed past him and flung the door open again. I knew the closet had been empty before—empty and clean. But now a length of electric cord with a plug at one end and a bulb on the other lay on the floor.

"The missing cellar illumination," I breathed reverently.

"Just call it the missing light," Tony advised. "You're wasting your breath, trying to impress me."

"We must phone Mack Brewster—or Albert Hahn," I said excitedly.

"What about Froby? He's out to clear this thing up by himself."

"Well—but I think the other two are in charge of it," I said doubtfully.

"Doesn't matter. We'll phone Froby."

He started off down the stairs, and I followed him.

He did the phoning himself—explaining to me that if he let me do it my tongue might slip when I gave the number and I might find myself talking to one of the prosecutors instead of to Froby.

Timothy was not at home, as it turned out, but his mother promised to send him along as soon as she could get in touch with him.

"I suppose I'll have to stay with you until he comes," Tony said resignedly. "Your parents should hire one of these women—fifty cents for the evening, I believe the charge is—to look after you when they go out."

I was just about to tell him to go off, and be damned, and send us a bill for twenty-five cents, because he wasn't in the top rank of the profession yet, when I had a brilliant thought.

I smiled at him nicely, and asked, "Won't you let me get you something to eat? I'm going to have my own supper now, anyway."

He gave me an odd look, and after a moment said politely, "Thank you. I'd appreciate that."

I nodded graciously. I felt confident that he would start by helping me and end up by doing it all himself—as he always had done when we were married. It was quite a weight off my mind, because I knew nothing about cooking, and I was getting pretty hungry.

"Will you come out to the kitchen and watch me while I prepare it?" I asked casually.

"I wouldn't miss it," he said earnestly, "for a hundred dollars. Is there a comfortable chair out there?"

I began to feel distinctly uneasy, and when we got to the kitchen, I looked at him anxiously and asked him what he'd have.

"Nothing fancy," he said airily. "I don't want you to fuss just for me. A small steak-and-kidney pie, perhaps, and a french pancake for dessert." He sat down on one of the kitchen chairs, and tipping it back against the wall, watched me lazily.

My idea seemed to be going sour. I walked into the pantry and stood looking at the shelves rather helplessly. I knew Mother avoided canned stuff as much as possible, and there was not so much as a Bismarck herring. I came out again, empty-handed.

Tony gave me a green-eyed look of sympathy and concern. "Not having any trouble, I hope?"

I kept my temper and said, "Oh no," but as I passed him on my way to the ice chest he went crashing to the floor, owing to the leg of his chair having got in the way of my foot. He made some statement in which only the word "bitch" was at all clear.

To my great relief, I found the remains of a cold chicken in the ice chest, and I hauled it out joyfully.

"Set the table, will you?" I said to Tony.

He resumed his seat on the chair but kept the four legs on the floor. "No," he said, "that's woman's work. Men don't do those things."

I started to make some coffee. "Then you weren't a man during the time you were married to me?"

He said, "No—I was a mice. But the next time I marry, it's going to be different. I shall start things off properly each morning by hauling my wife out of bed at six-thirty and giving her a smart slap in the face to go on with."

I found some cheese, pickles, jam, bread and butter, and put them on the table, along with the chicken.

"Isn't there any little thing that your status as a man would allow you to do?" I asked, foraging for cutlery and chinaware.

He got up from the chair, and taking the coffee percolator from the stove, deliberately emptied the entire contents into the sink. "I'll make the damn' coffee. I can't drink dishwater."

"How do you know it's dishwater, when you didn't even wait to taste it?"

"Two teaspoons of coffee to six cups of water," said Tony, "is the recipe for dishwater."

When his coffee was ready, we sat down at the table and ate like a couple of hungry wolves. And there was no doubt about that coffee—it was the best I had had since my divorce.

"When I marry again," I said, looking at him admiringly, "I certainly hope I get someone who cooks as well as you do."

"When *I* marry again," said Tony, busily buttering bread, "I want a blonde—a quiet, refined little woman who keeps the house in perfect order and knows her place."

"She'll have exactly two children—no more, no less," I supplied interestedly, "entertains charmingly, ancestors are all Mayflower, loves only fine things, and hasn't made a faux pas since it went out of style with her set after they left school."

"Oh hell!" said Tony. "I don't think I'll marry her, after all."

"Who is she?" I asked, snooping.

"Nobody. I was trying to make up an antonym for Lissa."

"Don't be bitter," I said reprovingly.

"The human flesh is so weak," he said, hacking away at the chicken. "I have to remind myself constantly not to get stuck with another of your ilk."

"What's so wrong with me?"

"You're a spoiled brat," he said promptly. "Whatever you want, you must have—and you must have it at once. Your only asset is your cheerfulness—and even that gets to be a pest at times. Everyone wants to gloom a bit occasionally."

I began absentmindedly to hum the "Volga Boat Song" while I thought this over, and in the middle of it the front doorbell rang.

We both jumped up and ran—but Tony beat me to the door, and ushered in D.S. T. Frobisher. He nodded to me, and then he and Tony went into a low-voiced conference and ignored me completely.

They started up the stairs after a while, and I followed along, muttering, "Only a woman. I guess I'll go and faint."

I edged into the attic room after them, and watched Frobisher clasp the electric extension to his bosom as though it were a long-lost brother. He and Tony had a few more words together, and then they turned toward the door again.

"Wait a minute!" I cried. "Didn't you notice the cards? Or did you move the nine yourself?"

Frobisher popped his head back around the door. "Don't, on any account, touch those cards. They have not been moved by anyone, and are not to be moved. They are there for a special reason."

He flew off again after Tony but a piece of the electric cord must have tripped him, because he fell all the way down the stairs—I heard him go. I shook my head and murmured, "Haste makes waste."

I looked at the cards again, and decided that if Froby wouldn't listen to me I'd have to tell Hahn or Brewster about it. After all, there might be a fingerprint on that nine of spades. Of course it might turn out to be Father's—I'd have to remember to ask him about it the minute he came in.

I glanced around the room, and thought longingly that I'd give my eyeteeth to find some vital clue that I could wave under the noses of Tony and Frobisher, and pay them out for slighting me.

I searched the room thoroughly, with that idea in mind, but all I found was a small piece of tin foil that might or might not have come from a chocolate bar.

I could not find anything else, so I took the tin foil downstairs and placed it carefully among my other clues. I hoped—though not very vigorously—that it would turn out to be the deciding factor in the case.

I went in search of Tony and Frobisher then, and was disconcerted and annoyed to find that they had disappeared. I searched and called—and even peered into the blackness of the cellar—but there was no answer and no sound. I hoped, piously, that Froby had hurt himself falling downstairs and that Tony had taken him to the hospital.

The doors and windows were still locked, and I figured that they were both too big to get through the broken pantry window, so that they would have to ring if they wanted to come back in—and I could admit them, or not, as I liked.

I went up to my bedroom, locked myself in and stretched out on the bed with a cigarette. I was not at ease, though. I kept thinking of all sorts of dark deeds that might be going on in the house, on the other side of my locked door.

I got up from the bed and wandered restlessly around the room, looking for my book, but I could not find it.

There was a small sitting room directly across the hall from my bedroom, and thinking I might find a book there, I cautiously opened my bedroom door, flew over to the sitting room and—determined to take no chances—locked the door behind me.

It was a bit of a blow to find that the only books the room contained were *Tom Swift in the Underground City of Gold* and *Things Every Young Girl Should Know.*

I sighed, and wandered over to the window.

The rain had stopped, so I opened the window and rested my arms on the sill. I was immediately conscious of the light in the attic cutting into the darkness above my head, and I regretted that I had not turned it off. There was something eerie about it, shining all by itself up there.

I glanced at my watch, and saw that it was ten minutes to ten— still pretty early. The Reed house was lighted from top to bottom; the Potter house in darkness. Rick still seemed to be sitting in a drunken stupor in his dinette, and the Drucker house showed one small light on the second floor. Tony's place was in darkness.

I yawned, and decided to read Tom Swift, since I probably knew all the things a young girl should.

I was just about to turn away from the window when the light in the attic went out.

CHAPTER 17

I DREW BACK into the room, and stood quite still, for a moment of horror—and then I flung myself at the door, and made sure that the lock was fast.

I retreated to the middle of the room and listened stupidly to my teeth banging together.

I pulled myself up, and decided grimly that the best thing to do was to make a run for it and get out of the house. I took a step toward the door—and heard someone coming down the attic stairs.

The sitting room was right beside the back stair well, and I could hear the footsteps clearly. They were quiet but quite distinct. They went all the way down the stairs and out to the side door—and I heard the door close after them. There was no mistaking the sound of that door closing— and I was never to hear it, afterward, without a faintly sickish feeling.

I clenched my teeth, to keep them from chattering, and turned back to the window. I crouched down by the sill and peered out—

and an instant later I saw a dark figure making its way rapidly in the direction of the cottages. It kept carefully within the shadows of the trees and shrubs, and I could not see it clearly at all, but I managed to keep track of it, and followed it with my eyes straight to the back door of the Reed house.

The Reed house was still brightly lighted—and I suddenly lost a great deal of my fear. There must be people there—it looked as though some sort of a party were going on—and I determined to go over and see what I could find out.

I unlocked the door and went out into the hall—and then I hesitated. I wanted, badly, to see if anything had been done in the attic—and the idea of going up there had me shaking with fright.

My nervousness yielded to my curiosity, and I turned about and ran up the stairs to the attic. I jerked on the electric switch and looked about me fearfully. Nothing seemed to be changed or out of place, though, and I was conscious of a faint disappointment.

I walked over and looked down at the solitaire game—and felt my eyes pop. The nine of spades had been taken off the red ten and returned to its original position.

I stared at the cards, and felt completely at a loss. What possible reason could anyone have for coming up and moving that nine of spades?

My teeth started to chatter again, and I felt a sudden loathing of the room and everything in it.

I backed out and ran quickly down the stairs and let myself out at the side door. I examined the lock, but it did not seem to have been tampered with in any way.

I knew that I had no keys with me, but nothing would have persuaded me to go back into that house again just then. And in any case the pantry window was still available. I shut the door firmly behind me and made for the Reed house.

I went around to the front door and rang the bell—avoiding the back door for no better reason than that it made me shudder.

Gertrude admitted me, with a nice smile, and as I walked into the hall Catherine came down the stairs. She greeted me without undue enthusiasm, and the three of us went into the living room.

The table from the dinette had been brought in and covered with a green cloth, and Edith, Wilbur, Sr. and Ben were seated around it, playing poker.

They gave me a mass welcome and urged me to sit in.

"Take Mother's hand for a while," Catherine suggested. "Maybe you can change her luck."

I slid into the chair indicated, and Gertrude and Catherine sat down, too. There was still another chair, and a small stack of chips left, which I took to be Mrs. Potter's place.

There was a smell of coffee from the kitchen, and I could hear Mammas Reed and Potter chatting amiably out there. I threw away a hand composed of king, nine, seven, four and three, in what looked to be about six different suits, and stood up abruptly.

"I'll go and say hello to your mother," I murmured, with a glance at Catherine.

She nodded, and I went out to the kitchen.

Mrs. Reed and Mrs. Potter were putting a supper together, and they greeted me in a friendly fashion.

"Did anyone just come in the back door?" I asked, feeling silly.

They looked at me blankly.

"I mean—I've been looking for Tony and the detective sergeant," I stammered, "and I believe they're together. I thought I saw someone come in the back door—and—well, I guess they're not here, though."

They spoke more or less together. Mrs. Reed said, "No, we haven't seen anyone," and Mrs. Potter declared that no one had come through the kitchen while they'd been working there.

I left it at that, and returned to the poker game.

Presently I had what seemed to me a clever idea. I looked around and said casually, "Too bad it's still raining so hard."

Catherine rose to it. She said, "But it isn't. It's perfectly dry now."

I mentally catalogued it as another clue, and stored it in my mind with a few dandelions of various colors, a piece of tin foil, two pencils, one match folder, something peculiar about a suitcase and the nine of spades and a red ten.

The two mammas presently appeared with a delicious supper, and the table was cleared of cards and chips. We all sat around and dug in—and though I took time to enjoy the food, I kept an eye on Catherine.

She was gay and full of sparkle—her face flushed and her eyes very bright—and she opened up to Ben like a flower. It made me feel a bit sick, somehow, to watch her. She had always given the impression before that Ben was much the same to her as a pebble in her shoe—and here she was, carrying on as though he were Rick himself. Ben was positively pathetic. He hung eagerly on her words, and touched her arm, and even her hair and cheek, whenever he thought it would not be too obvious.

Gertrude was quiet. She had made her poker bets in a business-like fashion and had dispatched her supper promptly—but she had very little to say, and her mouth and eyes were grim.

Edith Drucker was a bit tight. She told dirty jokes at intervals, and shrieked with laughter at the denouements—and then snapped viciously at Wilbur when he tried to shut her up.

Mammas Reed and Potter deplored the dirty jokes. They shook their heads at each other, and clicked their tongues at each performance.

After we had finished the supper we cleared the table and went on with the poker game—and we had not been at it for more than ten minutes when Catherine suddenly went into hysterics.

There was no warning. One minute she was sitting there, looking at her hand, and the next, she was making enough noise to lift the roof.

We had quite a trouble getting her up to bed, but we finally left her there, with Mrs. Reed and Mrs. Potter working over her competently.

They got her quiet at last and came down to report to the rest of us that they had given her something to make her sleep.

"I can't understand it," Mrs. Reed said unhappily. "I've never known Catherine to be hysterical before."

"Too repressed," said Mrs. Potter firmly. "I thought she was much too calm during all that dreadful business about Charlie—and now, you see, it comes out."

We left in a body. It was not quite one o'clock, and I knew Mother and Father would not be back. I kept with the others, hoping that one of them would ask me in for a while, but Gertrude and her mother said good night briefly and turned at once toward their house.

The rest of us went the other way, and in another moment Ben muttered a farewell and disappeared into his front door.

I stayed in among the Druckers, but I had no luck with them, either. Edith began to sing in a shrill soprano, and Wilbur, with the sweat on his brow, ran her up their steps and into the house, and forgot even to say good-by to me.

I was left alone, and I did some fancy cursing as I made my way home. Tony's place was still in darkness, and I wondered whether he and Timothy had gone out on a binge.

I went straight to the pantry window and climbed in, and crept through my own house as though I were a criminal. I locked my bedroom door after me, and then threw off my clothes and fell into bed. I thought that I was dead tired, and would go straight to sleep, but my brain was instantly wide awake and unpleasantly active.

I began to wish that I had brought Tom Swift with me—any reading matter would be better than just lying there, thinking.

I rolled out of bed, put on the light and made a hasty dash across the hall to the sitting room.

The book was lying on the window sill, and I raced over and snatched it up.

Rick's dinette was still flooded with light, and I glanced over there—and then paused, to look again.

He was still sprawled in his chair, and there was something peculiar—something about his face

I put my eyes close to the screen and stared.

That was it—the lock of hair that had been lying untidily across Rick's forehead seemed, somehow, to have grown— it appeared, now, to be covering all of one eye.

CHAPTER 18

I WAS SUDDENLY in a cold sweat of fear and horror. That was not hair over Rick's eye—it was something else—something ghastly. He'd been sitting there too long—and he was much too still.

The front doorbell rang stridently, and with a little gasp of relief I flew to my bedroom for a dressing gown. I pulled it around me and stumbled down the stairs, still trying to fasten it. I did not care who was at the door—all I wanted was company.

It was Frobisher, and after hastily averting his eyes from my sketchy attire, he stammered an apology for disturbing me at such an hour. "But I've just thought of something, and I must look into it now."

"Rick! Take a look at Rick!" I jabbered incoherently.

Frobisher stared at me, and his mouth dropped open.

I tried to explain more quietly, but I could see that he thought I was indulging in one of woman's little hysterics. "I'll go and have a look," he said reluctantly. "I'll be right back." But he did not darken the door again for nearly two hours.

I went to one of the drawing-room windows and watched him make his way to the still-lighted dinette. He hoisted himself up to the sill and peered through the window—and then he jumped—or fell—to the ground again, and ran to the back door and started pounding on it.

I had to leave, then, because Mother and Father came in, and I could hear them arguing about an end play, in the hall.

I went to them, and put bridge completely out of their minds by giving a fevered account of the night's events.

Mother looked positively gray when I had finished. "It's utterly absurd," she said, "that we should be made to stay here. We shall leave tomorrow—I'm going to insist on it."

I took them to the drawing-room window, and we all peered over at the dinette. There seemed to be several people there now, and I thought I saw Froby's sparse, blond hair—but we could not make out much of what was going on.

It was too much for Father. Before Mother had time to forbid it, he slid away, and yelled back from the front door, "Just find out what's happened."

Mother opened her mouth, but the front door slammed immediately, so she said "tch, tch," and turned back to the window.

It was not long before we could catch glimpses of Father milling around in the dinette with the others—but we could not make head or tail of what was going on, so Mother, always practical, decided on bed.

I went upstairs with her, but I stationed myself at the window in the small sitting room and stared over at Rick's house until my eyes ached.

I began to think that Father would never come back. He seemed to have been gone for hours—but it was actually only half an hour before I heard him slam the front door and come puffing up the stairs.

Mother and I hurried to meet him, and pounded him with frantic, impatient questions while he got his breath back.

Finally he waved us to silence and panted, "Shot! Shot in the forehead—not very close—no powder burns—probably from across the room, some hours ago—that's according to Frobisher, anyway. The medical examiner arrived just as I left." He took a long breath, and gave me a faintly accusing glance: "You were wrong about the fella's name, Lissa. It isn't Hitler—it's Rickford."

I laughed. In fact, I laughed so shrilly, and for so long, that Mother told me sharply to go to the bathroom and wash my face with cold water. She came along to see that I did it, and Father trailed in the rear, patting first her shoulder and then mine.

"Just keep calm," he said, "and I'll get you both away from here tomorrow. They can't stop us—it's criminal! Why should we sit around here waiting for one of those damned cottagers to come over and put a bullet in us? I'll see the mayor in the morning."

"We'll discuss all that at breakfast," Mother said firmly. "Let's go to bed."

We started off toward our bedrooms—but it was not to be. The front doorbell rang long and insistently.

"Pay no attention," Father advised us in a raucous whisper. "Just let them ring."

Mother said briefly, "Go down and answer it, Hammond."

Father started down the stairs, and I followed him. We opened the door together, rather timidly, and Albert Hahn, Mack Brewster and Timothy Frobisher flowed into the hall.

Father regained his confidence immediately, and started to roar. He wanted to know what they meant by it—assured them that our house was not a hotel and ended by making some sort of reference to their shoes and our oriental rug.

Hahn and Brewster quite obviously did not know whether to push him in the face or adopt a "yes sir," line. Frobisher, looking a trifle smug, stood back a few paces and left them to it.

Hahn said at last, "I'm sorry to bother you people again so soon—but it was Mrs. Herridge who first discovered Mr. Rickey, and we must have her statement. It's important to have it now, before the morning; it may make all the difference in our actions during the night."

"Surely it can't make much difference," said Father, "on which side of your faces you snore." This piece of supposed wit completely restored his good humor, and he laughed quietly to himself for at least ten minutes.

I told them what I knew about it, beginning with the hands that drew on a pair of gloves, and ending with Rick's hair, that seemed to have grown too quickly.

"Were they the hands of a woman or a man?" Hahn asked eagerly.

I said I didn't know.

Brewster almost pleaded with me. "Surely you have *some* idea?"

"I thought, at first, that they were a woman's hands," I said slowly, "but I realize, now, that they could easily have belonged to a man."

Brewster made a restless movement, and said, "What man would wear gloves in the summer?"

Timothy cleared his throat, and spoke for the first time. "A gentleman," he said.

Brewster glared at him.

"Those gloves were black," I said thoughtfully, "or dark, at any rate, and very few women wear dark gloves in the summer out here. Now, in New York—"

"Save it for *Vogue*," said Albert Hahn.

I thought they were going to arrest me when I told them about going into Rick's kitchen and hearing his visitor, and I'm sure that they did not believe me when I swore that I had not gone in and looked at him.

They tried to force me to give an opinion as to who the visitor had been but I told them I had not the slightest idea. I hated to tell them about Catherine, but they drew it out of me somehow.

They kept me on the mat until four in the morning, and even then, I remembered, just as I was getting into bed, that I had not told them about that nine of spades.

I dropped into an exhausted sleep at once, but it was shot through with lurid and exciting dreams. Among other things, I thought that I opened Charlie's suitcase and looked through the contents again, and with this still in my head, I woke to hot, bright sunlight streaming into the room.

I lay thinking it over for a while, and suddenly I understood about that suitcase. Frobisher had said there was something odd about it, and Father and I had supposed that he was merely showing off. But it *was* odd—because if Charlie had really intended to go away with it he would have found several things missing—brush and comb, toothbrush, pajamas. Then, apparently, he did *not* intend to go away—and the suitcase was only local color, to make it look as though he did.

So he went up to our attic, started to play solitaire and was suddenly interrupted. And the next thing he was sitting in a chair in the cellar, with five bullets in his face and a blue dandelion lying at his feet. Further, according to Tony, the blue dandelion meant a clandestine meeting between Catherine and Rick.

Now Rick was dead, too—and if Catherine had conceivably done away with Charlie—what earthly reason could she have for doing away with Rick ? And yet I had seen her run across the strip of lawn between Rick's house and her own last night. The police had been very interested in that brief glimpse I had had of Catherine. I gave it up, and decided to get dressed.

Father went out early that morning, to call on the mayor, but the visit was a dismal failure, since it turned out that Tom Baker was the mayor, and Mr. Baker it was who had sold his ground for the erection of the cottages.

From what I could make out, Father completely forgot the original purpose of his call, and it was never mentioned. Instead, he had a tremendous row with Mr. Baker on the subject of the cottages, and very nearly landed in jail. He told Mother and me all about it with great gusto, but Mother merely compressed her lips and said she was glad to hear that he had made such a good job of arranging to get us away.

"I'm going to my room," she said firmly, "and I'm going to lock the door until lunch. I simply cannot face either police or reporters. Since I cannot persuade you two to do the same, you'd better keep out of mischief by going over to East Orange and doing some shopping. There are some things we really must have for the house. You can take a taxi."

She gave us a list and then retired to her bedroom—although I don't believe she actually locked the door.

I collected my hat and bag and then went downstairs to phone the station for a taxi.

Father backed out of the hall closet with his Panama, and whispered sharply, "Psst! Put that phone down, Lissa. I'm going to drive over—I've bagged a car."

I dropped the telephone back into its cradle, and felt my hair rise under my hat.

Father's driving is a menace—although he loves it.

"Where'd you get the car?" I asked suspiciously.

"Matter of fact, it's Tony's car. He loaned it to me."

"Tony's? But you're not speaking to him, are you?"

"No, no, no," said Father hastily. "Certainly not. Wouldn't give the fella houseroom. But he pressed me to take it—said he wouldn't be using it today. Felt obligated, probably."

I let it go at that, because I knew if we were to get any of Mother's shopping done I couldn't stand there all the morning, listening to Father's lies.

We plowed through an encampment of reporters, got into Tony's car and shot off up the road like a bat out of hell. We heard, later, that Mack Brewster thought we were trying to make a getaway, and started phoning in a description of us, but Mother heard him, on the extension, and put him in his place.

Much to my surprise, we had only one small mishap on the way to East Orange. Father misjudged a corner a trifle, and hit a tree. There was very little damage—Father's hat was knocked over his eyes and one of the fenders was rumpled— but immediately there were about fifteen cars stopped all around us. Father backed up and made off, and after we had got some distance away I looked back over my shoulder. Cars were still stopping, and there was quite a crowd collecting.

When we got to East Orange Father parked beside a hydrant, but the cop who appeared turned out to be his old friend, Jack. After a few words of bonhomie Jack persuaded Father to park the car elsewhere.

I got out, while Father and Jack shifted the car, and wandered idly to a drugstore window I looked in, and saw Edith Drucker standing at the counter—and she appeared to be buying a large, flat nail file.

CHAPTER 19

I FLATTENED my nose against the windowpane and stared. I knew I had seen a file just like that very recently, but it took me a moment or two to remember where. It came to me at last that I had picked one up from under the step of the side door and had put it in the kitchen.

With my mind more than half-occupied by the idea that Edith's clothes were all wrong for her, I did a fine piece of sleuthing on the side. I deduced that Wilbur, Jr., had snitched his mother's nail file and taken it outside to dig dirt or something, and had finally left it under our steps. And so Edith, missing her file, and unable to find it, was forced to buy a new one. Of course the one I had picked up had been rusted and had apparently been lying around for some time—but then a nail file was just the sort of thing that you'd keep forgetting to buy.

I was jerked out of my reverie by a rude bellow from Father. I flung around, half-afraid that he had run over somebody or was picking a fight—but he was merely trying to get my attention. He explained, peevishly, that he had called me decently three times, before he opened his mouth and let me have it.

We went off about our shopping, and I had to drag Father away from every automobile showroom.

When we got back to the car Jack appeared again, as if by magic. His corner was the best regulated in East Orange, and I guess he didn't rely on Father to get safely out of the neighborhood by himself.

With some low soothing speech and the holding up of a bit of traffic here and there he effected a perfect getaway for Father, and Father was so pleased at what he thought was his own cleverness that he wanted to take a drive out into the country.

"No, you don't," I said grimly.

He gave it up, and went straight home. He put the car into Tony's garage and we collected our bundles and walked across the garden and around to the back door. The reporters were still holding services at the front door, and Mother was keeping the side door locked.

She approved our shopping, and while she was disposing of the various articles Father started agitating to buy a car. Mother merely asked him, with deceptive friendliness, what we would do with a car in the city.

I left them to it, and went along to my bedroom.

Timothy Frobisher was standing by my bed, looking down at it—and he had each and every one of my clues spread out neatly on the counterpane. He glanced up at me, put his finger to his lips and said, "Shh. Come in and shut the door."

"Thanks," I said coldly. "I do hope I'm not intruding. I'm sure you have every right to come into my bedroom and look through my things."

"No right whatever," said Timothy calmly. "I'm in your hands, and I shall do as you say. If you want me to go to Hahn and Brewster with the story of how you found the blue dandelion, you've only to mention it."

I murmured, "Blackmail, Froby," and sat down on the bed. For a while we both gazed in silence at my array of clues.

After a while I said, "How do you make a dandelion blue, anyway?"

"It's quite simple," said Timothy. "You paint it."

My mouth dropped open, and I stared at him. "Then why was I wasting time messing around with ink?"

"I've wondered myself," said Froby mildly.

I thought it over for a minute, and then asked eagerly, "Have you been through the cottages yet? To look for a paintbox, I mean, with the blue well used?"

He gave a dry little cough and said, "No, I haven't yet. No time." He glanced at his watch and added, "We are going to question Ben Amherst again—in about ten minutes—so I must go. I'll drop in this evening and see you for a few minutes."

I understood him perfectly. He wanted me to look for the paintbox, and tell him about it in the evening. He went off, and I fell to wondering, idly, why it was that Ben had not discovered Rick. He must have seen the light from the dinette when he went in after leaving us—and you had to take only a step or two to see into the dinette from the front door, anyway.

I heard Mother and Father go downstairs, and I took a hasty wash and brush-up, and followed them down to lunch. Dora was moving sedately around the table, and I asked her if she had found a nail file in the kitchen. She produced it at once, and Mother asked rather sharply what it was all about. I told her that Edith Drucker had lost the file, and she seemed satisfied—but I saw Father's eyes gleam, and I knew I'd never be able to shake him for the afternoon.

I did try. I crept out the side door, after lunch, and made a quiet, speedy dash for the Drucker house—but Father was right with me.

I shrugged resignedly and rang the bell, and Edith admitted us. I showed her the file, and asked her if she'd lost it, and she said, "Well, it certainly looks like one of those I lost. I hadda buy two lately."

"What happened to the others?"

"Oh, I don't know," she said. "Where'd you find that one ?"

I told her, and suggested, "Maybe little Wilbur took it outside."

The kid was standing in the doorway, staring at us, and Edith turned on him and asked him if he'd been taking her files out of the house, but he said no without listening to her question.

"I'll bet he did, though," Edith said. "I bought a brand-new one this morning, and now maybe the other one will show up, and I'll have three."

She laughed heartily, and then turned to Father and asked him if he'd have a drink.

I said no, and hastily inquired if Wilbur, Jr., was fond of painting.

"Painting?" said Edith, looking first at me and then in complete bewilderment at the kid.

I felt that I had showed a lack of finesse, and I stammered foolishly, "I thought I saw him painting in the yard once."

Edith shook her head. "No. We gave him a box of paints for Christmas, but he's never used it."

Father spoke up then and said he thought he'd change his mind about that drink. Edith said the weather made you thirsty, didn't it, and winked at him.

I stood up and asked to be directed to the ladies' room, and Edith, pausing on her way to the kitchen to make the drinks, carefully explained the exact location of the bathroom. Once upstairs, it was an easy matter for me to invade Junior's bedroom and dig out his paintbox. But Edith had told the truth. Junior had never used his paints—not even the blue.

When we left the Drucker house Junior trailed after us, and we could not shake him. I made a virtue of necessity, therefore, and taking him for a short walk across the back yards of the cottages, tried to dig out the truth about the lady who had allowed him to dip dandelions in ink.

I got absolutely nowhere. The kid gabbled on about the lady who apparently had treated him white, and allowed him to dip dandelions to his heart's content, but he could not or would not put either a name or an address to her—he seemed to think it didn't matter. And the whole thing put ideas into his head. He ran off and gathered a bunch of dandelions in his hot, grubby little fist, and insisted that I lead him to some ink.

Father lost all patience at this point. He said to let him know when I intended to do something more constructive than trying to get sense out of a half-witted child, and stamped off home.

That left me with only Junior hanging around my neck, and I presently disposed of him by telling him that his mother wanted to give him some candy.

I wended my way to the Reed house. Mrs. Reed suffered me to come in—but she was far from cordial. She said that Catherine had a headache and was lying down.

She looked ill herself, and I felt sorry for her. I tried a little delicate sympathy, but she brushed it aside and reproached me with having told the police about Catherine's flight across the grass between Rick's house and their own. "I think you might have left that out—it has made things look so bad for Catherine. And it was all so innocent. She went to the Druckers' to get poker chips—we were a bit short—and Edith told her exactly where to find them. She wasn't gone more than a minute or two, and came right back with the chips—but the police as much as told us that she had plenty of time to go into Rick's house "

She broke off abruptly, and I supposed she meant that the police suspected Catherine of having detoured, on the way to or from the Druckers', and shot Rick

I set her right on it. "Rick was shot some time before Catherine went for the chips."

"What!" She clutched at the arms of her chair and asked feverishly, "Do the police know?"

"Of course they know. If they gave you any other impression, they were fooling you."

She relaxed completely and closed her eyes for a moment. "Oh, I am relieved," she murmured.

"I'm sorry about it all," I said uncomfortably, "but when they start asking questions they have you turned inside out before you know it."

"Oh, I know," she said, much more warmly.

I asked her, then, if I could go up to the bathroom, and she said, of course, and gave me directions.

I climbed the stairs, feeling a bit silly. If Catherine had a paintbox it would almost certainly be in her bedroom, and since she was lying down with a headache I could hardly intrude on her, or start searching her room, even if I did.

Her door was closed, and just for the looks of the thing I went into the bathroom.

The paints were there. Just a child's paintbox, on the window sill—and the blue was the only color that had been used.

CHAPTER 20

I WENT ON to the Potter house and hung around for a while, uncertainly. I was beginning to feel like a house-to-house canvasser, and I wondered what they would all think of me if they ever got together on my round of visits and checked up on the fact that I had made an excuse to go upstairs each time.

A couple of reporters sneaked up on me, while I was thinking it over, and started to ask questions. I kept repeating "I really don't know," without listening, and just as my head was beginning to ache, the Drucker dog, Cato, and a visiting Scottie started a free-for-all. The reporters said they'd better go and watch, so as to see fair play.

I hurried to the Potter door and rang the bell urgently. Mrs. Potter let me in, and I murmured something about being sorry to intrude. She said "Not at all," rather frostily.

I explained about the reporters, and she loosened up a bit. "Dreadful," she agreed. "They don't give a person a minute's peace."

She was in the midst of polishing silver, so I started in to help her, and after we had finished she asked me to have tea with her.

She chatted quite amiably over the tea, and after I had finished my second cup I asked if I could go up to the bathroom.

She said it would be quite all right, but told me to please not notice how untidy it was, because what with all the upset and everything her housekeeping had been disorganized.

The entire second floor was scrupulously clean and tidy, of course—people who apologize for the state of the house are usually morbid about every tiny fleck of dust.

I found a box of paints in what was obviously Gertrude's bedroom. It was a good set, with tubes and an assortment of professional-looking brushes. The box was clean and orderly except for one patch of bright blue paint on the inside of the lid.

I put the box away where I had found it, went and flushed the toilet for the proper sound effect and rejoined Mrs. Potter for my third cup of tea.

I asked her if she did any painting.

"No," she said, "but Gertrude has quite a talent. I wanted her to go on with her art studies, but she says there's no money in it. Still, I don't feel that she's wasted her time. It's a nice hobby for her—and she's made some wonderful Christmas presents and bridge prizes—painting things, you know."

I knew. I'd had a friend like that when I was married to Tony—only her hobby was woodburning—or something like that. I remembered how embarrassing it had been.

I worked the conversation around to Catherine and Ben, and asked, rather crudely, "Is Ben in love with Catherine?"

"Oh yes," she said easily. "Has been for some time—head over heels. He makes quite a bit more than either Charlie or Rick did, too. It wouldn't surprise me a bit if she ended up by marrying him now."

"But he's not at all attractive," I suggested.

"No—but Catherine is nearing thirty—and I know she wants to marry."

"Isn't it odd that she hasn't married before this, then? She's stunning," I said sincerely

"Oh well, no—she was engaged to a man for quite a long time—six years, I think—and they were waiting until he made enough money. And then, quite suddenly, he married some other girl. I always think a girl is foolish to consent to a long engagement."

"I don't see why they should have had to wait six years," I said. "After all, Catherine and her mother have an income and the three of them could have lived together."

She nodded. "Mrs. Reed wanted that—but Catherine wouldn't consent. She wanted her own home and to have everything just right, I guess."

"Doesn't always work out," I said absently. "Look at my wedding. Everything just right—and a year later the whole outfit is on the rocks."

"Oh, my dear!" she said, melting into sympathy. "I'm so sorry."

I laughed. "It's quite all right. I really don't mind, at all."

I got away shortly after that and went on home. I tried the side door first, out of habit, and then remembered that Mother was keeping it locked. I turned away, with my eyes on the ground, and spotted another nail file. I picked it up and stared at it. It looked very like the first one I had found, except that it was not so rusty.

I went around to the back door and, in the kitchen, I showed the file to Dora and Grace and asked if either of them had lost it.

They said no, and Dora added, "Don't you remember, Mrs. Herridge, you asked us before?"

"This is another one," I explained, and could feel them exchanging questioning glances about my sanity as I walked out of the kitchen.

I went up to my bedroom and tossed the file among my other clues. I stretched out on the bed then, with a fan and a cigarette, and tried to do a little constructive reasoning.

The second nail file, lying on the ground by the side door, was completely baffling to me, and I decided reluctantly that Wilbur, Jr., had probably snitched them both and had abandoned them, one after the other, in the same place

There was a light tap on the door, and at my call Timothy Frobisher drifted in, smiling vaguely. I told him about the various paintboxes, and he nodded his head quietly for so long that I began to get dizzy watching him. He eased it to a stop at last, and said, "Then the Drucker house and Tony's are out of it."

"What about Rick's?"

"Mr. Rickey had a fine, big box, with the blue all used up."

"Then I suppose Tony was right about Rick and Catherine," I said thoughtfully.

Timothy said "Yes."

"Did Catherine admit it?" I asked. He nodded absently, and I could see that he was thinking furiously about something else.

I continued to pump him, in the hope that he would answer automatically.

"Were they meeting in our house?"

He nodded again.

"Then how did they get in?" I demanded.

He shrugged, still with a faraway look in his eyes.

"You mean you don't know?" I asked incredulously. "But you ought to know by this time how they got in. What kind of police are you?"

He came out of his abstraction then, and defended himself and the force rather hotly, before he realized that he really should not be talking to me about it at all.

"There are several ways they might have got in," he ended lamely. "It isn't important, anyway."

"I think it is."

He shot me a rather fierce look, but after a moment of silence his shoulders drooped, and he said in a discouraged voice, "I've thought and thought—but there are no signs of any of the doors or windows having been forced."

"Didn't Catherine tell you how they got in?"

"Miss Reed," said Froby, rather pompously, "when confronted with our knowledge that she had been having an affair with Mr. Rickey, denied everything and burst into tears."

"But you said she had admitted it."

"Circumstances and her own actions made the admission for her," said Froby, still pompous.

I said oh, and had a very faint, fleeting idea that I was being led up the garden path.

He changed the subject and asked, "Did you try out any of the blue paints on a dandelion?"

"No. I didn't think it was necessary."

"Well, it is. It's always necessary to be sure about things. Will you make those tests for me?"

My intangible breath of suspicion vanished, and I said "Certainly." I wondered importantly what Hahn and Brewster would think if they knew that Timothy Frobisher had made me a deputy sheriff. I knew that Father would be green with jealousy.

Froby made one of his quick, silent disappearances, and in a glow of friendliness toward him I went out into the garden to pick some dandelions. But I could not think of any reasonable excuse for getting into any of the cottages again, and I wandered around in the garden, racking my brains to no purpose. It was very quiet, and I realized, with a sense of peace, that the reporters had disappeared. "The cocktail hour, perhaps," I thought idly.

Unexpectedly, in a far corner of the garden, I came upon Catherine. She was sitting on a rustic bench, her hands lying listlessly in her lap and her face blank. But there was something tragic about her eyes.

The bench was on our property and belonged to us—but I felt very much an intruder.

She glanced up at me and said "Hello," dully, but made no other movement.

I sat down beside her, and felt helplessly inadequate to express the sympathy I felt for her. "You ought to go away somewhere," I said, after a moment. "I don't suppose you care one way or the other, right now, but I think it would be the best thing for you. I'm going to speak to your mother about it."

She gave a short bitter laugh. "Disregarding anything else, I don't believe the police would allow it. They like to keep the chief suspect underfoot until the case is solved, you know."

"Chief suspect!" I gasped.

She twisted her hands together in her lap and said painfully, "They know that Rick and I were—attracted to each other, when I was engaged to Charlie—and they think I wanted to get rid of Charlie. They think"—her voice rose to a higher note, and I could see the imprint of her nails on the palms of her hands—"they think I knew about Charlie's having left me his money. But I *didn't*—he never told me—I had no idea of it."

"Charlie left you his money?" I said stupidly.

"Yes—but I tell you, I didn't know. He was the finest fellow I've ever known—and if anyone thinks I'd have thrown him over for Rick, they're insane."

"Of course you wouldn't," I said soothingly, and added after a moment, "Rick was kind of fascinating, wasn't he?"

"Yes. Oh yes." She gave a little moan and closed her eyes. "They think I killed him, too."

"But that's absurd," I said, in astonishment. "If they think you killed Charlie for Rick, what possible reason could you have had for killing Rick?"

"They say I quarreled with him—about you. Well, I did." She was silent for some time, and I waited quietly. After a while she said slowly, "Rick was just a philanderer. As soon as Charlie and I were engaged he began to pay attention to me—and last Saturday, after Charlie was killed, he couldn't see me at all."

I nodded. "Scared-of-matrimony type."

"But I had nothing—absolutely nothing, to do with his death," she said shrilly.

I thought she looked ripe for another attack of hysterics, so I soothed her as best I could and urged her to go home and lie down.

She went docilely enough, and I escorted her to her door. I was longing to make the experiments with the blue paints, but I could not force myself to intrude any further, so I took myself and my dandelions home.

I remembered a box of paints that I had had as a child, and that I believed to be in one of the storerooms in the attic, and I decided to go up and paint one of the dandelions to see how it came out.

I found the box easily enough. It was clean and new, except for the bright blue color—and that had been used and smudged around the edges.

CHAPTER 21

THE THING frightened me for some reason. I left the box where I had found it and ran downstairs.

Mother gave me a long lecture that night at dinner. She insisted that I stay in the house, or garden, until things had died down or been cleared up. She declared that she was worried about me, because she knew very well that I was poking into all sorts of things that did not concern me, and that sooner or later, if I did not heed her warnings, I'd be certain to run afoul of the law. And that, said Mother, would be a nice thing for us all.

Father, looking smug and virtuous, coughed and said, "Quite right."

I told Mother that there was really nothing to worry about, and after dinner, just to prove it, I settled down in the library with a book.

It didn't last long, though. I caught sight of Froby, after a while, standing motionless in the hall. He was out of sight of Mother and Father, and as soon as I looked up he beckoned to me silently.

I got up, yawned, said good night to my parents and quietly followed Froby to the side-door lobby. He asked me about the dandelions, and I put him off by telling him about the paintbox in our attic. He galloped up, taking the stairs two at a time, and I trotted after him. He wrapped the paintbox up with loving care and took it off with him, after first making me promise to get a dandelion painted with a sample of blue from each and every box in the cottages.

I went slowly down the attic stairs and paused, in the hall outside my bedroom, to think Froby over. I supposed he was ambitious, and working secretly against Hahn and Brewster, and I quite understood why they were going to slap his ears off when they caught up with him.

I opened the door of my bedroom and went in—determined to give Mother one peaceful night by going straight to bed and to sleep.

I looked around at the comfort and luxury of my room as I slowly removed my dress, and wondered whether I would ever again be really at home there. There was something tense and sinister about the whole house these days—as though some horror were waiting in the dark corners and behind the doors.

I flung my dress onto a chair, and at the same time something crashed against the screen at one of the windows. I let out a startled yelp, and after a moment of nervous indecision went over and peered out.

I could not see anything, but Tony's hoarse whisper came floating up to me. "For God's sake, Liz, are you deaf?"

"What's the matter?" I whispered back.

"Come on out the side door."

"Why?"

I heard him swear to himself, and then he said impatiently, "I *must* speak to you."

I said, all right, mentally apologized to Mother and went back for my dress. I slipped it on and went quietly down the back stairs. The maids had gone, and the house was very still. I was conscious of a feeling of pleasurable excitement, and by the time I got to the side door I realized that the prospect of Tony's company was responsible. I stopped in some surprise, with my hand on the knob, and considered it. "Pleased to be in the company of that bum?" I asked myself, and was promptly answered, "What bum?" I shrugged, and gave it up.

As soon as I got outside the door Tony grabbed my arm, and said shh rather sternly in my ear. He led me straight off to his house, sat me on a couch in the living room and poured me a drink, all without a word. He poured another drink for himself, and sat down, facing me.

"As I said before," he remarked, "you seem to be getting very hard of hearing."

"I'm nothing of the kind," I said shortly. "I hear as well as anyone."

"Well, dammit, I must have thrown a dozen small stones against your screen, and couldn't get a rise out of you. So I heaved the rock at last."

"And just like you, too. You ought to learn to control your temper. I suppose I didn't notice the small stones—they probably sounded like those insects that bang against the screen at night. That rock might have broken the screen and done some damage."

"It might have hit you on the head and killed you," he said, staring into his glass. "Might have been the best thing all around. *My* troubles would be over, anyway."

I was surprised, and obscurely pleased.

"How am I a trouble to you, Tony?" I asked curiously.

He got up abruptly and refilled both our glasses, and instead of returning to his chair sat down beside me on the couch.

He rattled the ice against the sides of his glass, and after a short silence he said slowly, "I brought you over here to warn you about Froby."

"Froby!" I repeated. "But we're the best of friends."

"That's what you think. As a matter of fact, Froby has the case against you all sewed up—except for one thing—and he's your intimate friend until you spill that one thing." He paused to rumple his hair fretfully. "I don't know what he's after, either. You can't dig anything out of him, if he wants to keep it under his hat—he's a cagey devil. You might give him what he's looking for at any time—and then he'll pin the whole thing on you and you'll have a hell of a time getting out of it."

I stared at him—or at his profile, because he was gazing across the room—and I was so dumfounded that I could not find two words to put together. I concentrated on Tony's profile for so long that he turned and looked at me.

"Do you know," he said, almost gently, "there's only one other time that I can remember seeing you look so serious— and that was when I killed your dog."

I looked away quickly. That dog had been the cause of our divorce. Tony had run over him when he was backing the car out of the garage—and I had accused him of doing it on purpose. The ensuing row was really awe-inspiring—in fact, it was hardly fair to blame the divorce on the death of the dog—it was the stinging art istry of the subsequent arguments that did the damage—and toward the end we had practically forgotten about the dog.

Somehow, remembering the childishness of the whole thing, I couldn't help laughing.

"That's right," said Tony bitterly, "laugh about it all. Maybe you can find something to amuse you when they stick you in the clink."

"Nothing funny about that," I said hastily. "Why does Froby think I had anything to do with it? Catherine says she's the chief suspect, so how do they work us both in?"

"Catherine is the favorite as far as Hahn and Brewster are concerned—but Froby is being brilliant all by himself—and he has his money on you."

"He's insane," I said scornfully. "I hardly know those people — didn't know any of them until we came here this summer. As for Charlie, I saw him once."

"That's where you're wrong, as it happens. You went to school with Charlie—and Catherine, too."

"I did?"

He nodded. "No reason why you should remember it, of course. Catherine was a couple of classes ahead of you, and Charlie was one ahead of her."

"Oh no," I said. "It's—it's impossible."

"Why? Just because you don't remember them? Think back a bit, and see how many of the kids you can remember who were in

classes above you—or even in your own class, for that matter. Froby
has looked up the records—and the three of you were very definitely going to the same school at one time. He told me that much,
because he thought I'd be glad to see you in trouble—but he would
not come clean on just how or why he figured you'd done it."

"Childhood triangle," I suggested.

Tony said, "Probably," and sat staring at his drink.

He was silent for so long that I touched his arm and said, "I'm
still here."

"Quite all right," said Tony. "I don't mind at all."

I got to my feet and put my glass on a table. "I'm going," I said,
in an offended voice.

He caught my arm and pulled me down beside him again.

"Don't be rude," he said. "You can't go before the refreshments."

"Who's preparing them?" I asked suspiciously.

"I am."

"I thought you were a man?"

"I'm a divorcee," he said with dignity. "What will you have?"

I said promptly, "Steak-and-kidney pie, and french pancakes."

"You're mistaken. Sandwiches and coffee, waffles and coffee—
or go hungry."

"Waffles," I said cheerfully.

He sighed and stood up. "Waffle iron's down in the cellar. Be
back in a minute. And remember—don't have any more talks with
Froby. Avoid him—duck around corners when you see him—and
above all, keep your father away from him."

"That means I'll have to keep Father beside me all the time," I
said gloomily.

"Worth the sacrifice," said Tony, lighting a cigarette. He went
off, and I heard him tramping down the steps into the cellar.

I indulged in some rather bitter reflections about Froby and his
two faces. I felt that he had taken me over properly, and I was thoroughly resentful.

It was not until about ten minutes later that I suddenly realized
that Tony had not returned from the cellar.

CHAPTER 22

I STOOD UP, my breath coming faster, while the silence seemed to
pound in my ears. I was suddenly terrified, and I fled into the kitchen,

and stumbled, half-falling, down the dark cellar stairs. I kept calling "Tony, Tony," in a hoarse whisper.

At the bottom a pair of arms caught me and my mouth was muffled against a tweed shoulder. "What's the matter? Don't make so much noise," Tony muttered into my ear.

Relief surged over me, and before I could think up a decent lie I said childishly, "I thought you'd been murdered."

"I was looking at something," he whispered. And then instead of releasing me, he tightened his hold and kissed me. I relaxed, and enjoyed it for what it was worth.

After a while he said quietly, against my ear, "Poor old Liz. So you're still in love with me."

I backed away a step and hissed, "Nothing of the sort."

"Lizzie," he said reasonably, "there was urgency, and a tear in your voice, when you came boiling down those stairs, thinking I'd been murdered."

"I was worried for your uncle Horace," I said feebly. "He's fond of you."

I heard him laughing quietly, and I longed to slap his face, but it was so dark that I didn't know where to find it.

"What about you?" I asked furiously. "You kissed me, didn't you?"

"Unless there's someone else down here," he agreed amiably. "I was testing your response."

"And I suppose you think it was warm?"

"Hot," said Tony, in a satisfied voice.

"What kept you down here so long?" I asked, changing the subject in a bit of a hurry.

"I was watching someone out of the window—but probably whoever it was has gone, after all the noise you made."

He reached for my hand and led me to one of the small windows on the side and toward the back of the house.

We could see the Drucker back yard and a patch of light on the grass from the Drucker dinette.

"Do you see those two trees, just beyond the light? They're rather close together."

"Yes."

"Something was going back and forth between them every few seconds."

"What do you mean?" I whispered sharply.

"I think it was a woman—but I'm not sure. It was just a dark figure. Anyway, it came out from behind one tree, moved across to the other and slid behind it. And then back to the first one again, and so on. I was wondering how long it was going to keep it up, and hoping it would advance as far as the light, where I might recognize it. But right in the middle of everything you spoiled the show and revealed your undying love for me by falling down the stairs."

"I did not fall down the stairs."

"We might as well put the light on," said Tony, "and find the waffle iron. If these murders are ever solved, it will be in spite of your earnest efforts to help."

We took the waffle iron up to the kitchen, and I sat on the table while Tony enjoyed himself messing around with batter.

He had just completed the first waffle when there was a sharp rap on the back door. I slid off the table and opened up, to find Father standing there.

"Lissa! What does this mean? Your mother's nearly frantic. She sent me out after you." He looked past me into the kitchen, and added weakly, "What are you doing?"

Since he could see for himself that we were preparing to have waffles and coffee, I didn't bother to answer him.

Tony said, "Set another place, Liz."

Father walked into the kitchen and eyed the completed waffle. "Count me out," he said. "I wouldn't break bread with the fella— and anyway, I'm on a diet."

"Phone Mother first," I said, setting an extra place, "and make some excuse."

Father went to the telephone in the living room, and I could hear him making one of his silly, theatrical excuses. "It's all right," he said, "I've found her. The little Reed girl is ill, and Lissa's helping out. Eh? How did Lissa know she was ill? I don't know, Janice—you'll have to ask Lissa herself. Yes, I'll bring her back within half an hour."

I felt that I could see Mother's face as clearly as though it were in front of me: lips compressed, eyes cold and unbelieving.

The waffles were delicious. Father and Tony ate an enormous number and had a polite scuffle over the last one—which they finally halved.

Father sat back in his chair then, lit a cigar and asked sternly, "What are you doing in this house, Lissa?"

"Eating the one or two waffles I've been able to snatch from you and Tony," I said crossly.

"I got her over here to warn her against Frobisher," Tony explained. "He has her under suspicion for some reason."

Father swelled up, and started to roar. "What the hell does that silly, four-eyed alligator think he's doing? I'll have him fired. Suspecting my daughter of murder!"

"You'd better stay away from him," Tony warned.

"Do you think I'm afraid of the miserable skeleton?" Father shouted. "I'll find him first thing in the morning. He can't go around suspecting Lissa like that."

"All right," said Tony, "but he can cause you a lot of trouble if you don't handle him with gloves."

"Tony's right, Father," I said impatiently. "For heaven's sake, keep away from the man."

I formally thanked Tony for the supper, then collected Father, and we went home. I looked around for the lurking figure on the way but could not see anything.

When we got to the house we found the doors all locked, and of course neither of us had keys.

We went to the front door and rang the bell—timidly, and with a certain tattoo, so that Mother would know who it was and understand that we were sorry about having forgotten our keys.

We had to wait while Mother got into a dressing gown and came downstairs—but at last she flung the door open and confronted us.

We slipped in, making ourselves as small as possible, but she merely observed, "I'm going to have your ears pierced, Hammond, and hang your keys there."

We diverted her mind by telling her about Frobisher's suspicions, and she was instantly furious. "I knew that man was not to be trusted— I was sure there was something behind all that vague stupidity."

"Oh well," said Father, "he's nosing into the wrong garbage pail this time."

I went off to bed, after saying good night to Mother and thanking Father not to compare me to a garbage pail.

I was up fairly early the next morning, and I put on a dress of a soft green color, with some sort of idea that it would merge in with the foliage.

Froby did not appear, however, and though there was no reason why I should continue to help him, I went out and picked a dandelion, and then made for the Reed house. I decided that I wanted to make the experiment for my own satisfaction.

Mrs. Reed admitted me and was quite gracious. "Hello, dear, you're out bright and early, this morning."

"I dropped over to inquire about Catherine," I smiled. "She didn't seem well yesterday—and I'm so sorry for her."

"It will take time," Mrs. Reed said, with a faint sigh. "You don't get over things like that so quickly. But I guess she'll be all right."

She led me to the dinette, where she seemed to be having breakfast alone. "Poor Catherine," she said, as we sat down. "All the disappointments she has had!"

She poured me a cup of coffee, which I did not want, and added, "I'm beginning to think I shall never see her safely married."

Her eyes filled with tears, and I buried my face in my coffee cup in some embarrassment.

"It's tragic for her just now," I said presently, "but she'll get over it in time. And Catherine is so attractive—I'm sure she'll be able to marry whenever she chooses."

"I know—but she seems to be jinxed—she really does. She was engaged for six years—very much in love with the man—and she would not go out with anyone else during all that time. She turned down several promising chances. And then he suddenly married someone else—after she had waited all those years for him to make enough money. Then you see what has happened here."

I nodded, feeling sorry for them both. They had had some bad breaks.

The doorbell rang, and Mrs. Potter breezed into the house. She gave me a cordial good morning, which was faintly tinged with suspicion.

She eased herself into the dinette and accepted a cup of coffee, and I gathered that it was a regular morning ritual— sometimes at the Reeds', and sometimes at the Potters'.

After we had talked for a while, I found an opportunity to go upstairs—and all the way up I reflected on how those two women must be shaking their heads and saying it was too bad that I had such weak kidneys.

I went straight into the bathroom, closed the door and started the water running into the basin. I took the dandelion from my purse, and using the paints that were still on the window sill I set to work. It took time and care, but in the end I had a nice, bright blue dandelion. I admired it for a while, and then I turned the water off and opened the door.

Catherine stood directly outside, facing me. She looked furious, and I knew she was working up to saying something nasty. I waited, in guilty silence.

"Good morning," she said. "I hope you found what you were looking for this time."

I blushed furiously, and said rather feebly, "I wasn't looking for anything, Catherine. I came up to see how you were."

I slipped past her, without waiting to hear any more, and ran down the stairs. As I approached the dinette, Mrs. Reed was saying, "I can't imagine what's happened to my large nail file. It seems to have disappeared, and I can't find it anywhere."

CHAPTER 23

SUDDENLY, in that cheerful, sun-filled little house, I shivered, and felt desperately afraid. What did those nail files have to do with it all? And what sort of queer, furtive things were going on around us?

I shook the feeling away from me, and went slowly back to the dinette, where Mrs. Reed hospitably refilled my cup.

I was thinking furiously, and although I was aware that Mrs. Potter had started to talk to me very seriously, it was a few minutes before I realized that she was giving me some good advice about how to keep Father from getting inebriated.

"I'm so sorry for your poor mother," she said, "but as I tell you, I used to think up little ways of keeping Mr. Potter amused, and you'd be surprised at how well it worked."

I struggled with a desire to laugh, and told her I'd try it. The two of them got at me then, very skillfully and subtly, and really saying nothing that I could take amiss. But they wanted to know my exact status with Tony—why was I seen going into his house, why was I seen being run out of his house, by Tony himself—and were we still divorced? If we were, I really should not go into his house, unchaperoned, at any time.

I told them that Tony and I were properly divorced, but that he and my parents were still very good friends. I added that when he ran me out of his house it was in a spirit of fun, and that I looked upon him more in the light of an uncle than anything else. And I assured them that Father got drunk only once a year—and as long as he kept it down to that, Mother and I really did not mind.

They agreed, gravely, that once a year wasn't so bad.

Mrs. Potter tactfully changed the subject then, and asked, "Did you know that Ben is having a bit of trouble with the police?"

Mrs. Reed and I were satisfactorily eager, and she continued: "Well, when he went into the house, you know, when Rick was— Well, you can almost see the dinette from the hall, and they think it's funny that Ben didn't discover Rick before he went upstairs. Of course Ben told them that he went straight up to bed, and just called out 'Hello.' He admits he got no answer from Rick, and they think it's peculiar that he should have gone right on up to bed—living with Rick like that, you know—without stopping for a word or two. It would be only natural for him to alter his course a bit and glance into the dinette."

"Ben ought to tell the truth," Mrs. Reed said, after a moment.

"What's the truth?" I asked quickly.

Mrs. Potter nodded. "You're right—he should. But he's afraid. He thinks if they know he and Rick were not speaking, they'd suspect him of having had something to do with it."

Mrs. Reed said, "Rubbish!" and I asked, "When did they stop speaking to each other?"

Mrs. Reed said she didn't know exactly, and Mrs. Potter declared it was at least two weeks before Charlie was killed.

"What was the trouble?" I asked.

Mrs. Reed shook her head. "That's the funny part about it— nobody knew. We all talked about it, and Rick himself declared he had no idea what was wrong. He said Ben simply refused to know him all of a sudden."

They started to talk about Charlie's funeral then—he was being buried that afternoon, but his body had been shipped to his sister, in upstate New York. The sister, it developed, had criticized Catherine for not attending the funeral, and Mrs. Reed was indignant. She declared that Catherine was not fit to travel, and I agreed with her.

I made my escape and went off home. I walked straight to the side door and looked under the step. I did not have to look very far—the nail file was there, as I had fully expected it to be.

I picked it up and looked at it. It seemed to be exactly the same as the other two, and told me exactly nothing. I turned it over in my hand and began to walk slowly back to the Reed house.

I had decided that I might as well return it to Mrs. Reed. I was not going to give it to Froby—I was trying to keep out of his way—

and, in any case, I was mad at him. I could not face all the complicated explaining that would be necessary if I handed it to Hahn or Brewster—and anyway, it was quite possible that the Drucker child was responsible for the whole thing.

Mrs. Reed was surprised and pleased to get her file back. "Wherever did you find it?" she asked.

"Lying in our yard," I told her. "Do you think Willie Drucker could have wandered off with it? Has he been here lately?"

"Edith had him here for a while yesterday," she admitted.

"I guess he took it, then." I said, speaking as much to myself as to her. "He seems to have a weakness for them."

Mrs. Reed laughed, and Mrs. Potter shook her head and declared that the child was spoiled.

I went off home again, then, and as I crossed the side garden I caught a glimpse of Froby, around at the front. He saw me and called out, but I doubled back and sneaked into the basement entrance. I went in, surprised to find the door unlocked, but glad of any refuge.

I went up the cellar stairs in a bit of a hurry, and continued on to the second floor. I felt safe from Froby for the time being, but I realized that I was depressed and unhappy. There was no telling what the silly ass was concocting against me—it might be something that I'd find pretty difficult to break down.

I went toward my room with the intention of putting the dandelion away—and solemnly vowing, the while, to have nothing further to do with the investigation.

I opened my door, to find Froby standing at the foot of the bed with a diffident little smile.

I frowned at him. "If you boys really need this room, I'll be glad to move out and take another one."

He said, "Tch, tch—what's the matter now? Have you done any dandelion-testing yet?"

I swallowed my fury, put on a false smile and produced the dandelion. It was a perfect job—bright blue, faintly flecked with yellow, and exactly like the original.

Froby took it and asked, "Where did this come from?"

"Reed house," I said shortly.

"Did you get samples from the other two houses?"

"No," I said. "I didn't think it was necessary."

Froby removed his glasses, polished them and replaced them on the bone that served him for a nose. "In an investigation of this sort," he said, enjoying himself, "no stone should be left unturned. Every clue should be sifted so thoroughly that there can be no possibility of a mistake."

"Yes," I said, "and when the state starts paying me a decent salary I'll be glad to turn stones over from morning until night."

Froby actually blushed. "Mrs. Herridge!" he protested. "You can't think I was suggesting that you do any of this! *Absolutely* not. And I am very grateful for the one or two things you have done to help me out. I thank you profoundly."

I nearly laughed at him, in spite of the nagging need to be wary.

"It's quite all right," I said, watching him. "I'll get the other samples for you, if you like."

He said "Thank you," and there was a moment of silence, while we looked at each other like a couple of tomcats.

"What about the paintbox in the attic?" I asked presently. "Did you find any fingerprints on it?"

"Yours," Froby said smoothly.

Well, of course my fingerprints would be on that box—I'd handled it, and Froby knew I had. I shrugged, but I could feel the prickle of hair along my scalp.

He started to question me, again, about Sunday afternoon. "You were walking in the grounds with Mr. Rickey early in the afternoon, were you not?"

"I was," I said formally.

"He left, after a while, and you wandered around for a bit by yourself—right?"

"Yes," I said, keeping my eyes on his face.

"Now—he left you to keep an engagement at his club—right?"

"Right," I agreed.

"And then he went in and changed his clothes?"

"Did he?" I asked.

Froby looked distinctly annoyed. "He changed to a blue suit, from sport flannels."

I said, "Oh yes—it was a bridge club."

"Right," said Froby.

"So he changed his clothes, and then didn't go?"

"Right," said Froby again. He gave a little cough, and adjusted his glasses. "Mr. Rickey was expected at his club— three men were waiting for him at four o'clock. But he never went—although he had changed into a dark suit and was, apparently, all ready to leave.

Now, none of the people in the cottages stopped him. I think I have fairly conclusive proof that not one of them could have gone into Mr. Rickey's house between four and five o'clock. It was around five, was it not, when you saw that pair of hands?"

I stared at him, feeling more acutely uncomfortable than I ever had in my life before. If he had alibied all the cottages, then I was the only one left.

I heard myself saying, in a voice almost as precise as his own, "Yes, around five. But what on earth could have stopped Rick ?"

"That," said Froby, "remains to be seen." And I breathed again.

"Now, at five," he continued, "Mr. Rickey had a visitor. We don't know whether it was a man or a woman—and you say you cannot tell from the appearance of the hands. But a woman's hands would be smaller than a man's, would they not?"

I wrinkled my forehead, and said slowly, "They were squarish gloves—sport gloves, I think, if they belonged to a woman—but just ordinary gloves, if a man's."

He turned his glasses on me and gave me a long stare which told me very plainly that I could not possibly tell the difference between sport and dress gloves at such a distance. I felt my face grow hot, although I knew I had told him the truth to the best of my ability. I was strongly of the impression that those hands had been encased in sport gloves, and were the hands of a woman.

Froby let it go, and changed his course. "Mrs. Herridge, do you possess any sort of firearm?"

I caught myself on the edge of saying no, and remembered Father's birthday gift to me when I was eighteen. He had bought it himself, without telling anyone, and I had been very thrilled about it—a tiny pearl-handled automatic, glittering and initialed. I had wanted to put it in my purse, and carry it around with me, but Mother had stepped in and laid the law down. I could remember her saying, "Nice, suitable sort of toy for a child, Hammond—I commend your taste and judgment. But now that Lissa has looked at it, and enjoyed it, it is going up to the attic, and it's going to stay there."

Over my protests, and Father's, she had put it away in an old tin cashbox in one of the storerooms.

I told Froby all about it. I hated to, but I was afraid that he might have snooped it out.

He had, too. He pulled it from his pocket, looking badly disappointed.

"This it?" he asked briefly.

I nodded.

He sighed, and looked down at it as it lay in the palm of his hand.

"You may be interested to know," he said slowly, "that it was used for both murders."

CHAPTER 24

I LOOKED from Froby to the silly, glittering little toy in complete astonishment. It seemed impossible, somehow, that the thing could look so frivolous and yet be so deadly.

"Did your father provide you with bullets when he gave you the gun?" Froby asked, making it obvious he agreed with Mother about Father's judgment.

"Of course. The thing would be useless without ammunition."

Froby nodded, and as the luncheon gong sounded through the house, he slipped the revolver back into his pocket and turned toward the door.

I stood up and moved after him. "Where did you find it?" I asked.

"In that chair in the drawing room."

"Oh!" I drew a quick, frightened breath. "You mean the chair I saw that—that shape bending over?"

Froby held the door for me. "That's the one."

"But we searched it. There was nothing—not one thing— but some old pencils."

Froby closed the door again before I could get out, and faced me with his back to it. "Pencils?"

"Old pencils," I repeated, exasperated. "The sort of thing you always find under the seat cushions in a chair."

"May I see them?"

I flung around impatiently. "All right—I did keep them, as it happens." I went to my dressing table and jerked open the drawer. "Tell me," I said, "when did you find that gun—and whereabouts in the chair?"

"I found it yesterday morning—stuffed down behind the seat cushion. I had it examined, and there is no doubt that it was used in both cases."

I selected the pencils from my collection of clues with a growing sense of fear. Froby had had that gun since yesterday morning, and had not questioned me about it, nor even mentioned it, until now. I looked down at the pencils in my hands—and was jerked abruptly from my abstraction. They were labeled, in modest gilt, "Anthony Herridge, Architect." I closed my fingers on them and took an involuntary backward step away from Froby.

He was after me like a flash of lightning, and had the pencils in an instant—without actually having snatched them.

"They've been in the house for ages," I said desperately, watching them disappear into his pocket. "Absolute ages. Tony had them done some years ago—as an advertisement."

He opened the door for me again, and said, "By the way, are you quite sure that your gun was not in that chair when you searched it?"

"I'm positive," I said grimly. "I took everything but the stuffing out of that chair—and there was no gun. It must have been put there afterward."

He nodded absently as we started down the stairs. "Are you also sure that those gloves you saw on the hands were black?"

"They were black, or very dark-colored."

Froby said, "Hmm," and added pleasantly. "A thorough search of the immediate neighborhood has failed to bring to light any such gloves."

I left him in a huff and made my way to the dining room. I saw him head for the rear of the house, and wondered if he was snitching our food at mealtimes.

Mother spoke to me on the subject of tardiness at meals, but I hardly heard her. I was trying to untangle in my mind the gun and the chair, and the dark figure bending over it. I had seen that dark figure by the chair, and afterward there was no gun. Then, later, the gun was found there. Had I scared it away? And had it come back later? The explanation dawned on me suddenly. It was Saturday night when I had seen that dark figure—and it must have taken the gun at that time, and subsequently replaced it—because Rick was shot on Sunday.

"Lissa!" Mother said sharply. "What on earth are you mooning about? Father has spoken to you three times."

"I'm sorry," I said guiltily. "What did you say, Father?"

He frowned at me, and said "Never mind" in an offended tone.

"Don't lose your temper, Hammond."

"Dammit! I'm not losing my temper! But if no one wants to listen to me, I'll keep quiet."

"We are all attention," said Mother. "You may give the Gettysburg Address if you wish."

"Lot of fuss for nothing," Father muttered unreasonably. "I merely wanted to know if Lissa would like to go to East Orange again this afternoon."

I groaned inwardly. "Do you have to go?" I asked pitifully.

"Certainly not," Mother said decidedly. "It's neither necessary nor advisable."

I drew a breath of relief, while Father turned sulky and said no more.

I realized that I was more than uneasy by this time—I was definitely frightened.

After the wretched gun business, I felt that it would probably be a matter of hours before Froby pounced on me.

I decided that I might as well paint up a sample dandelion at the Potter house—I had nothing else to do, and my willingness to help him might possibly cast a doubt into Froby's mmd.

I was thoroughly annoyed at my carelessness about the pencils, too. If I had properly examined them when I first pulled them from the chair—as any third-rate sleuth would have done—Froby would never have known of them. As it was, I supposed that Tony would probably be dragged into the mess. I picked a dandelion from the lawn and walked on into the side garden, where Father quietly joined me.

"You know that light extension that was used in the cellar?" he asked, in the voice of a conspirator.

"Yes."

"They couldn't find any fingerprints on the thing."

"They can't be sure it was the one that was used in the cellar, though," I said thoughtfully.

"Yes, they are—it fits exactly. But they said it was a crude job. It hadn't been clipped onto the wall or the floor or the ceiling—simply attached to the socket outside, dropped onto the floor, run through the corner of the doorjamb and then hung over a hook on the wall. The socket had no switch, either—you'd have had to loosen the bulb to turn it off."

"Was the cord covered by all that coal outside the door?" I asked vaguely.

"Why don't you listen?" said Father impatiently. "The cord was doubled back close against the wall, after it came out of the doorjamb, and run along the wall to the corner, and then taken straight to the socket."

I remembered the socket, and had a misty idea that there was always a cord hanging from it.

I nodded. "But I don't see why it was removed after Rick and I left, and before the police came. It's always been there, as far as I can remember."

Father shrugged his indifference to that point, and as we had arrived at the Potter back door by then, I absentmindedly rapped on its panels.

It was opened suddenly, and Gertrude stood before us with a look of chilly inquiry.

I was a bit confounded. My mind had been so full of other things that I had not made any preparations for effecting an easy entrance. I stared back at Gertrude helplessly.

Father flung himself gracefully into the breach. "How do you do, Miss Gertrude? I have a message from my wife, for your mother."

Gertrude stood aside and said briefly, "Come in."

We filed through the kitchen, and I wondered what she was doing at home on a weekday.

Mrs. Potter was asleep in an easy chair in the living room, and Gertrude woke her up. "Visitors," she said, in the same voice she would have used to announce the exterminator.

Mrs. Potter started, blinked and fussed uneasily with her hair.

"Shame to wake you up," I murmured.

She said "Not at all" rather stiffly, and added, "Won't you sit down?"

We sat, and she looked as us warily out of small suspicious eyes while Gertrude stood silently in the dinette.

There was an uncomfortable pause, and because I could not think of anything else to say, I turned to Gertrude and asked brightly, "Are you on vacation?"

She said, "No. Just taking a day off."

The silence fell again, oppressive and heavy, and my mind began to dart wildly about, in search of small talk.

Father came to the rescue again. He said, "Mrs. Potter, my wife sent me to ask you to drop in to tea this afternoon."

A thaw set in at once, and Mrs. Potter gave us a pleased smile. "Why yes, thank you very much—I'd love to."

I went dizzy at the thought of Mother's reception to this, but since the thing was done, I turned recklessly to Gertrude and asked, "Won't you come, too? I know Mother would be pleased."

She smiled faintly, and said, "All right. Thanks."

Silence again.

I carefully folded and unfolded my handkerchief, cleared my throat, coughed a couple of times and said desperately, "Mrs. Potter, when you and Mrs. Reed were preparing the supper on Sunday night, are you sure that no one came in? I'm certain I saw somebody open the back door and disappear inside."

"Why—I couldn't be sure, of course. We were in and out of the kitchen quite a bit, you see. I suppose it would have been possible for someone to come in."

"Did either of you go upstairs?"

She got a bit red in the face, and stammered, "Why, yes— I think so. I think we both did, at different times."

"Would you mind timing me, while I go upstairs, so that we can see how long it takes ?" I said, feeling inspired.

Father pulled out his watch, studied it carefully and said, "All right. Off you go."

Gertrude moved out from the dinette, and her eyes followed me as I mounted the stairs.

I went straight to her bedroom and found the paints. The blue had been washed off the cover, but I found the matching tube. I took some water from the bedside table and hastily painted my dandelion.

I held it up, for a moment, to admire it—and was conscious of a faint movement behind me. I flung around, to find Gertrude standing at the door, looking at me.

CHAPTER 25

I STARED AT HER, with my heart in my mouth, and made a silent vow never to snoop into other people's affairs again, as long as I lived.

She said, "I knew you were up to something—but I didn't think it was anything like this. Painting a dandelion blue! You must be quite crazy."

"No," I said, "I'm not, really. Crazy, I mean. I'm—doing this for someone else. As a matter of fact I'm in a jam, and I'm trying to work myself out."

"I'm not convinced," she said flatly. "I don't see how sneaking up to my bedroom and painting a dandelion blue can get you any-where, except into the insane asylum. It seems to be becoming a habit, too—you've done it before. I found my box messed up with blue paint the other day."

"I didn't do that, Gertrude," I said feebly. "Someone else did. Have you any idea who it could have been?"

"Yes," said Gertrude. "You."

I started to speak, but she interrupted me sharply. "You've been snooping around at the Reeds', too. Catherine says you're always over there on some flimsy pretext or other."

"The police suspect me," I said patiently. "I'm trying to prove that I had nothing to do with it."

"By painting a dandelion blue," she said, with heavy sarcasm.

"Don't you know about the blue dandelions?"

"No," said Gertrude, "and I don't want to. Not if it makes you behave the way you've been doing."

It seemed to me that we weren't getting anywhere, so I slipped past her and went on downstairs. I collected Father, murmured, "See you at four o'clock," to Mrs. Potter, and left the house.

We went straight home and put the dandelion away with the one from the Reed house. We went in search of Mother, then, and I be-lieve we were holding hands by the time we found her. But Father seemed to be inspired that day. He had another brilliant idea.

"Janice," he said, "how did you come to invite that old Potter bore over to tea today?"

Mother gasped, and said, "What on earth are you talking about, Hammond?"

"Well, she's getting into her best bib and tucker," Father said airily, "and heading this way at four o'clock."

"Gertrude's coming, too," I added, avoiding Mother's eye. "She has a day off."

"Most definitely, I never asked either one of them," Mother said indignantly. "I've a good mind to go out—" She stopped suddenly, and gave us a long, suspicious look.

We must have borne it pretty well, because she shrugged her shoulders, turned away and called for Grace.

The telephone rang then. I was halfway upstairs when I heard Mother answer it, and after a pause she said frigidly, "Of course, Mrs. Potter, bring Mrs. Reed if she'd care to come—yes, I under-stand—Catherine, too—of course."

The telephone clicked back into its cradle, and Mother gave an ominous little cough. I flew up the remaining stairs and went quietly and quickly along to the small sitting room opposite my bedroom.

I stationed myself at the window and watched Tony's back yard and his garage. I thought that since he had taken the trouble to warn me about Froby, I ought to warn him about the pencils.

For a while I sat in peace, and then I heard Froby's pattering feet come down the hall and slip into my room. I didn't move—I knew he'd dig out the two dandelions, and they were both labeled.

I turned my attention to Tony's back yard again, and saw that Wilbur, Jr., had materialized there, and was picking the choicest flowers in a furtive fashion. He collected a fancy bouquet, and then he sat down and amused himself, while he was cooling off, by pulling the flowers to pieces. After he had made a thorough mess of them, he threw the stalks away, and proceeded to kill some time by walking straight through the hedge that divided Tony's yard from the Druckers', some four or five times. When he had made a fairly sizable hole in the hedge he suddenly disappeared around the side of the house.

He presently reappeared in his own yard, carrying a pail and shovel. He made straight for a tree, and began to dig in the rough earth beneath it. While I watched him, fascinated, he dug up a man's necktie, some toy soldiers, two empty bottles—and a pair of black gloves.

I was out of my chair in an instant, and went flying down the stairs.

By the time I caught up with the kid he was burying the things again. I snatched at the gloves, and at the same time he threw back his head and let out a fearful howl.

I made a panicky effort to shut him up. "Look," I whispered, "I'll give you a dollar if you'll let me have the gloves."

He gave another howl and said, "Naw! Gimme 'at—'at's mine."

I gave it up, and watched him gloomily while he buried the gloves and patted the earth neatly above them. They were a woman's sport gloves of a black fabric—but I could not possibly identify them as the ones I had seen on those hands. Froby had said there were no such gloves in the neighborhood—and yet, here they were. I noted the spot carefully, and decided to come back and dig them up later.

I smiled at the kid, and tried to pump him about the mysterious lady who had let him dip dandelions in ink. "Shall we play at putting flowers in the ink?" I asked, feeling like a super-fool.

He sat there, with two dirty tears drying on his cheeks, and looked at me blankly.

"You know," I encouraged him. "Like you did with the other lady."

His expression became, if anything, a bit more stupid.

"Don't you like to play with ink and dandelions?" I cooed.

The kid shoved his fingers into his mouth and blinked at me, and at that moment Edith Drucker opened the back door and looked at us with coldness and suspicion. I nodded brightly, and throwing all caution to the winds, invited her to tea.

She relaxed, and accepted, and I pushed off. I decided not to tell Mother about it—there were so many coming, by this time, that she probably wouldn't notice any extras.

I went around to the side door and looked under the step — and was mildly surprised when I found no nail file.

I hung around in the garden until I saw Mrs. Potter emerge from her back door, decked out in what must certainly have been her Sunday dress. I went up to my room, then, to pretty up a bit.

When I got down to the drawing room, four of them were there, but the Drucker woman had not arrived Either she was busy titivating, or had decided to be fashionably late.

Mother did not know that she was coming, of course, and ordered tea at once. She had an air of cool abstraction with the faintest hint of poised superiority, and her guests were ill at ease without exactly knowing why.

It turned out later that she was merely composing, mentally, a few crisp words for Father, once she got him alone, because Mrs. Potter had spilled the beans during her telephone call. She had explained that when Father delivered the invitation for tea, she had completely forgotten having asked the Reeds over for the afternoon. Mother, with her back to the wall, had been more or less forced to make the invitation wholesale.

Edith Drucker and the tea arrived at the same moment— and three minutes later Froby appeared on the scene.

He looked us over with a coldly official eye, and then, without actually putting on a false beard and whiskers, he donned his gentleman's disguise.

He put his heels together, bowed slightly from the waist and said, "Good afternoon, ladies. May I join you?"

Mrs. Reed and Mrs. Potter smiled graciously, Catherine and

Gertrude gave him a couple of cold, hostile glances, Edith Drucker gave him the glad eye and Mother slightly elevated one eyebrow, and said distantly, "I don't believe you would find a ladies' tea party very amusing, Mr. Frobisher."

Froby bowed a little lower. "I am longing for a cup of tea, Mrs. Vickers—and I promise to be very quiet and inoffensive."

Mother rang for another cup in a fury, and Froby made his way to the window seat, kicking a delicate little table on the way.

After he had been supplied with tea Mother said, "When did you come in, Mr. Frobisher? I did not hear the bell." She allowed her eyes to wander from him to the little table— although it really hadn't been damaged at all.

"I, er—arrived about half an hour ago," Froby explained.

"But I'm sure I never heard the bell. Perhaps you came in the back way?"

Froby squirmed, and admitted, "I had something to discuss with the maids."

"Still," said Mother, continuing to ride him, "they should announce you when you come. I like to know when you are here."

That was exactly what Froby did not want. He frowned, studied his tie for a space and then came out of his disguise. "I'd like you ladies to show me, as soon as possible, all the nail files in your possession."

CHAPTER 26

THE VISITORS opened their mouths and stared, Mother tightened her lips and began to tap her foot, and I looked at Froby with startled interest. I had found the nail files—but evidently he knew more about them than I did.

Too late I dropped my mouth open and tried to look amazed along with the rest of them. But Froby had been watching me, and he pounced.

"What do you know about this, Miss Herridge?"

"Either call me Mrs. Herridge or Miss Vickers," I said, playing for time. "I answer to both names."

"Very well, Mrs. Vickers," he said impatiently. "I am waiting to hear what you know."

I felt that he was pushing me deeper into trouble all the time, but I decided that the truth was my safest course. I told him all about it, and Edith Drucker and Mrs. Reed backed me up.

Froby asked Edith if she kept her nail files in a place where Wilbur, Jr., could not reach them, and she told him, pertly, that there was no such spot in the house. She added that she had lost two files, and that I had returned one to her.

Froby turned to me and pounced again.

"And the other?"

"The other," I said promptly, "is in one of my drawers—as you know full well. Unless you have it yourself."

He uncrossed his legs and recrossed them the other way—kicking Mrs. Potter's ankle and the piano.

"I have not seen it anywhere," he observed, placing the tips of his fingers together.

"Then you haven't looked."

He ignored me, and turned his attention to Mrs. Reed.

She was slightly uncomfortable, but she answered him readily enough. "Why, I just noticed, suddenly, that my file was missing."

"Do you know how long it had been gone?" Froby asked.

"No. I've no idea."

"Would you have any idea, Miss Catherine?"

"None whatever," said Catherine shortly.

"Now, Mrs. Reed, your file was returned to you by Mrs. Herridge?"

"Yes."

"Have you any idea where she found it?"

"Yes she has just told you   under the step of the side door."

"But when she returned it to you?"

"No, she didn't say, then, where she had found it."

Mother reached the limit of her endurance at this point. "Mr. Frobisher," she said firmly, "I must ask you to leave. This is a ladies' tea, and your presence here is in the worst possible taste."

Froby blushed and untangled his legs—kicking Mrs. Potter's ankle again. He bowed coldly, and walked out of the room.

"Good for you, Mrs. Vickers," Edith Drucker applauded stridently. "That ape certainly needs to be told where to head in."

Mrs. Reed laughed. "He can be annoying. It seems to me that his questions are sometimes entirely irrelevant. For instance, he asked me if I were fond of solitaire. I told him I had played it, on occasion, but I would not go so far as to say that I was fond of it."

They all laughed, and it appeared that they had all been asked the same question.

I wondered a little at Froby's method. If he had really wanted to find out, I felt that there were better ways than asking them all outright. I supposed that he trusted to what he thought was his keen sense of observation when they gave their answers.

The tea broke up shortly afterward, and they all went at the same time. I went with them, because I thought that Father and I had better face the reckoning together. I walked with the guests to their various homes, and was on my way back when I saw Tony come in. I raced after him and caught him at his back door.

"Tony," I said breathlessly, "I want to warn you."

He handed me a cigarette. "What is it? Are you setting your cap for me?"

"You'd better take it seriously. I think I've got you in Dutch with Froby. Only, I didn't mean to."

"Come in and have a drink—and you can tell me about it."

"Lissa!" said Father, stepping out of a bush. "If you think I paid out good money for a divorce, simply to have you—"

"How about a couple of drinks?" Tony interrupted. "We can finish the fight inside, where the neighbors won't enjoy it."

"Come on, Father," I said impatiently. "You can't dictate to me—not with that tea party on your conscience."

He skulked into Tony's house without further argument, but once inside he turned on me. "I invited one—and one only—the rest of the push was your fault."

"Save it for Mother," I said briefly.

We sat down in the living room, and while Tony mixed drinks Father fell silent. I could almost hear the wheels going around in his head. "It's one of his good days," I explained to Tony. "He's had two brilliant ideas so far—and those things usually go in threes."

"What is he going to do with it when he catches it?" Tony asked, bringing the three drinks on a tray.

"Garnish it skillfully and serve it up to Mother. He's in the doghouse, you know."

"Damn it all, Lissa," Father exploded, "anyone would think you'd had no hand in this business yourself."

Tony sat down and looked at me inquiringly. "What particular brand of Dutch have you got me into?"

I told him about the pencils, and watched him anxiously while he sat back and thought it over. After considering it for about two minutes he began to laugh.

"Is this hysteria?" I asked.

He shook his head, still grinning. "I was thinking of Froby's probable reaction."

"Well—what?"

"He thinks I am your pet aversion, and he'll take those pencils to be a clumsy attempt, on your part, to cast suspicion my way."

I said, "Oh!" and felt an instant conviction that that would be exactly Froby's reaction. "All wrong," I muttered feebly. "Wilbur, Jr., is my pet aversion."

"You're getting hard," said Tony. "I can remember a time when you loved all children, including the Scandinavian."

"Wilbur, Jr., picks your flowers and then tears them apart."

"I'll kill the little bastard!" Tony shouted. "Just let me see him— once!"

I leaned back in my chair, shaken with helpless laughter, and at that moment the doorbell rang. Tony went to the door, still muttering, and admitted Ben Amherst.

Ben wandered in, caught sight of me, blushed and edged back. Then he saw Father, still sitting in the attitude of The Thinker, and relaxed a bit.

Tony got him a drink, and he swallowed it almost at a gulp. "God!" he muttered. "I can't stand that house any longer—it's awful."

"Pretty grim," Tony agreed. "Why don't you move out?"

"I'm liable for the rent until July first. I'll move then."

"If you stay that long, you'll probably be used to it and won't want to move," Tony suggested.

"I don't want to move—if I can stick it out," Ben said, almost to himself.

I supposed it was because he wanted to be near Catherine.

Father suddenly came out of his abstraction, drained his drink and stood up. "Come on, Lissa—time for dinner."

Tony took out his watch. "Hmm. Twenty minutes to six. But go, by all means, if you're bored."

"Yes, of course," said Father heartily, but with his mind on other things. "Thanks for the drink, old man."

We went home, and Father was whispering to himself most of the way.

"All set for the Big Lie?" I asked.

"It's a wonder you wouldn't do your own work," he said bitterly, "instead of leaving it all to me."

Mother was stretched out, elegantly, on the chaise lounge in her bedroom, with a book. She gave us a look that was several degrees below zero, and turned a page.

"Janice," said Father, "I have a confession to make."

Mother glanced up from her book and murmured, "Not really?"

"Yes, I have. Matter of fact, I invited all those women to tea."

"I don't believe it," said Mother, dripping sarcasm. "You're shielding someone."

"Now, wait a minute, Janice. I've been worried about your state of mind—all this murder, and so on—and I thought if you could be thoroughly bored it might be good for you."

"That was sweetly thoughtful of you," said Mother, turning another page. "And now, if you could see your way to giving your mind a rest, I think we should all benefit."

I sneaked off at that point and left them to it.

At dinner I could see that Father was making progress, although he was only partly out of the woods even then.

We went into the library after dinner, and Father induced Mother to play some sort of card game with him while I stretched out on the couch with a book.

I lost myself completely in the book for an hour or two, and then I became sleepy. I heard Mother and Father go up to bed, bickering over the cards, and I must have fallen asleep immediately afterward.

I was brought slowly to consciousness again by the insistent clatter of the doorbell. I shook the sleep from my eyes and glanced uneasily around the room—and then I looked at the clock. It was ten minutes past two.

CHAPTER 27

I SHIVERED in the close heat of the night, and sat still for a moment, hoping that the bell had roused Father—but there was no sound from upstairs.

I crept out into the hall. The bell had stopped ringing, but there was a soft muffled knocking on the door now.

I hesitated, and was conscious that my hands were clammy and my forehead damp.

The knocking came again, and I moved cautiously along to the door and poked the letter slot open.

"Who is it?" I whispered shakily.

"It's Ben—Ben Amherst. Please let me in."

I drew a quick breath of relief and opened the door. Ben slipped in, and I looked at him curiously. He was not wearing his usual vague smile, and his face was strained and gray. He was sketchily dressed.

"I'm sorry," he said simply, "but I cannot stay in that house any more tonight. I saw the light on here, and hoped you were still up."

I led him back to the living room and told him to sit down. "What happened?" I asked.

He took out a cigarette and lit it with shaking hands, and then inhaled nearly a third of it at once. The smoke poured out in two thin streams from his nostrils, and he seemed to relax a little.

"When I came down to breakfast this morning," he said slowly, "I found a deck of cards laid out on the table in the dinette—as though someone had been playing solitaire."

I gasped, and reached for a cigarette myself.

Ben continued painfully, "I asked the colored woman if she had been playing, but she said no—she thought I had. I gathered the cards together and put them away—and thought no more about it until tonight. I read until late, and when I finally turned out the lights, I went out into the hall and I—I thought I heard cards being shuffled." He stopped, and swallowed convulsively.

"Are you *sure* it was someone shuffling cards?" I whispered.

"No, I can't be sure, but it sounded like that. And after seeing those cards on the table—" He huddled back into his chair and stared at the tip of his cigarette.

"Go on," I said, and found that I was shaking with nervous excitement.

"I called down the stairs, but there was no answer, of course, so I went down. The doors were locked, and the screens all latched at the windows, as I had left them. But there was a game of solitaire on the table—half-finished." He took out a large handkerchief and mopped unsteadily at his face. "It wouldn't be so ghastly if they hadn't told me that Charlie had been playing solitaire—when he—" His voice trailed off, and he crushed out his cigarette just before it burned his fingers.

I looked uneasily around the shadowy room, and wondered what I could do. It would be inhuman to send Ben back to all that horror—and yet I did not know what Mother and Father would say if I told them we were harboring one of the cottagers. I wondered why he had not gone to Tony's—or even Gertrude's—or Catherine's place. He was much more intimate with them all than he was with us.

I think my doubt must have showed on my face, because he burst out almost hysterically, "There's something queer going on among the people in those houses! I thought I knew them—but there's something— Things keep happening that I don't understand.

"But you people here—you're right out of it. I'm sure of that."

"I don't think any of them know what it's all about," I said soberly.

He shook his head fretfully. "But this—somehow, it's at the back of my mind. I know there are—and have been—things going on that I don't understand." He rumpled his hair, and added rather pathetically, "if you'll just let me stay here—I can sleep on the couch, or anywhere. I can't go back."

"Wait here a minute," I said. "I'll call Father."

He nodded, and I went upstairs.

Mother was awake in an instant, at my knock, but Father had to be dragged out of his sleep, and he came to in a bad temper.

After I had explained, for the fifth time, that Ben Amherst was downstairs, he sat straight up in bed and glared at me. "If you must entertain callers at three o'clock in the morning," he raved, "at least have the common decency not to come up here and announce them to me. I don't care if you have Vanderbilt, himself, down there—"

Mother said, "Hammond," and there was peace and quiet for a minute. Then Father lowered his voice and said sulkily, "The fella's yellow. Why should he come and bother us, when he has his own friends over there?"

"He doesn't want them to know that the house is getting too much for him," Mother said shrewdly.

"He saw my light," I explained. "I was reading downstairs, and I fell asleep."

"He may be the murderer," Father said darkly.

We had to consider it, of course, but Mother decided, at last, that we could not turn him away, and she directed me to put him in the small guest room at the back of the house.

Father came downstairs with me, and we found Ben sitting where I had left him, nervously adding butts to the ash tray in front of him.

"Well, young man," Father boomed, "this is all very irregular— but I think we can put you up for the rest of the night."

"Thank you, sir," Ben whispered hoarsely. "My house has—it's getting on my nerves."

"Yes, yes—so I understand. But the thing to do with nerves is to control them," said Father, who'd been born without any.

We went upstairs again, and I showed Ben his room. He was quietly grateful, and just before I left him he said, "Don't tell anyone that I slept here tonight. I don't think anyone knows, now—and if you let me sleep here again—they won't know where I am. I have a queer feeling that someone is after me. Maybe I'm nuts—I don't know."

I promised to say nothing, and went off to my bedroom, where I carefully locked the door. After all, we didn't know much about Ben— and it did seem foolish to let anyone into the house after what had been going on. And yet, it didn't make much difference, because they seemed able to get in anyway. And if Ben were telling the truth, they were getting in there, too—with the doors locked, and the windows latched!

The next day was hotter than ever, and we were all languid and inclined to be cross.

Grace told me that Ben had gone off early, and had had only a glass of milk for breakfast. She had seen him go into his own back door, and he had come out again, shortly afterward, in a change of clothing, and evidently bound for the station.

After breakfast I took a book and went out to the shade of a tree in the garden. The spot had looked cool and pleasant from the house—but once established there, I found it anything but comfortable. It was hot and humid, the grass was prickly and the ground hard. I could not read, and I presently went off into a doze.

I woke up to find that the sun had shifted around a bit and was staring me in the eye, I had a sprinkling of ants all over me, and Froby was seated on the grass a few feet away, watching me.

I sat up, and began to brush frantically at the ants. "Lovely day," I suggested.

"Too warm," said Froby.

I disposed of the last ant. "Maybe it will be cooler tomorrow."

"Paper says warmer," said Froby, unyielding.

We fell silent, and I fingered the pages of my book nervously, and hoped that he would not suddenly produce handcuffs and clamp them on me. I silently cursed Father for a silly ass on his choice of a birthday present for an eighteen-year-old girl.

Froby scratched his ankle. "You know those blue dandelions?"

"We've met," I admitted cautiously.

"You painted two, and I did the other two."

"Well?"

"They have dried now, and the one most like the original was painted from the box in your attic."

I had a distinctly gone feeling in the pit of my stomach. I stared at Froby, and he stared back—evidently waiting for me to say something wrong.

I swallowed twice and said in a squeaky voice, "Then my paintbox was used for the same reason that my gun was used, I suppose. To— to cover up."

Froby shifted his eyes from my face to the lower branches of the tree, and I felt the tension ease a little.

He said presently, "When you were locked in the cellar room that night, how long did it take Mr. Rickey to get in and release you?"

I thought back, and said slowly, "Why—not very long, I guess."

"Yet he had to break in."

"I don't know," I said guardedly.

"Why not?"

"There might have been a door or so left open—I wouldn't know."

Froby clicked his tongue about six times, and I interrupted him at last. "I don't see why it's important, because if Tony's story is true Rick had his own way of getting into our house."

Froby let it pass, and changed the subject. "Now, when Mr. Rickey left you on Sunday to keep his bridge date—some little time elapsed before you saw him sitting in his dinette?"

"Yes—quite a while."

"But he intended to go to his club—he was expected, and they were waiting for him. It must have been an important interview that delayed him—an interview with someone who wore dark-colored gloves."

"The gloves!" I gasped, and struggled to my feet. How could I have forgotten them! I should have taken them from Wilbur, Jr., and allowed him to yell his head off.

I began to run toward the Druckers' yard while Froby loped along beside me. "I think I know where those gloves are," I panted. "At least they looked as though they might be—"

I clawed at the soft earth in Wilbur, Jr.'s, treasure-trove, knowing all the time, somehow, that those gloves would be gone—and they were. I turned up the tie, the toy soldiers and the bottles—but there were no gloves. I sat back at last, and pushed the hair from my damp face with the back of my wrist.

Froby was watching me with an angry frown—Edith Drucker stood at her back door, watching both of us and vigorously chewing gum, and Wilbur, Jr., clutched at her skirt, whining.

Froby, disappointed in what he had hoped was to be a good catch, flung at me furiously, "Mrs. Herridge, you may as well know that there are only a few nail files between you and real trouble!"

CHAPTER 28

FROBY STRODE AWAY, his long legs looking like a pair of shears, and I got slowly to my feet and wiped the earth from my hands with an inadequate handkerchief.

So it was those mysterious nail files that kept the hand of the law from my shoulder! But how? And why?

I gave it up with a shrug, and silently prayed that in a wilderness of my weapon and my paintbox having been used in my house, the trusty nail files would not desert me.

Wilbur, Jr., left his mother's skirts, advanced across the yard and looked down at the shambles I had made of his cache. He went into a tantrum on the spot. Edith followed him, shook him violently and ordered him to shut up.

"She took my sings," he howled, pointing at me.

"What sings?" Edith yelled.

"Goves!" he blubbered.

Edith let him go and stared at him. "What are you talking about?"

"Black gloves," I translated. "Maybe they're yours?"

"Gloves?"

"Wilbur had a pair yesterday—he was playing with them in the yard. I figured I'd better tell you—they might be yours."

"*Black gloves?*"

"Yes."

"Not mine," said Edith, putting her gum into motion again. "I never wear black gloves. I wonder where he got them."

"Let's ask him," I suggested hopefully.

Edith had to promise him a lollipop in order to get his attention, and then she asked him where he had found the gloves.

He led us out of the yard, across our side garden, around to the side door, and pointed to a clump of bushes close by.

"Maybe one of your maids threw 'em out," Edith said, losing interest.

The kid started to whine again, and said he wanted his "sings" back. In a moment of brilliance I told him that the lady who had let him dip dandelions in ink had probably taken them—and why not ask her?

The kid stared at me with a faint gleam in his eye. He appeared to consider it for a moment, and then his face clouded again and he whined afresh. Edith took a step in his direction and murmured something in which the word "hairbrush" was ominously clear, and the kid turned and shot around the corner of the house with astonishing speed.

Edith sighed, "Tch, tch, children are a trial. Well—I'll be seein' you," and went off at a more leisurely pace.

I followed her around to the back and absently watched her disappear into her house. I yawned, idly shot the butt of the cigarette I had been smoking and was mildly surprised at the distance I made. I was conscious of sleepy regret that I did not have another butt so that I could try it again.

I started back toward the side door, and was brought up short by the sight of Albert Hahn and Mack Brewster—who appeared to be examining the lock.

I eased back around the corner of the house, without them having seen me, and ran full into Froby. He had a lilac bush more or less draped around him, and both ears flapping.

I winked at him, and he blushed all over and tried to pretend that he was measuring the bush. I watched him with a superior smile, and at last he gave it up and turned on me. "Why didn't you tell me you had Mr. Amherst staying with you last night?" he whispered savagely.

I was a bit taken aback, but I put on one of Mother's airs, and said coldly, "Mr. Amherst was hardly staying with me! He was my parents' guest."

Froby waved it aside impatiently. "What I'm trying to get at—"

"All right," I said hastily, "I'll tell you." I recited the events of the night, and ended by assuring him that I would have told him about it sooner had I not felt certain that he would know all about it before breakfast.

He gave me a coldly reproachful look. "Everybody is so secretive," he alibied.

I left him, and went in the back door. The kitchen was deserted except for Father, who had his head in the icebox.

"What are you doing?" I asked sharply.

He said bitterly, "I am engaged in morning prayer."

I watched him concoct an enormous ham sandwich and open a bottle of beer.

"You'll ruin your lunch," I suggested mildly.

He took a huge swig of beer, and relaxed comfortably "If you refer to that assortment of grass and weeds they serve at one o'clock— I can eat that at any time."

"And Mother wonders why you gain, instead of losing, on your diet!"

I went on upstairs. Dora was busy in my room with an assortment of mops and dusters, so I established myself in the small sitting room opposite and gazed drearily at the five back yards. I wondered, with a little thrill of fear, how long it would be before Froby came after me with the Black Maria and a warning that anything I said might be used against me.

Wilbur, Jr., appeared in Tony's back yard, and I watched him idly. He made his way to where Tony's garbage can and wastepaper basket awaited disposal, and began to grub around in the waste paper. He examined each handful of rubbish carefully as he pulled it out, and then flung it to the ground. He was nearly knee deep in the stuff when he came upon something dark—and I think he and I must have recognized the gloves at the same instant. A split second before I left the window I saw him streak away with his treasure clutched tightly in his hands. I flew out the back door, narrowly missing a collision with Grace, and began to search frantically—but the kid had disappeared.

The end of our property, at the back, was wooded, and it was there that I finally ran Wilbur, Jr., to earth. He emerged from the trees with a satisfied look on his dirty face—and minus the gloves.

When he caught sight of me he put on a ferocious scowl. I knew it would be hopeless to make a direct inquiry about the gloves, since he was convinced that I wanted to rob him of his "sings," so I dropped onto the grass, and said casually, "Hello, there—hot, isn't it?"

He came to a halt and stared at me—warily.

I wondered whether I ought to go and start searching, then and there, and let the kid rouse the entire neighborhood with his shrieks—or wait until he had gone.

Lunch was called before I could make up my mind, and I went reluctantly back to the house. I made a brief search for Froby, Hahn and Brewster—but they had disappeared completely—which was usual when I had anything to tell them. Wilbur, Jr., continued to stand where I had left him, uneasily guarding the new cache for his "sings."

At lunch Father ate his grass with unusual gusto, but Mother was too preoccupied to notice. It developed that Mrs. Potter had called during the morning, and had diffidently offered a sure cure for drunkenness. You put it in the soup, or the coffee, without the drunk knowing anything about it, and it worked wonders. It had been worked on the late Mr. Potter with outstanding success.

"The woman's a damn' busybody," Father said, munching celery, with his ears a bright scarlet.

"But why should she pick on me?" Mother persisted. "Once or twice I had the impression that her solicitude was aimed at you—but surely that isn't possible? You haven't been intoxicated since we came here, Hammond?"

Father and I exchanged a fleeting guilty glance, in which the memory of his superb performance on Tony's front lawn, with a representative audience on the Drucker property, stood out clearly.

Mother was looking at us, with sudden and ominous concentration, when the doorbell rang She took no apparent notice of it, but I knew that she was listening, and that the showdown was temporarily postponed.

A minute later Tony appeared in the dining room, with Dora trailing behind him.

Mother lowered her fork, raised her eyebrows and said, "We do not receive guests in the dining room, Dora."

"No, ma'am," Dora agreed emphatically.

Tony said, "I understand that Ben Amherst slept in this house last night."

Father opened his mouth but Mother got in ahead of him. "Mr. Herridge, we are at lunch. I must ask you to leave."

"Are you going to let him stay here again tonight?" Tony demanded.

"If you will not leave of your own accord, I shall call the police," said Mother.

Tony laughed. "The police will be accompanied by thirty or forty reporters."

Mother drew in her breath sharply and her eyebrows came down a notch or two. She weakened to the extent of calling upon Father. "Hammond! See Mr. Herridge to the door at once."

Father got to his feet, and Tony pulled up a chair and sat down. He took my glass of iced tea and drained it while Father looked at him helplessly.

Tony replaced the glass. "Mrs. Vickers, it may be—I think it is—extremely dangerous for you to have Ben Amherst staying here. You must realize that you know nothing about him."

"Very kind of you to give us the benefit of your opinion," said Mother in a faraway voice.

"I want your assurance that you will not allow him to stay here again."

"I shall give you no such assurance," said Mother definitely. "You must allow us the privilege of managing our own affairs."

Tony stood up abruptly, his eyes flashing green fire "Then you can expect me, too. I'll have the buff room—and please see that there is ice water left there."

He departed, having worked himself and Mother into a fine fury.

CHAPTER 29

MOTHER drew a long breath and murmured, "Impertinence."

"Are you going to put ice water in the buff room?" I asked.

"Don't be silly. Of course not."

"You don't think he'll come?"

"Certainly not—I'll see to it myself. If it's dangerous to have the Amherst man here, I should say it was doubly dangerous to have Tony Herridge as well."

I laughed. "I'll bet on Tony. If he says he'll be here—he will."

Father hooted. "If Janice says he's not coming—she means it. I'd bet on her any day in the week."

"How much?" I asked.

"Five."

"Five it is."

"Betting on a thing like that!" said Mother. "It's vulgar."

After lunch I went straight to the woods at the end of our property, and started to search for the gloves. I made a casual survey at first, which was unsuccessful, and then I decided to do it systematically. I started at one side and walked slowly up and down, keeping my eyes on the ground and hitting at the undergrowth with a stick. I had done only a small section when a noise of breaking twigs brought me sharply about face.

Wilbur, Jr., was watching me with his lower lip stuck out in a sullen scowl. I ignored him and continued on my way, and the little brat started to follow close on my heels.

I persevered for a while, but in the end, I gave up and said to the kid, "Let's sit down."

He lowered himself to the ground and began to chew on a piece of grass, while I sat on a stone and fanned myself with my handkerchief.

I looked over at him, and to my surprise he suddenly gave me a broad grin. I smiled back at him and said tentatively, "What shall we play now?"

"Cops," said the kid promptly, "and wobbers."

"All right," I agreed, feeling as transparent as a piece of glass. "You go and wob those gloves of yours—and I'll be the cop and try to catch you."

"Oke," said the kid, his grubby face lighting up with pleasure.

He scrambled to his feet, started off confidently and suddenly stopped. I saw him look over his shoulder, and the next minute he was streaking across our lawn. He disappeared around the side of our house just as Edith came into my line of vision, after him in full cry, but not gaining any distance on him.

I thought, "Oh well—that's children for you—bless their little hearts," and hoped piously that Edith and the hairbrush would overtake him before long.

I made a halfhearted effort to go on with my search, but the heat was too much for me. I left the woods, and finding a couple of cushions under a tree on the lawn I settled myself comfortably and promptly went off to sleep.

I slept heavily, weighed down by the heat, and awoke at last feeling thick and stupid. The hands of my wrist watch stood at four o'clock, and I thought about tea but lacked the energy to drag myself into the house.

I lay near a tall hedge that Father had started years ago, with the idea of building a maze, and I presently became conscious of a murmur of voices that seemed to come from behind it. I listened for a while, mopping languidly at my damp forehead, and then got slowly to my feet and went around to investigate.

It appeared to be a conference in which Ben Amherst held the speaker's chair. Mrs. Reed, Mrs. Potter, Edith and Catherine were grouped around him. I supposed that Gertrude had not yet returned from work and wondered why Ben was home so early.

They were listening round-eyed while he told them that every morning, when he came downstairs, he found a deck of cards laid out in solitaire formation on the table in the dinette. I noticed that he made no mention of his flight to our house. They all greeted me pleasantly with the exception of Catherine—who barely nodded. But I could not make up my mind as to whether her coldness was intentional or merely the result of apathy. She appeared to be taking in what Ben was saying but she seemed listless and indifferent.

Ben was enjoying himself. It wasn't often that he could take the floor and hold it, and it had gone to his head a bit. He began to boast. He declared that Rick had entrusted to him all his private papers—had once told him that if anything ever happened Ben was to go through them and after returning certain of them to the people most intimately concerned, destroy the rest.

According to Ben this was a task of no mean proportions, as Rick's private papers had filled to capacity a good-sized desk. There were letters from numerous women—love letters for the most part—and quite a number from men, containing odd bits of gossip and scandal. "And," said Ben, visibly swelling with importance, "there was a diary. Rick's own diary, which he had kept under lock and key."

Gertrude joined us at this point, but she was so quiet about it, and we were all so excited about the diary, that we hardly noticed her.

"Have you actually got it?" I asked Ben eagerly.

He drew it proudly from an inside pocket of his coat—a fat little book bound in red leather, with a gilt lock. He would not let us touch it though, and he returned it to his pocket almost immediately. "I keep it with me always," he announced rather primly.

"Have you read it?" Mrs. Reed asked.

"No—not all of it—it has taken all my time to go through the other papers. And of course the police went through everything before turning them over to me. But I'm going to finish it, and then I shall probably destroy it."

I felt a sudden, sharp distaste for any further discussion of Rick's affairs, and I annoyed Ben by abruptly changing the subject. "Where is Wilbur, Jr.?" I asked Edith.

She said she hadn't seen him, but when she caught up with him he'd know it.

Mrs. Potter gave me a look of impatience and steered us straight back to Rick. "How many love letters did he have from local ladies?"

Ben immediately became very male and very noble, with a touch of severity. He could not answer the question. Rick's affairs were inviolate and most of the letters and papers were to be destroyed.

"You could get quite a good price from the newspapers for them," I suggested dryly.

Ben, still noble, sneered proudly at such a low idea and told the entire audience that Rick's sacred trust was safe from betrayal by Ben Amherst.

Edith, chewing languidly, said he was quite right, but how about reading aloud just a page or two from the diary? He could select parts that would not betray anybody or anything.

Ben shook his head. "There is no part that I would care to read. Rick left it in my care—and he was my friend."

Mesdames Reed and Potter nodded solemn approval.

"You're quite right," said Mrs. Reed. "Rick knew what he was doing when he left his things to you."

Ben colored happily, and Edith smothered a yawn. "I'm going to look for that kid," she announced, and got to her feet.

She brushed grass and a couple of ants from her dress, slapped at a mosquito on her arm, yawned again and went slowly but surely home. It was the beginning of the end of Ben's little hour in the sun. The others found various excuses to take them off until only Catherine and I remained.

Apparently we looked pretty hopeless as an audience, for Ben sighed, stood up and wandered away, murmuring something about an errand he had to do before dinner.

Catherine and I sat in a silence that suddenly became electric as our eyes fell together on the oblong of red lying in the green grass. Rick's diary had evidently, in some fashion, slipped out of Ben's pocket.

I reached a tentative hand, but Catherine's arm shot across me and her fingers closed over the book.

I looked at her curiously and saw that her eyes had lost their apathetic stare and were glittering feverishly.

"Now I can find out," she whispered, "whether he did love me—or whether it was you."

I laughed at her and said easily, "Don't be so silly—of course he was in love with you. Why, he barely knew me."

She shook her head impatiently. "That wouldn't make any difference to Rick."

She opened the book and ruffled the pages until she had got into the middle, and then she started to read.

I lay flat on my back, with my arms folded behind my head, and watched her face. Wild horses could not have dragged me away. I had a faint, feeble hope that she would let me read it when she had finished.

She read quietly for some time, and I had an idea that she was pleased with it—and then her expression changed abruptly. She raised her head and stared straight in front of her for a moment, and then turned back a page and read again.

As I watched her face it was suddenly and startlingly drained of every particle of color, and her eyes had a queer, dazed look of shock. She got to her feet and the book fell to the ground.

I sat up hastily, and she stared at me without seeing me. Her consciousness seemed to be turned inward on her own helpless suffering.

I tried to say something, but she turned away without any sign of having heard me and began to run toward her own house.

CHAPTER 30

THE DIARY HAD FALLEN face down on the grass at about the place Catherine had been reading, and without so much as a twinge of conscience to stop me I pounced on it.

I began to read the two pages that lay open, and I was a little surprised at the text. It seemed that the cynical and sophisticated Rick had had his own little flights of poesy.

He had written, "Poor Charlie! How he would have loved today! Sunshine and flowers and color—Charlie could get drunk on color. I must try to see it all through his eyes, now that he cannot.

"Senseless, appalling destruction—the life of one so young, and so good. It gives me a sharp, half-fearful realization of how wonderful a thing it is to live.

"I have nothing on my conscience as regards Catherine—I knew she could never marry. But I think the cards should have produced the ace of spades rather than the nine of spades."

That was the end of the two pages, and I noticed that the date was the Sunday of Rick's death. He had written several more pages under the same date, but it was all flights of fancy, and he did not refer to anyone by name.

I started at the beginning of the book and read the whole thing— and as far as I could make out there was nothing of any significance.

He mentioned people occasionally, but always in a vague way, and it was often difficult to understand what he meant.

I went back to the original two pages, and studied them carefully. What did the reference to Catherine mean? And why could she never marry? Or was it only that she could never marry Charlie? And if so—why?

I gave it up for the moment and turned my attention to the bit about the ace of spades. Almost undoubtedly it had some connection with the games of solitaire, and I had a vague idea that in fortune-telling with cards the ace of spades meant death—but I had not the remotest notion of what the nine of spares was supposed to represent. And yet that nine of spades had been mysteriously moved around from time to time on the table in our attic.

I got up, closed the book and slipped it into the large, appliqued pocket on the skirt of my dress. I made straight for the back door and went into the kitchen. Dora and Grace were putting the last artistic touches to the evening meal, and after a couple of appreciative sniffs I asked, "Do you tell fortunes?"

They both said no.

"Do you know anybody who does?"

They both said yes.

"What does the nine of spades stand for?"

Grace said "Quarrel," and Dora said "Let me see "

I waited while Dora saw, and at last she said slowly, "Yes—quarrel."

I thanked them and went on into the dining room. I was sitting at my place deep in thought when Mother and Father appeared.

Mother was pleased. "I'm glad to see you on time for a meal, Lissa—you must have listened to me yesterday after all."

I tried to think what Mother had said yesterday on the subject, but I could not remember one word. I gave my hair a furtive pat or two, hoped my face had no smudges and kept my hands as much out of sight as possible. I didn't want to spoil Mother's fun by letting her find out that my punctuality was mere accident.

Ben Amherst showed up at seven-thirty. We were having coffee in the library when he walked in with a small overnight bag and a confident, toothy smile. He seemed to take it quite for granted that we were going to let him stay and he told us, graciously, that he felt much safer, because nobody knew where he was.

I wondered idly how many of the cottagers, in addition to Tony, knew that Ben was spending his nights in our house. I still did not know how Tony had found out about it—unless it was through Dora or Grace. I thought that Froby would probably have kept it under his hat.

I knew that Mother would have turned Ben out—promptly and efficiently—and told him to go to a hotel, were it not for the fact that Tony had more or less ordered her to do that very thing. Mother has had to do all her own thinking, and a great deal of Father's and mine—with resultant dictator characteristics. If anyone tells her she can't do a thing she does it at once.

So Ben stayed and had coffee and brandy, and began to talk business to Father. Mother smoked a cigarette, stared at her ruby ring, tapped her foot and—I'm sure—wished Tony in hell for having brought it all on her. I knew, by nothing more tangible than the slight lift of her eyebrows, that she thought they were talking pure drivel, and although business is a closed book to me I did hear Father say, "I could put this country on a paying basis, if they'd let me at it. I'd pin their ears back!"

I slipped out after a while. I was tired of watching Ben smoke one of Father's cigars—and anyway I wanted to look for the gloves.

As I made my way over the lawn I patted the diary that still reposed in my pocket. I knew that Ben had not discovered his loss, as yet, because he looked entirely too smug and self-satisfied.

The diary had been a disappointment though—there really wasn't much in it that was helpful. I decided that Rick had merely used it to pretend to himself that he had culture, a soul and a higher nature.

It was pretty dark when I got into the wooded section, and my search was halfhearted from the first. I cursed my lack of forethought in not having brought a flashlight, and I cursed young Wilbur, Jr., for having the instincts of a magpie.

When I finally gave up I was not far from the Reed yard. I glanced over there—and came to a dead halt. A short dark figure, standing on an overturned box, was crouched under the kitchen window, and seemed to be peering over the sill into the lighted kitchen. I took a step closer and broke a twig—and the figure spun around, revealing itself as Mrs. Potter.

She hopped down from the box, carried it swiftly back to a spot beside her own back steps and disappeared into the house. I went straight over and picked up the box and carried it to the Reed window. I climbed onto it, got a run in my stocking, swore softly but luridly and peered into the window.

The thing was a flop. I had expected a family quarrel at the very least—but the scene was quite peaceful. Mrs. Reed was not in sight, and Catherine stood quietly coiling up a rope, with a cigarette dangling in her mouth.

I jumped down again, replaced the box where it would be handy for Mrs. Potter the next time she needed it and started for home.

I ran into Tony before I had gone very far.

"What the devil are you doing?" he asked companionably.

"I'm going home to change my stockings."

"If you could manage a sane interval," he said coldly, "I'd like to know why you were snooping at the Reed window."

"Just maneuvers," I explained airily. "Give me a cigarette, Tony."

He supplied me in silence and took one himself, and after we'd puffed up a small fog he observed, "I saw Ben go into your place— and that means that I go in, too. You're all borderline cases—you Vickers. Allowing that fellow to sleep in among you after all that's happened—and you don't know a damn' thing about him."

"It's your fault," I said equably. "You had to come shoving your oar in—and now, of course, Mother feels bound to show you that you can't run her affairs. In any case, it doesn't make much difference, since people seem to come in and out of our house at will."

"Who? And how?" Tony asked sharply.

"I haven't the slightest idea."

He took my arm. "Come on—we'll have a look around."

"You look around," I said, trying to pull away. "I'm going in."

He tightened his hold. "When you go in, I'm going, too. Lack of opposition is bad for your mother. But first I want to have a look at these doors that don't keep people out."

We went slowly around the house, while Tony tapped at windows and rattled doors in search of something defective. I began to limp after a while. "I'm tired," I complained. "I want to go in. Besides, I want to protect my parents—they're alone with Ben, the Fiend."

"They can look after themselves. It's you I want to keep from harm."

"Why?" I asked, burning with curiosity.

"Guess," said Tony cheerfully.

And then Father flung open a window right beside us, and nearly fell out of it.

"What the Goddamned hell do you think you're doing?" he raved. "D'you think it's Halloween, or what? Rattling doorknobs and tapping on windows! Are you trying to scare us to death—you blasted fools? For Christ's sake go on home and play with your paper dolls, or I'll get a shotgun to you!"

He banged the window shut, and Tony and I moved on peacefully into the dusk.

After a while I yawned, and announced firmly, "I'm going in now, Tony—and I'll yell if you try to stop me."

"All right," he agreed amiably. "I'll concede. But let's look at the side door first—then we'll go straight in."

I limped wearily after him, and watched him while he examined the side door. He seemed particularly interested in the frame and I thought he'd never finish with it, but at last he straightened up and said in an absorbed voice, "Have you a largish nail file handy?"

CHAPTER 31

"NAIL FILE!" I squealed. "Why do you want one? Tell me—quickly!"

Tony turned his head and looked at me. "Why the dramatics?"

"Please, Tony," I said, almost stamping with impatience. "What has the file to do with it? Froby says that only a few nail files stand between me and trouble—and I want to know why."

Tony laughed and turned back to the lock. "This door is a pretty crude affair, you know."

"Mother wanted it put in some years ago," I said anxiously, "and Father asked her to let him handle it, because he knew where he could get it done wholesale or something."

"It looks like one of your father's undertakings," Tony admitted. "It opens inward, doesn't it?"

I nodded.

"Well, this frame, which keeps the door from opening outward, was put on badly to begin with—and someone has tampered with it, just beside the lock."

I looked at it closely, and he showed me where the wood was chipped in the crack between the frame and the doorjamb.

"You see, one of those large nail files would be perfect for the job. It's flat and wide and long enough to be inserted between the frame and the doorjamb, and if it's pushed firmly it will ease back the spring lock. I think that's what has been done—and that's the way people have been getting into the house. Rick probably thought of it first. He was more or less mechanical-minded anyway."

"Do you want to try it?" I asked. "I have a file upstairs—one of those I found lying around here."

"Oh, you found some?" he said. "Well, that settles it."

But he wanted to try it, anyway, so we went around to the back door, and passed Grace and Dora who were on their way out. They never spent any more time in our house than they could possibly help.

We managed to reach my bedroom without being seen by anyone else, and I went to the drawer where I kept my clues. Tony leaned against the footboard of the bed while his green eyes roamed the room.

"If you're looking for your picture," I said, pushing the contents of the drawer around, "I threw it out."

"You always were impulsive," he said, bringing his eyes back to me. "I'll send you another."

I could never be sure that my clues were all there, as Froby seemed to take them and put them back at will, but I did find the file at last.

I had it in my hand and had just turned away from the drawer when Mother walked into the room.

She gave us one comprehensive look, and immediately became Mayflower, Puritan fathers and lavender and old lace.

"I suppose it would be trite to say that I'm surprised, and disappointed in you, Lissa," she said, arching her eyebrows delicately. "Recriminations would be a waste of time, I am sure—and since the presence of this man in your bedroom seems to indicate that you still care for him, we must simply plan for you to be remarried as early tomorrow as we can make the arrangements. I trust that Tony will be gentlemanly enough to spend the night elsewhere—and I shall send Mr. Amherst to a hotel."

There was an uneasy pause, while we stared at her speechlessly. I stammered, "But—wait a minute, Mother—I don't—I mean—"

"Don't try to explain, darling," Tony broke in smoothly "there's really nothing to say, is there? Your mother is right. I'll take Ben home with me tonight—and when tomorrow dawns, it will be the beginning of a new life for us."

He took the nail file out of my hand, winked at me and bowed low to Mother. "You will arrange to have the minister and guests here tomorrow—I shall get the license and the flowers. Lizzie can use the same rings I gave her last time—no sense throwing money away."

He walked out of the room, and Mother watched him go with narrowed eyes. Mother is no fool.

She rallied quickly, and said in a matter-of-fact voice, "Perhaps he'll stay away for a while now. Nothing frightens a man quite so much as a threat of marriage."

We went downstairs, and I laughed quietly all the way to the library.

Father and Ben were in the midst of a loud, animated discussion on the modern girl, Father shouting that he had had experience because he had me, and Ben insisting that a father never really knew.

When Mother and I walked in, Ben raised quite a dust placing chairs for us and getting us seated.

He relighted his pipe then, to Mother's obvious annoyance, and announced as a good joke, "Tony wanted me to go home with him tonight." He laughed heartily, while we all looked at him blankly.

I suggested a game of bridge at that point, in an earnest endeavor to head off any more discussions of business, the modern girl or anything else.

We settled down to it, and I found within five minutes that every card I played, and every bid I gave voice to, was wrong. Mother, Father and Ben concentrated on telling me about it, and the going began to get pretty rough. As early as I dared I suggested that we stop, but they overruled me firmly, and it looked as though we might go on all night.

Ben saved the situation. He accidentally placed his hand on the pocket in which he had kept Rick's diary and discovered his loss—and the bridge game was over.

I wanted to look through the diary again, so I did not tell Ben that I had it—but I assured him very earnestly that it would certainly turn up again.

He was not convinced. He said he was afraid it had been stolen—but in case he had just been careless, and dropped it somewhere, he felt in honor bound to make a thorough search.

I knew he was afraid to go outside, and he confirmed me by telling us that he would go through our house first. He was not a methodical searcher, and Mother was furious inside of three minutes. She began to threaten him with expulsion, but he went doggedly on and took no notice.

I slipped upstairs and left him to it. I thought he might insist on searching our persons next—and I still had the diary in my pocket.

I walked into my room and found Tony lying on the bed smoking a cigarette, with one arm folded comfortably behind his head.

"I thought you'd gone," I said, frowning at him.

"Quite right—I had. But I came back via the side-door and nail-file route."

"Then it really works!" I exclaimed breathlessly.

"I told you it would work, Lizzie," he said patiently, "but evidently you weren't listening."

"I'll get an ear trumpet," I said coldly. "What are you doing here anyway?"

"That ass, Ben, refused to budge—and until he goes, I stay."

"All right," I said wearily. "I don't care. But for God's sake go and pick another room."

He heaved himself off the bed and, going to the door, opened it and peered out. Then he closed it again and turned to me. "I think," he said politely, "that Ben is looking for something."

"Yes, I know."

"What?"

"It's Rick's diary," I explained reluctantly.

"Where did he lose it?"

"Out on our back lawn."

He looked full at me. "Then why the devil is he hunting for it in your upstairs hall?"

"Well, he—he doesn't know where he lost it."

"I see." He advanced a step. "But you do. Are you sure he lost it? Or was it, perhaps, a steal?"

"I didn't steal it," I declared hotly. "You can ask Catherine."

"Where is it?"

"In my pocket," I said, beginning to back away.

"Give it to me."

"Certainly not!" I said, and backed into the wall.

He advanced with his green eyes fixed on my pocket, and the

next instant there was a short tussle and he was standing with the diary in his hand.

"Thanks," he said. "You can have it back when I've read it."

"Will you get out of here, Tony Herridge!" I said bitterly. "I want to go to bed."

He slipped the diary into his pocket. "Well—I'm off now, Liz. I can take a hint as well as anyone." He went to the door, opened it cautiously and peered out, and then disappeared, closing it softly behind him.

I undressed and went to bed in a temper. I could hear Tony moving about in the next room, and I laughed nastily, all to myself, because I knew that the bed in there had not been made up and there was only a spread over the mattress.

After I had turned out my light I could not deny to myself that the presence of Tony in that next room was decidedly comforting. Even though I had locked my door, the thought of Ben being in the house was disturbing, for I disliked and faintly distrusted him.

I heard him give up the search, and say good night to my parents, and a moment later Father came to my door and called through to ask if I were all right. I reassured him and he went off to bed.

I had a great deal of trouble in getting to sleep. First, the Drucker dog howled until someone threw what sounded like a garbage lid at him, and after he became quiet the heat seemed to pour down over me like a great steamy blanket.

I tossed uncomfortably for a while and at last fell into a troubled, restless doze.

I was brought out of it sharply by a succession of hoarse masculine shouts.

CHAPTER 32

MY FIRST IMPULSE sent me out of bed, and I struggled frantically into a negligee. I flew to the door, but with my hand on the key I paused and waited, with my breath coming in short gasps, until I heard Father in the hall.

I went out then. The hall light was on, and Father and Tony were just disappearing into Ben's room. Mother stood at her door, her eyes looking very big and dark in her pale face.

She joined me, and we followed the others into Ben's room. He was sitting on the side of his bed, jabbering wildly, and holding a bronze bookend in his hands. There was a nasty gash across his fore-head.

Father hastily relieved him of the bookend and said, "Come, come, young man! Pull yourself together, and try to give us a clear account of what happened."

Ben replied hysterically and with a great deal of bitterness that he was together, and that he had already given us three clear ac-counts, and if we would not listen to him it wasn't his fault.

We finally got out of him that he had been brought out of a deep sleep when the bookend hit him on the forehead. He had heard the closing of a door immediately afterward—but he was certain that it was not the door into the hall, because he had naturally looked in that direction as soon as he could collect his faculties, and it was closed, and had remained closed until Tony opened it.

There were two other doors in the room. One opened into the closet—which was empty—and the other into an adjoining bedroom. Father and Tony went through, and we could hear them moving around in there searching the room.

Mother had gone to her bathroom for a first-aid kit, and she presently returned and began to bandage Ben's head.

"Have you sent for a doctor?" he asked shrilly.

Mother said no, in a voice that she might have used to a frac-tious child. "It's just a surface wound. It does not require any stitches, and I can quite easily attend to it myself."

Ben was obviously disappointed. I think he had hoped for more serious damage and corresponding importance—but he allowed Mother to fix him up, and probably hoped that a couple of days would see her in the wrong.

I wandered uneasily about the room, trying to keep my teeth from chattering. I found the mate to the bookend on a desk close to the door that opened into the next bedroom.

It was the figure of a nude woman paddling in a brook. I re-membered that Father had brought the pair home—and Mother and I always had a certain amount of trouble in finding a place for Father's purchases.

Whoever had struck Ben must have come in from the adjoining bedroom, picked up the bookend, and either walked up to Ben and hit him, or else thrown it from the door.

I asked Ben what he thought about it, and he seemed pretty sure that it had been thrown, because he had awakened and sat up as soon as the thing hit him, and he had heard the sound of the door closing almost immediately. "If anyone had been right beside the bed I'd have seen him before he managed to get out of the room." Which sounded reasonable enough.

Tony came back and said, "Detective Sergeant Frobisher is on his way over."

Mother looked at him coldly. "It seems odd that we had no trouble with Mr. Amherst yesterday—when you were presumably sleeping in your own bed. Yet all this occurs tonight, when you force your company upon us in direct opposition to my expressed wishes."

Tony said, "There's a foul insinuation wrapped up in all those pretty words."

"I am merely stating facts," said Mother, giving him a chilly stare. "May I venture to ask for an explanation of your presence here?"

Tony glanced at Ben, and hesitated. Mother knew as well as I did that Ben was the explanation, but she waited perversely for Tony to get out of it as best he could.

He said at last, "I'm trying to protect you from harm."

Mother thanked him, with delicate and biting sarcasm, just as Froby burst in.

Froby was evidently in a hurry. He galloped around the room, searching and measuring with lightning speed, and he flung his questions at us as he went. He seemed distinctly put out at Tony's presence, and Tony was unable to explain himself properly, because Ben was still in the room. He passed it off by telling Froby that he had known us all for a long time, and for the sake of auld lang syne he had come over to see that all was well.

Froby said, "Auld lang syne or no—you've no right to be here. As a matter of fact you're in the way, and I want you to go home at once."

"Not a chance," said Tony composedly. "I'm staying."

"You won't go?"

"No."

Froby disappeared into the adjoining room, but a minute or so later he popped his head back and observed, "You may be sorry for this, Herridge."

Tony made no reply—possibly because Froby's head had disappeared again.

"Absurd creature," Mother murmured. "Why is he in such a hurry?"

"It's his precious clues," Tony explained. "He wants to cover the ground before Brewster and Hahn get here and mess things up."

As it turned out, Froby need not have worried himself about Brewster and Hahn. They did not show up until the next morning— and then they had something else to worry about.

Mother decided to go back to bed. She said no more to Tony— probably because she knew how stubborn he was— and didn't feel up to fighting it through to a finish.

Ben did not want us to go, and it was fairly obvious that he was afraid to be left alone. I found a couple of keys for him so that he could lock both doors, and we left him firmly clutching the bronze bookend, and apparently with every intention of taking it to bed with him as a weapon in case of further trouble.

Tony and I went slowly along the hall toward my bedroom, and presently met Father emerging from the door that gave onto the back stairs.

"That blasted side door was open again," he said uneasily. "I had to shut it."

Tony nodded. "I supposed it would be."

"I'd give a lot to know if that nine of spades has been moved," I said after a moment, "or whether it's still on the pack where it was the last time we saw it."

"Let's go and see," Father suggested promptly.

We all went up to the attic, and on the way I thought of Catherine, and wondered whether Rick's reference in his diary to the ace and nine of spades was what had upset her so much. I made up my mind to tell Froby all about it in any case.

The room in the attic did not seem to have been disturbed, and the nine of spades was on the deck as we had seen it last time. I think we were all a bit surprised—and I know that Father was definitely disappointed.

When we got back downstairs Father declared that he had had enough of mystery and sleuthing, and was going to bed. He and Tony escorted me to my room and waited outside while I locked the door, and then I heard Father say good night, and walk off.

I waited for a while, but there was no sound of Tony's retreating footsteps, and I was beginning to wonder whether he'd dropped through the floor, when he said in a loud whisper, "Lissa."

"Oh," I said, "you're still alive."

"I was going to mount guard outside your door for the rest of the night, but I find I'm too sleepy. For God's sake keep your door locked, and don't do any wandering around."

I said, "Good night, Herridge. And the next time you get a noble impulse I hope it lasts longer."

"Me, too," he whispered equably. "I don't see how the military and the constabulary manage to do it."

I heard him go away, and I got into bed and snapped off the light. If I had taken his advice and stayed there, I'd have saved myself a particularly ghastly experience.

But I could not sleep, and I became very restless; and after a while I switched on the lamp that stood on my bedside table and reached for my book.

I remembered quite clearly that I had left it on the edge of the table nearest my bed—and now it was on the farther edge, where I could hardly reach it.

I sat up in sudden alarm and sent a frightened glance around the room. There was something. My underwear! I had thrown it over the back of a chair, and it now lay draped over the seat.

I flew out of bed in a panic, and opened one or two of my drawers. There was no doubt about it—my room had been thoroughly searched.

CHAPTER 33

WITH THE BLOOD pounding in my ears, I looked under the bed, behind the various pieces of furniture and at last in the closet—and was relieved to discover that at least there was no one locked in with me.

I sat on the end of the bed and rested my chin on the footboard, to keep it from chattering. Someone had been in my room since Ben's shouts had taken me out of it—and whoever it was had made a thorough search.

But who would want anything of mine? There was nothing but my clues—and Froby had most of those, anyway. I went to the drawer where I kept them, and jerked it open with a faint clatter. There were only a few inked dandelions and some bits of tin foil. I supposed that Froby had the rest of them—and of course Tony still had the nail file.

I remembered the diary with a sudden clammy, cold sweat of fear. Ben's house had been broken into while he had the diary in his possession—and now they were after me because I had it. But who could possibly know that I had it? Catherine, perhaps—when she had recovered sufficiently to remember that I was sitting near her when she dropped it.

Well, supposing she did remember—and for that matter, supposing they all knew that I had the diary—why was it important? I had read the thing from cover to cover—and there did not seem to be anything that mattered much.

I wondered why Ben had been hit with the bookend, and after puzzling it over for some minutes it came to me rather suddenly. It must have been calculated that Ben's shouts would bring me out of my room—and leave it clear for the search.

But what a dangerous thing to do—and how desperate somebody must be to get possession of the diary!

The bookend had evidently been-thrown from the connecting door, and the door closed again immediately. Then what? Out into the hall? No—the window, of course. The flat roof of the porch was directly below it and extended all the way to one of my windows. Quite simple, of course, to climb out that window, watch at mine until I left the room, then climb in, lock the door for greater safety and search comfortably. Then, back to the other room again—and what? How could any murderer get out of the house, with Froby kicking around? Moley had turned up, too, and it seemed a wonder to me that they had not already caught up with this intrepid hunter of diaries.

Froby had made a rapid search of the house. He had started in Ben's room, I remembered, and gone from there to the adjoining room. I did not know the order after that—but my murderer could easily have slipped out onto the porch roof when Froby got to my room. It would be dangerous to stay there, though, because Moley would probably be patrolling the grounds outside. Back to the room adjoining Ben's, then—since Froby had already searched it—and possibly into the closet, there to wait until the excitement died down.

Perhaps this dark figure of mystery was still there—waiting for another opportunity to search my room! The idea brought me to my feet in a panic. I crept to the window that gave on the porch roof and looked out fearfully—but there was no one on the roof—no one in sight below.

The locked room seemed to be closing in on me, and after a moment's hesitation I unlocked the door and went out into the hall.

It was dark and empty, and quite silent—and I faltered a little in my decision to wake someone. I went across to the little sitting room instead, and looked out of the window.

I heard a faint click, below, and looking down I caught a glimpse of a dark figure as it sped into the shadows of the trees from the side door. I gasped and strained my eyes, but the thing was gone—and though I tried desperately to put a shape and identity to it, it remained in my mind as just a shadow.

I opened my mouth to call Froby—and closed it again. If that figure had been making for one of the small houses, it was safely inside by now—and what was the use of stirring up more excitement? Froby had pulled a boner—but the damage was done.

I returned to my room, searched it carefully, locked the door and went to bed.

I was dead tired, but I could not sleep. My mind was uncomfortably active and it would not let my body rest. I found myself thinking of Tony—and the more I tried to put him aside, the more I thought of him. I decided to get Mother and Father to take me to Australia as soon as possible

Then the Drucker dog started to howl, and the sound seemed to parade all the horrors I'd ever known before my eyes.

The room began to get gray, and I saw that the dawn was breaking. I was still wide awake, and the house seemed to weigh down on me—and I suddenly decided to dress and go out into the garden. It was rapidly getting lighter, and most of the shadows had disappeared.

I put on a few clothes and went quietly downstairs. I saw no sign of Froby or Moley, and I let myself out the back door.

The air was cooler and fresher in the garden, and I took several deep breaths and was glad that I had come. Cato had stopped howling and was giving voice to an occasional injured whine—which sounded not unlike Wilbur, Jr., when things had annoyed him.

I walked slowly among the flower beds and came at last to the wooded section. I thought of the gloves at once—and it seemed an ideal opportunity for an uninterrupted search. I plunged in and set to work.

To my surprise, I caught sight of one of the gloves almost at once. It seemed to have caught on the bark of a tree and was apparently hanging there, some distance from the ground. The light was poor and I could not see it very well—and as I got closer, there seemed to be something peculiar about it.

I had actually reached out and touched it before I realized that the glove had a hand in it.

CHAPTER 34

AS I TOUCHED that black-gloved hand it swung away from me—slowly and almost lazily. My arm fell back to my side, and I felt as though every drop of blood in my body had gathered around my heart and would burst it.

A faint breeze stirred my hair—and the hand swung idly back. Quite without my own volition I took an automatic step forward and looked up—and recognized the body of Catherine Reed. It hung by a rope from a lower branch, and swayed back and forth, carelessly, in the early morning breeze.

I turned around and began to stumble frantically back toward the house. The numb horror that had paralyzed me gave way, and I screamed, shrilly and senselessly, over and over again.

Froby appeared in front of me, jabbering excitedly, but I could not tell him anything. I pointed to the woods, and he gave up trying to get anything coherent out of me and loped off. I collapsed in a huddle on the back steps and sobbed helplessly.

Father and Tony came out with various odd bits of clothing on them, and after giving me a certain amount of conventional comforting and back-patting—with their eyes straying constantly to the woods—they hurried off after Froby.

The cottages were astir, too. Several windows had been raised, and it was not long before Mrs. Potter and Mrs. Reed appeared on our lawn.

They were headed toward the woods, and I pulled myself together sufficiently to realize that Mrs. Reed must be stopped. I mopped hastily at my wet face and went after them.

They questioned me eagerly, and I admitted to having done the screaming. "But you can't go in there," I said desperately. "It's—it's Catherine."

Mrs. Reed went very white, and put a groping hand on Mrs. Potter's arm. "Catherine? Catherine is in bed. She's asleep."

I said miserably, "No—she's—in there."

Mrs. Reed suddenly broke away from us and ran, stumbling and awkward, into the woods. Mrs. Potter hurried after her, but I stood and waited—and wanted to put my hands over my ears.

The scream came almost immediately—a queer, high wail that started my teeth chattering.

Father and Tony took her home. As they neared her house she went out, and they had to carry her, with Mrs. Potter opening the doors for them.

I was only vaguely conscious of events after that. Hahn and Brewster appeared; the medical examiner came and went; and eventually poor Catherine was taken away in an ambulance.

At seven Mother appeared, beautifully dressed, and blessedly calm and matter-of-fact. I told her what had happened, but she refused to let me to dwell on it. She said that we would have breakfast at once, and sent me out to collect Father.

I found him smoking a pipe on the lawn and apparently thinking furiously. He followed me docilely enough, and when Mother saw him she sent him straight up to get properly dressed. We went along to hear what he had found out—and he shouted out an account of the proceedings from the bathroom, where he was shaving.

He said they had come to the conclusion that it was suicide. Hahn and Brewster had had a heated argument—Hahn insisting on suicide—and Hahn had finally won out.

His argument was that Catherine was big, that she was hanging from a branch well above the ground, and that there were no marks beneath the tree with the exception of a few vague footprints which had been identified as her own. Brewster, yielding reluctantly, had searched the ground for signs of the imprint of a ladder or a box—but there were none—and he was forced to admit that the tree was one that was very easily climbed. Hahn summed it up rather crudely by saying that Catherine had lost two beaux—and there you were.

I felt sure that their conclusion was right. I had seen Catherine folding that rope in her kitchen—and I knew that Rick's diary had shocked her badly in some way.

As Father finished dressing, Ben came charging along the hall with his clothes awry and his hair on end.

"Grace told me—she woke me—it isn't true, is it? For God's sake—say something!" he shouted at us.

"You mean you slept through all that disturbance?" Father said.

"She just woke me—I haven't heard anything—I don't know anything."

He looked rather wild, so Mother started to tell him about it, very quietly. After she had confirmed Catherine's death he did not wait to hear any more, but plunged down the stairs and clattered out of the house, with doors slamming behind him.

We went down to breakfast then. I drank two cups of black coffee and smoked a cigarette, but I could not eat anything, and several times I felt the tears sliding over my cheeks. Mother glanced at me once or twice and talked quietly of everyday affairs, but I could not keep my mind away from Catherine. What awful despair she must have felt to have done such a thing.

After breakfast I put in a long and weary session with Hahn and Brewster—and Froby.

I told them about having seen Catherine coiling up a piece of rope in her kitchen—and of course they wanted to know how I came to be looking in the kitchen window. I simply told them that I had seen Mrs. Potter doing the same, and was curious to know what was going on.

They departed in a body for Mrs. Potter's house then. I watched them with a feeling of superior scorn. Third-rate, amateur sleuth I might be, but I knew, at least, that Mrs. Potter would be in the Reed house nursing her friend for some days.

I saw Gertrude open the door and reroute them, and they disappeared into the Reed place.

Gertrude had stayed home from business then. And so had Ben—for I presently caught sight of him frantically searching our garden. I knew he was looking for the diary and I felt a bit guilty about it. I should return it to him—only I'd have to get it back from Tony first.

I searched the room Tony had occupied during the night but the diary was not there, so I went in search of Tony.

I found him in his dinette' breakfasting rather soberly on coffee and toast. He halved his meal with me, and after a rather keen look into my face advised me to eat it. I nibbled dispiritedly at a piece of toast, and asked him about the diary.

He said he had finished it and would give it to me, so that I could put Ben out of his misery.

We were silent for a while, and I reflected dully that I was getting to the point where I could put away eleven-o'clock coffee without turning a hair.

Tony said presently, "I don't understand those gloves."

"Catherine? The black gloves, you mean?"

"Yes, I can't see any possible reason for them—and I don't think they were hers. They—didn't fit."

"They were in the woods there. I suppose she found them."

Tony glanced up at me. "What do you mean, 'they were in the woods'?"

I explained about Wilbur, Jr., and his "sings," and Tony thought it over for a while. "Perhaps she found the gloves, and put them on to save her hands while she was arranging the rope," he said without conviction.

I shook my head. "She would have had no thought for her hands at that time."

He said, "I know," and sighed. "But she must have had some reason for putting them on. I wonder where the damn' things came from before that kid got hold of them."

I shook my head, and made a mental resolution to clear the point up before the day was over.

Tony gave me the diary then. "You know," he said, "it more or less explains the why of the blue dandelion—that diary. Rick obviously thought he had the soul of a poet, and devised that ridiculous signal of the blue dandelion to indicate a rendezvous in order to prove it."

I nodded absently and stood up. "I'll give it back to Ben now—and relieve his mind."

I found Ben pacing up and down in the woods. I thought at first that he was still searching, but when I got close to him I saw that his eyes were blank, and that he was muttering to himself in a troubled, feverish sort of way.

I gave him the diary, and told him that I had found it on the ground. He thanked me without really seeing me, slipped the book into his pocket and continued his animal-like pacing.

Tony, who had propped himself against a tree at the edge of the wood, called, "Come on, Liz," and I walked slowly away.

Tony took my arm companionably. "We'll go and have a nice little visit with Edith Drucker."

"Why do you want me along? The Shadow?" I asked coldly.

"You have a one-track mind, Lizzie darling—all Love and Intrigue. But this happens to be business. Edith is the number one fortune-teller around these parts, and we want to find out from her why the ace of spades should have turned up in Catherine's fortune instead of the nine of spades."

CHAPTER 35

EDITH USHERED US into her living room, offered us cigarettes or a stick of gum, and then, chewing rhythmically and mournfully, settled herself for a long talk about Catherine.

"She was such a lovely girl," she observed conventionally. "So attractive—and wonderful to her mother. I've been thinking all morning about that time she was engaged to Jeff. Jeff wasn't the only pebble on the beach then, either. There was this fella—Dan, I guess his name was—and he was crazy about her, too. But she wouldn't look at anyone but Jeff— they were cracked about each other. And then out of a blue sky he went off and married Bunny Thompson. You could of knocked me down with a feather!

"Everyone knew Bunny had been trying to get him—she had corns on her feet from chasing him—but Jeff never gave her a tumble. I saw him and Catherine three days before he eloped with Bunny— and they were so devoted to each other they couldn't see anyone else! Well, I always say you never can tell, can you?"

"What happened to Dan?" Tony asked.

"I'm not sure if his name was Dan," Edith said, staring into space and still chewing. "Anyway, he was a swell guy, and lots of the girls would have given their eyeteeth for him—but I guess Catherine told him to go fly his kite. She wouldn't see him or have anything to do with him, and we all thought it was because she was so disgusted with men, after Jeff doing a thing like that on her."

"Where is this Dan now?" I asked.

"I think he lives in New York."

"What about Jeff?" Tony asked.

"They live right in town—couple of blocks from here."

"Did his marriage turn out all right?" I asked, feeling like a full-blown gossip.

"Yeah, I guess so," Edith said reluctantly and disapprovingly. "We all thought they'd split up in a month—but they seem to get on all right, and they have two nice-looking children. Honestly, the people who ought to be hung seem to get all the fun," she added darkly.

Tony said suddenly, "Did you ever tell Catherine's fortune?"

"Well, sure—I guess I must have. I've told all their fortunes around here."

"Do you remember what you predicted for her?"

Edith accelerated her gum and went into a huddle. Tony, waiting patiently, gave me a cigarette and took one himself.

"I know," Edith said presently. "I remember now. She was going on a journey—we all decided that was her honeymoon with Charlie—and she was going to get a present. Wedding presents, you see? Then there was a disappointment— she had that, all right—and I think it finished up with great riches in connection with a blond gentleman. I don't know just how that fitted in. Let's see now "

"Never mind," Tony said hastily. "Who else tells fortunes around here?"

"Nobody."

"Are you sure?"

"Certainly I'm sure," Edith declared. "I taught some of them a few things, and they've tried their hands at it a bit, but they made awful mistakes. They couldn't learn to read the cards right."

"To whom did you teach the technicalities?" Tony asked.

"Oh—Mrs. Reed, and old lady Potter—and Catherine. Gertrude wouldn't be bothered with it."

"Who was the best pupil?"

Edith laughed. "They were all lousy. They knew what the cards meant but they never could tie it all up together."

Tony turned his cigarette around in his fingers for a moment of silence, and then asked, "Did the nine of spades turn up when you told Catherine's fortune?"

"Quarrel? Hmm—let's see. No—I don't think so."

Tony killed his cigarette and stood up. "Thanks very much, Edith—you've helped a lot. Come on, Lizzie."

"No kiddin'," said Edith, "are you two really divorced? You sound just like holy wedlock—or Tony does."

"It's a carry-over," I explained. "He never allowed me to live my own life. When we went out, he always started nagging to go home just when the gossip was getting hot."

Edith made some sort of reply, but I was jerked through her front door and never heard it.

"We have to work fast," Tony said, hanging on to my arm. "Unfortunately, I'm going to need your help."

I laughed hysterically. "Tony, let me give you some advice. Leave the investigation to the police. I dabbled in sleuthing myself, and where it got me was a few thin nail files away from the county jail."

Tony, making straight for Ben's back door, nodded abstractedly and muttered, "I suppose it's locked."

It was. Tony examined the lock and the doorjamb, grunted, pulled the nail file from his pocket, and had the door open well inside of two minutes.

He shook his head. "I'm rather ashamed of that."

I said, "So you should be. But I suppose you had to put locks on the doors just for the looks of it. Only, it seems a waste of money."

"Interesting," said Father's voice behind us. "Lissa, the next time you're in a drugstore buy me half-a-dozen nail files, will you?"

"If you're in a hurry," Tony said politely, "you may borrow this one."

"No hurry," said Father airily. "I'll wait until I get my own. I'm going to put them on a key ring."

Tony closed Ben's door, and we walked down the steps to the yard. "I suppose Mrs. Potter is staying with Mrs. Reed?" he asked.

I nodded.

"Come on, then—we're going to inquire after Mrs. Reed's condition. And you are to find out from Mrs. Potter, quite casually, if the two of them have been telling each other's fortunes."

"Why can't you do it yourself?" I asked peevishly.

"I want you to do it."

"Tony," I said, "for God's sake leave the thing to the police."

He said slowly, "I can't, Lizzie. There was a remark passed between a couple of these people—months ago. I had not thought of it again until it came back to me just lately—and I can't get it out of my head that it's terribly significant. It's given me an idea—a ghastly one—and I can't tell the police because I may be all wrong, and I won't risk getting an innocent person into unnecessary trouble. I want to dig up something on my own that will prove me right, or deny the whole thing."

I said eagerly, "What was the remark, Tony? Please tell me."

"Not in front of your father."

"What the hell do you mean?" Father exploded. "Do you think I'm a damn' gossip?" He added more mildly, and with an assumption of careless indifference, "Go ahead and tell her—I won't repeat it."

"No, of course you wouldn't," said Tony. "Come on." He took my arm again and steered me in the direction of the Reed house.

Father, thoroughly annoyed, but a victim of his own curiosity, trailed along close behind us and kept up a running mutter of conversation.

"You can't fool me," he said, "I know which way the wind's blowing. Young people these days are irresponsible and childish, and expect their parents to go on looking out for them until they have gray hair."

"Who?" said Tony.

"What?"

"Until who gets gray hair?"

"The children," said Father sourly. "And what's it to you, anyway? Here I spend a couple of thousand dollars on your first wedding—but no, it's not good enough. I have to fork over another fortune for a divorce, just so you can have another and bigger wedding. Last time I gave you a honeymoon trip to Europe—but this time I'll probably be asked to support a trip around the world."

"Thanks, fellow," Tony said cheerfully. "A trip around the world would just about hit the spot. And while we're on the subject—just a suggestion. Stick to champagne, this time, at the wedding. That bit of domestic sherry you had last time struck me as being distinctly gauche."

"If I could stand the muck myself," Father said viciously, "I'd order a case of sarsaparilla—and you could take it or leave it."

We walked in at the back door of the Reed house and found Mrs. Potter and Gertrude sitting in the dinette, lapping up the usual midmorning coffee. Wilbur, Jr., stood leaning against Gertrude's knee, eating a cookie. Gertrude smiled at Tony and gave Father and me a cold nod to divide between us. Mrs. Potter beamed impartially, and poured three more cups of coffee before we could stop her.

We all sat down, and Gertrude moved a little apart and lighted a cigarette. Wilbur, Jr., followed her, and announced to the room at large that he wanted another cookie. Gertrude supplied him. We inquired after Mrs. Reed and were informed that she was sleeping under an opiate. I was racking my brains to think of an approach to the fortune-telling business when Tony walked right in.

"Edith Drucker told me that she was the only person around these parts who could tell fortunes," he said, with a suggestion of challenge.

I relaxed, and reflected that it was just like Tony to tell me to do something and then butt in impatiently and do it himself.

Gertrude laughed—nastily—but Mrs. Potter took the hook. "Why, that's a deliberate falsehood," she said indignantly. "Helene Reed and I can do it quite as well as Edith—and probably better.

That girl is entirely too conceited!"

"Certainly is," I agreed encouragingly. "With all her so called skill I'll bet she didn't predict any of the terrible things that have happened."

"Of course she didn't. Although she's trying to say, now, that she did."

"Did you or Mrs. Reed predict anything of it?" Tony asked.

"Well, no—not exactly. But Gertrude did. We told her how to tell fortunes with cards one night—and she told poor Catherine's fortune and predicted the quarrel between Catherine and Charlie."

Gertrude's face was suddenly dyed with angry red, and she snapped, "Be quiet, Mother!"

CHAPTER 36

FROBY INSINUATED himself into the room at this point, and I caught myself looking at his ears and wondering how long he had been stretching them, listening to us.

He looked at Gertrude and said briskly, "You predicted the quarrel between Miss Reed and Mr. Carr?"

Gertrude, her color still high, gave him a look of defiance and tightened her lips, and Froby was preparing to wrap himself in the Law, and get stern, when we heard dragging footsteps in the living room.

Mrs. Potter flew out of her chair just as Mrs. Reed appeared in the dinette. "My dear, you shouldn't be down here. You must go back to bed at once."

Mrs. Reed brushed past her, advanced into the kitchen and sat down heavily. "Don't fuss, Martha," she said tiredly. "And don't give me any more drugs. They don't make me sleep—and they confuse me."

She dropped her head onto her hand and stared at the floor. Her eyes were feverishly bright, with dark smudges under them, and her face was haggard.

Froby cleared his throat and said, "Mrs. Reed. May I ask you a few questions?"

There was a general chorus of disapproval, but Mrs. Reed said desperately, "No, no—let him speak—let him question me. I must do something—I can't lie on that bed and look at the wall."

Froby said, "Thank you," very solemnly. He swept us to silence with a glance of mingled triumph and defiance. "Now, Mrs. Reed, I understand that you and your daughter had a quarrel last night?"

Mrs. Reed looked faintly startled, and I noticed that Mrs. Potter blushed furiously. I decided that they had put her through it, and made her own up to having peeped in the kitchen window.

Mrs. Reed said, slowly and painfully, "Yes—there was an argument. Catherine—had made up her mind to marry Ben Amherst."

We all showed surprise in one way or another at this, since Catherine had rarely troubled to hide her indifference, and even her scorn, for Ben.

"Ben took an unfair advantage," Mrs. Reed said defensively. "Catherine was feeling low and was getting a neurotic idea that her love affairs would always be unfortunate—and he knew it. Yesterday he asked her to marry him—at once, so that he could take care of her—and she had agreed to do it.

"I knew she would regret it later, when her outlook became normal again, and I tried to tell her so—but she was excited and hysterical. She told me to mind my own business, and even accused me of—of having tried to break up "

The recital ended abruptly, and Mrs. Reed began to cry quietly into her handkerchief.

Mrs. Potter and Father moved over to comfort her, and Wilbur, Jr., trailed after them. I had not noticed before that he was still there, and I had a guilty feeling that we should have put him outside long ago.

He put a grubby little hand on Mrs. Reed's knee and murmured something into her ear. She patted his head, and said faintly, "Not now, dear. You run outside and play, and someone will give you a cookie."

Wilbur thought it over, finger in mouth, for a moment, and then submitted to being eased out the back door by Gertrude. But he seated himself on the top step, and continued to stare at us through the screen door.

"I should never have opposed her," Mrs. Reed moaned, beating her clenched fist on the arm of her chair. "But I didn't know—how could I know, that she was so desperate!"

"Why did she put on the black gloves?" Froby asked.

Mrs. Reed half rose from her chair, and collapsed into it again. "Oh God!" she sobbed. "Those dreadful gloves! What were they? How long had she had them?"

"That's what I want to find out," Froby said.

Gertrude stirred, and threw her cigarette into the sink. "Aren't they your last year's gardening gloves, Mother? You bought them in the spring for that black-and-white dress—and then you used them all summer for working in the garden."

Mrs. Potter looked as though she were going to deny it, and Gertrude added impatiently, "If we don't tell the absolute truth about these things we'll never get anywhere."

Froby approved the sentiment wholeheartedly, and said encouragingly, "Mrs. Potter?"

"Well—yes, they were mine. But I discarded them early this spring."

"Where did you throw them?"

"I didn't throw them anywhere—I left them with the gardening tools in the cellar."

Froby nodded, and dropped the subject of the gloves. He fished around in his pocket, extracted a small square of folded paper and glanced at Mrs. Reed. "This note was found tucked in the belt of Miss Reed's dress," he said, and handed it to her.

Mrs. Reed opened it with shaking hands and, shamelessly, I looked over one shoulder and Mrs. Potter over the other.

The note ran, "Dear Mother, forgive me—I can't face any more—let the gloves speak for themselves. Catherine."

It was written in ink, which I was pretty sure had come from the Reed household. It had a greenish tinge, instead of the usual blue, and I remembered the color quite clearly.

Froby took the note and returned it to his pocket. "There does not seem to be much doubt," he said slowly, "that your daughter committed the two murders."

Mrs. Reed began to tremble visibly. She moaned, "Oh, the poor child! She was so emotional—highly strung!"

It was then that the thing hit me. The idea came so suddenly, and with such force, that I jumped.

I looked hastily around the room. Froby was waiting patiently for Mrs. Reed to control herself, probably because he wanted to question her further. I guessed that Hahn and Brewster had figured the thing finished and dumped the remaining bits and pieces into Froby's lap and told him to clear it up.

Gertrude was leaning against the sink with her arms folded, Mrs. Potter was trying to comfort Mrs. Reed, and Father, after a quiet and unsuccessful search for a chair, had perched himself on the garbage container and was staring at the floor with signs of incipient boredom on his face.

Tony was staring at me, his green eyes unusually serious. I stepped over to him and whispered hurriedly, "Keep them here. I'll be back in half an hour."

I took four cookies from their box on the table, and slipped out the back door, conscious all the time of Gertrude's scornful glance.

Wilbur, Jr., was still sitting on the step, and as soon as he saw me he made a grab for the cookies. I held them high in the air, and bargained.

"I'll let you have them all if you'll show me where you put those gloves. I won't take them away from you—I want only to look at them."

The kid stared, first at me, and then at the cookies, and finally made another grab for them.

"Show me the gloves first," I said firmly.

He shoved out his lower lip and started off toward the wooded section of our grounds. I followed him, and once I looked back over my shoulder and saw Edith Drucker disappear into the back door of the Reed house.

The kid went straight to the tree where Catherine had been, and before I could stop him he shinnied up a few feet and began to feel around in a small hole in the trunk. As soon as it had dawned on him that the hole was empty, he slid back to the ground, opened his mouth and howled.

I gave him the cookies and tried to shut him up. He accused me of having stolen his "sings," and I denied it, and at last in despair I took him into our house and tried to soothe him with an old pair of my own gloves. He refused them point-blank, and after pawing through my glove drawer rejected the lot, and opened his mouth to howl afresh. In the end I got him fixed up with a brand-new pair belonging to Mother, and I was able to push him out of the house without her seeing us.

I raced back to the telephone directory and looked up the address of Catherine's ex-fiance, the husband of the energetic Bunny. The house was only two streets away, and I ran almost the entire distance. Bunny was working in the garden, with a small child hanging around, and I shouted at her, "Will you please give me your husband's business telephone number?"

It took me five minutes to dig it out of her, and when I raced off again she stared after me with her mouth hanging open and her eyes popping.

I made my call and received the answer that I had expected, and then I went back to the Reed house, feeling hot and sick and miserable.

Tony was talking some sort of rubbish, in an effort to keep them all there, and I knew that he had guessed, too.

They all turned and looked at me as I walked in. Tony stopped talking and moved over to my side, and I gripped his arm and hung on feverishly.

I dropped my eyes to the enormous zircon ring that Mrs. Reed always wore on her left hand, and said slowly, "I don't think it's fair to leave the guilt of those murders with Catherine, Mrs. Reed. I saw your ring flashing on one of those hands—that night with Rick—when you were putting the gloves on."

CHAPTER 37

MRS. REED'S FACE was livid. She half rose from her chair, and then dropped heavily into it again. "How dare you?" she said, in an ugly voice. "I—I was not wearing it that day. I had loaned it to Martha Potter."

Mrs. Potter gave a little cry, and excitedly denied it in six different sentences. Gertrude put her arm around her mother, and said in a clear, cold voice, "I had not intended to mention it, Mrs. Reed, but I saw you manipulate that nine of spades so that it would appear when I told Catherine's fortune."

Edith Drucker, who had been giving her gum a stiff workout while her eyes snapped with excitement, now inserted her ten cents' worth. "You certainly did wear your ring that day," she said shrilly to Mrs. Reed. "I remember it, and I remember you saying it needed cleaning."

Mrs. Reed dropped her head against the back of her chair, and belligerence died out of her face. She looked haggard and old. "You are all against me. You're all telling lies about me."

There was a dead silence, and then I said breathlessly, "I can tell you what happened—the whole thing."

Mrs. Reed flexed the fingers of her left hand, and the zircon flashed in the sun. She said, "Don't—don't. You know nothing about it."

I took a firmer grip of Tony's arm, and said steadily, "You didn't want Catherine to marry. You broke her first engagement by telling a lie about her—and you had to kill Charlie because he would not believe your lies. You killed Rick, then, because you thought he was going to marry her, and because he suspected you."

"You don't know anything about it. You say those things, but you don't know the reason—the real reason."

"If you want to tell it," I said, "go ahead. If not, don't interrupt me."

"I'll tell it!" she cried fiercely. "I won't have you spreading lies about me, with your half-knowledge."

Froby stirred and made a forward movement, but Tony pushed him back.

Mrs. Reed said slowly, "We had this little house, and a comfortable income—but the income was in the form of insurance annuities—Catherine had one, and I the other, in equal amounts. That was one reason for her suicide—she knew her income would cease altogether.

"We had sufficient to live on, with enough over for certain luxuries and occasional short trips. But I knew that if she married, our resources would no longer be pooled, and I would have to live in a hotel in one dingy room, while she added her income to that of her husband and lived here—in my house—in comfort, and even luxury. My income alone was not sufficient to keep up the house—and Catherine would not consent to my living with her and her husband. She told me that, in my sweet way, I would cause innumerable rows. So, in my sweet way, I decided to prevent her from getting married at all. We had just moved in here, at that time, and she was engaged to Jeff. I went straight to him, and told him that Catherine was having an affair with the boy next door. Jeff believed it, too, because he had always been jealous of him."

Mrs. Reed took time out to laugh—but there was no sound or movement from any of the others.

"Jeff went into a fury," she resumed, "and married the girl that was nearest to him. I felt pretty safe then, for Catherine never seemed to get over fretting about him. It was some long time before she would even look at a man.

"Then this Charlie turned up. He was very persistent and would not be discouraged, and at last she allowed him to take her out. They went about together a lot after that—and he finally came here and rented the house next door. I wasn't really worried, though. Catherine used him as a companion, but I knew that she was not in love with him.

"Rick and Ben appeared later, and they all used the tennis court, and had a lot of fun together. Catherine cared more for Rick than she did for Charlie—I knew that—but I knew, too, that Rick was not a marrying man, and I felt fairly safe.

"Then this spring the blow fell. She suddenly announced her engagement to Charlie. I could hardly believe it. I told her she was not in love with him, but she declared that she cared very much for him, and that he would make a fine husband.

"I started hinting things to Charlie, but he just looked at me, without saying anything, and his attitude to Catherine never changed. I hated him after a while.

"I discovered that Catherine had a blue dandelion in her room every now and then—and once or twice I caught her going out with a blue dandelion in her hand. Always, during the same evening, she would slip out quietly, and would not return for some time. I followed her once, and saw her enter the Vickers house by the side door. She let herself in with a large nail file, which she picked up from under the step—and replaced again when she had the door open.

"I came to the conclusion that she and Charlie were having an affair—and I was desperate. I knew he was the type to marry her, after that, whatever the circumstances.

"I was furious about it—after having felt so safe—and I decided to do something drastic. I went into the Vickers house—using the nail file, as I had seen Catherine do it—and looked around. I found the little revolver and took it with me. Down in the cellar I came upon the small room—evidently long disused and almost hidden by the coal—and I knew it was an excellent place to hide a dead body. It might be there for years without being discovered.

"So I laid my plans accordingly. It took me some time to find out how to make the dandelion blue. I tried dipping them in all the bottles of ink that I could find—and no one caught me at it but the Drucker child."

I moved my cramped muscles at this point, and murmured, "He never told, either."

Mrs. Reed gave me a blank, uncomprehending stare, and went on with her story.

"The ink did not work, and it was not until I caught Catherine painting a dandelion that I realized how simple it was.

"My opportunity came when Charlie announced his impending trip to Washington. I went into the Vickers house, in the afternoon, and shoveled the coal away from the door of the small room just enough to allow the door to open. Then I discovered that the Vickers were coming back. It complicated things, but I determined to go on with it anyway.

"The morning of the day that Charlie was to leave I watched Catherine very closely—but she did not take any blue dandelion out with her. I had one ready—I had painted it from a paintbox in the Vickers' attic—and I put it in the driver's seat of Charlie's car. I did not know where Catherine habitually left their signals, but he would be pretty sure to find it in the car anyway. The Vickers arrived that morning, and I was desperately afraid they would spoil everything, and Charlie would not come because of them. But he did. I stood outside, with the little gun in my pocket, and watched him. He had a bit of trouble with the nail file, but he managed it eventually. He had the blue dandelion in his buttonhole—and he must have gone straight up to the attic."

"Wait a minute," Froby interrupted sharply. "How would Mr. Carr have known to go to the Vickers house, after receiving a blue dandelion? That signal was strictly between Miss Reed and Mr. Rickey."

Mrs. Reed looked up quickly, in obvious astonishment, and Tony broke in, "I guess Charlie knew all about that affair— I was afraid he did. I knew about it myself, and I was only a disinterested spectator. I suppose when he found the dandelion in his car he was curious enough to go over and see what it was all about."

Mrs. Reed's eyes darted to Tony.

"What are you talking about?"

"Continue with your story," Froby said coldly.

She smoothed her hair, and with something of complacency and self-satisfaction took up the tale again.

"I followed him into the house. I did not know where the usual meeting place was, but supposed he would go either to the cellar or the attic, because the Vickers were already occupying the house.

"I went to the cellar first, and groped my way to the little room. I had to turn the bulb to put the light on—there was no switch—and I forgot to put the gloves on first. I put them on immediately afterward, though. I had found them in the Potters' cellar, and had brought them to guard against fingerprints. Charlie was not in the cellar, so I made my way quietly up the stairs to the third floor—and found him there. He was sitting in one of the rooms, with the light on, calmly playing solitaire. He had nerve, all right.

"He stopped playing when he saw me, and put the pack down on the table. I motioned to him to be quiet, and he said, 'Why the gloves? Is this a formal party?'

"I went up to him, and spoke quietly into his ear. I told him that Catherine was downstairs, and wanted to get married right away— and I asked him if he were willing.

"He seemed thoroughly puzzled, but he said quite definitely, 'I'll marry Catherine at any hour or minute that she wants—but why do we have to talk it over here?'

"I did not say any more—my mind was quite made up then. They were determined to marry each other and push me out into the cold.

"I led him quietly down the stairs and into the little room in the cellar. I told him to sit down, and he did—and then I closed the door, walked around and faced him. I shot him—so quickly that he never even moved—though it seemed to me that he looked surprised. I shot him several times—I had to be sure, you see."

Mrs. Potter created a diversion at this point by fainting dead away.

CHAPTER 38

MRS. POTTER WAS SHIFTED to the couch in the living room and left there, with Gertrude in attendance, while the rest of us returned rather precipitately to the kitchen.

Mrs. Reed was thoroughly put out at the interruption. "I don't think I'll tell any more," she said sulkily.

Froby said, "All right. Come on up and get your things."

She changed her mind, then, and decided to go on with it.

"I made a mistake," she said, "when I left the light on in that room in the cellar—but you can't think of everything, I suppose. I went out and shut the door, and shoveled the coal back into position. I hid the little gun in a chair upstairs, and then slipped out the side door. I heard some of the Vickers coming downstairs as I went. I managed to get back to my bedroom without disturbing Catherine.

"Everything seemed to be all right for a while. No one was the wiser—and since that cellar window is on the far side of the Vickers house I never noticed the light that I had left burning until the night Charlie was discovered.

"There was some sort of a drinking party at Edith Drucker's that night, and I took a late walk to get some fresh air. First, I nearly ran into Catherine and Rick—and they were embracing. It upset me terribly. I did not know what to think—and as they had not seen me I hurried away I sat on a bench in the garden for some time, wondering how serious that affair was—and what I could do about it.

"After a while I got up and walked about restlessly—and happened around on the other side of the Vickers' house. I saw the light in the cellar almost at once, and I was horrified. I crept close and tried to look in, but I could not see much. I knew I would have to go in and get that light off somehow.

"It was just then that the Vickers girl started screaming. I had to run back behind the trees, and presently I saw Catherine and Rick hurry up.

"They got the girl out of the cellar, and it was right after that that I slipped in and took the light away. I remembered that I had originally turned the bulb with my bare fingers, and when I went back I could not find my handkerchief or anything else with which to wipe it. Charlie was still there—and there was no time for anything, so I simply ripped out the entire extension and flew home with the thing under my arm. I got back just in time to answer the phone when Mrs. Vickers called me to come over.

"I soon realized that it was stupid to have taken the extension home with me—there was nowhere that I dared to hide it—and I had to take it back again later.

"I gave a lot of thought to Catherine and Rick after that. I was worried about it, and I determined to settle the thing in my own mind. As a precautionary measure I went back and secured the gun again. I did not expect to have to use it, because I was still convinced that Rick was not a marrying man. I know I frightened Lissa when I went for the gun. Apparently she was wandering around, and I heard her scream.

"I was wondering how to arrange an interview with Rick when he phoned himself, on Sunday afternoon. He wanted me to come over at once. I told him I'd come as soon as I could—but I had some things to do which delayed me—and when I got there he was angry at having been kept waiting. I didn't care—I had the gloves and the gun with me and I was ready for anything. Without any preliminaries, he asked me point-blank if I had had anything to do with Charlie's death. I was utterly astounded. I did not see how he could possibly have tied the thing to me. I asked him why he thought so, and he replied that he knew I did not want Catherine to marry. He said that Catherine did not know it as yet, but that someday she would find out and turn against me.

"I asked him what reasons he had for such a belief, and he said that Jeff was a friend of his, and he knew what I had done about that affair. He added that he could put two and two together.

"I asked him if he was thinking of marrying Catherine himself. He said he was, for several reasons, and he did not mind telling me that one of them was in order to spite me.

"I did not wait for any more. He was lighting a cigarette, and I simply pulled out the gun and shot him in the forehead. He slumped back into his chair, and I put on the gloves and wiped off whatever fingerprints I might have left around.

"I went home, but I wanted to replace the gun and return the extension without further delay. The nail file had disappeared from its place under the step, at the Vickers' side door, and I was reluctant to use my own. Fortunately, the Druckers went out onto their porch at about that time, and I knew they were careless about locking their doors. I slipped into their house and took Edith's file. As a matter of fact, Edith's file disappeared later—I had left it under the step for convenience. I was forced to use my own then, but I made a point of telling Martha Potter that it had disappeared. Lissa heard me and brought it back to me, and I gave up leaving it under the step then, and kept it at home.

"Anyway, I took the extension back to the Vickers' house, and replaced the gun in the armchair. I took the extension up to the attic and put it in the closet—and then I did the third silly thing. I made the obvious move in the solitaire game—the black nine on the red ten.

"On my way out I hid the gloves in some bushes.

"When I got home, the poker game was just starting. I joined in; but later I happened to glance out the window and saw that I had left the light burning in the Vickers' attic.

"I waited until Martha and I were getting the refreshments in the kitchen, and when Martha went up to the bathroom I slipped out the back door and flew to the Vickers' house. I returned the nine of spades to its original position—I had already regretted that impulse—and I turned off the light.

"I hurried home and went right up to the back door, but just before I opened it I realized that it would not do for Martha to know that I had been out. I went around to the front then, slipped in without being seen, went upstairs and came down again—and Martha thought I had been to the bathroom.

"It was a shock to me to see little Wilbur playing with the gloves and Lissa trying to get them away from him. I went out later and dug them up, and put them deep into Tony's ash can. The next time I saw them, they—they were on Catherine's hands.

"I was terrified when I learned that Rick had left a diary, and that Ben had it. Ben kept his house locked, but I found that the nail file could be worked on the back door, and I went in twice—once during the day and once at night—and made a thorough search, but I could not find the diary.

"I started to lay out half-finished games of solitaire in Ben's house in an effort to frighten him out of the neighborhood. I supposed that he—and the police, too—had read the diary by this time, and nothing had happened. Therefore, if there was any reference to what I had done, it was not very clear. But I was desperately afraid that it might fall into the hands of someone who knew enough to read the truth from it—if the truth were there.

"And that is exactly what happened. Catherine got hold of it, and understood at once. She came home, and accused me hysterically and bitterly. I pleaded with her and denied everything, but she would not listen. She declared, over and over again, that she had nothing left to live for, that she was going to take her own life. I did not think she really meant it—she was always very emotional, but when she calmed down she was usually sensible enough."

Mrs. Reed cried quietly for a minute or two, and we all stood and waited in dead silence.

"I thought she would be herself again, by morning, and I told her to go to bed. She muttered something about going when she was ready, and I went upstairs and left her. I heard her go to the cellar, and then come up again, and she spent some time in the kitchen. She came up to her bedroom after that, but she did not go to bed. I could hear her moving around, and it began to get on my nerves. She was not pacing the floor—she seemed to be doing things.

"I could not wait any longer. I had hoped she would be asleep before I left—but there was no sign of her even going to bed—and I had to find that diary. It was too dangerous to be at large. If Catherine had understood it—other people might, too.

"I knew Lissa had it. I had gathered from Catherine's wild talk that she had dropped it on the ground practically in front of Lissa, and I hoped desperately that I could get it before she read it. I was sure she would keep it until she had read it."

Mrs. Reed dropped her head against the back of her chair, and sighed. "I'm tired," she said fretfully. "It was a hard night—last night. I went to the Vickers' house, and straight to Lissa's room. The door was locked, and I could not tell whether the light was on or not. I knew that she might be reading the diary at that very moment, and I was conscious of sheer panic.

"I made my way into the adjoining room and discovered the porch roof and its possibilities. The door leading to Ben's room was slightly ajar, and I could hear him snoring. I had not known that he was there, and when I peered in at him, and saw him lying in a flood of bright moonlight, I was completely surprised. I rested my hand on the bookend, quite by chance, and when I saw what it was, I lifted it and threw it at him on impulse.

"It aroused the house, of course, and I climbed out onto the porch roof. I'm a bit old for that sort of thing, but it was not so very difficult after all.

"Lissa left her room, and I slipped in as soon as she had gone. I locked the door that led to the hall and went to work —but it was all wasted effort, for the diary was not there. I unlocked the door and got back onto the roof. I stayed there for a while, but somebody appeared in the grounds with a flashlight, and I was afraid of being seen. I went back to the other room, and hid in the closet.

"I waited until things seemed to be quiet again—and then I simply made a dash for it. I got home safely, but I was tired—terribly tired.

"And Catherine was not there. I had a cold, horrid fear that she had done something dreadful, and I ran out, at once, to search for her.

"I found her after a while. You don't know—any of you—you can't—what that was like, for me. The pain of it—and the horror! And I dared not cry out or scream. I had to wait for someone else to find her.

"I don't know why she put the gloves on—she must have found

them somewhere. I did not touch them—or her. I knew she was dead, and I was too late to help her. I hated writing that suicide note—but it could not hurt her then. I went home and wrote it, and then I came back and tucked it into her belt."

CHAPTER 39

FATHER AND TONY and I went back to our house—silent, and rather subdued. We found Mother in the library, and we all sat down while Father mixed some drinks.

"You could not possibly have seen the zircon ring from that distance," Tony said to me.

"No—of course not. But I wanted to startle her into making an admission of some sort."

"How did you come to figure out that she'd done it?" Father asked.

"Well, I'd thought a lot about the diary's having upset Catherine so. And then Mrs. Potter had been peeping in the window at them— and she would hardly have gone to so much trouble unless they were quarreling. Therefore, they were probably quarreling about the diary. I knew the suicide note was wrong, too. Wilbur, Jr., was the only one who knew where the gloves were—certainly Catherine didn't. But they happened to be in a hole in the very tree from which she elected to hang herself. I figured that if she were going to write a suicide note she would do it before she left the house—and if she had not intended to write one, she would hardly go back to the house and do it after she had found the gloves. Yet she had to have the gloves before she wrote the note, because they were mentioned in it. She just put them on—that's all. I took a guess on that bit in the diary—'I knew Catherine could never marry.' I phoned Jeff and posed as a lady detective—and he told me what Mrs. Reed had said to him about Catherine. I was sure then.

"But, Tony—what was the remark you heard some time ago that made you suspect her?"

"Mrs. Reed had left Mrs. Potter's bedroom light on," he said, "and Mrs. Potter was annoyed about it. She said, 'Can't you ever remember to turn lights off after you?'"

Mother, sipping daintily at her drink, said, "I'm sure I don't know what you're all talking about—but I suppose I can read it in the papers tomorrow."

"I still don't understand what Froby meant by saying there were only a few nail files between me and jail," I said thoughtfully.

"He found out," Tony explained, "that the nail files were left under the step in order to make an easy entrance into the house. Before that, he had it all pinned onto you. Your paints, your gun, your house—and your suspicious behavior. But the nail files seemed out of the picture."

"Why was Gertrude using blue paint?"

"She wasn't—it was Mrs. Potter. I heard Gertrude giving her hell for it, and telling her to keep her nose out of other people's affairs. It was also Mrs. Potter who was dodging from tree to tree that night when you thought I'd been murdered in my cellar—and came pouring down the steps to save me. It seems the Druckers were having a row, and Mrs. Potter didn't want to miss a word, but they were moving around from the dinette to the kitchen, getting a late snack, and it kept her hopping."

"There are a couple of other things," I persisted. "Why was Ben not speaking to Rick? And why did Charlie leave his money to Catherine, when he knew that she was having an affair with Rick?"

"Ben was extremely jealous of Rick—he would have given anything to be able to take Catherine away from Charlie himself—and it was pretty galling to him to have to stand aside and watch Rick do it. That's why Mrs. Reed used Ben as an excuse for the quarrel with Catherine that Mrs. Potter snooped on. He turned noble over it eventually, and after calling Rick a few hard names refused to speak to him at all. As for Charlie—Catherine was his whole world, and had been for two years—no matter what she did."

I nodded. "Do you think Catherine was in Rick's house on Sunday night?"

"Undoubtedly. She must have discovered him. I suppose she realized the danger to herself if she raised the alarm, so she simply came back and tried to behave naturally. The strain was too much after a while, and she became hysterical."

We sipped our drinks in silence for a while, and then Tony said, "Hahn and Brewster are going to be burned over this. Froby will take all the credit."

"Well—he helped me a trifle," I said airily.

"Why was that suitcase only half packed?" Mother asked suddenly.

"Charlie was probably so excited that he just threw in what he remembered at the moment," Tony said. "You see he undoubtedly thought that the blue dandelion and subsequent rendezvous were about to be explained to him satisfactorily—he was probably quite happy."

Tony put down his glass, raised his eyebrows at me and jerked his head in the direction of the garden.

"I saw you," Father said bitterly, "go on out there and neck. If you want to—I give up." He turned to Mother. "I suppose you know that we have to come across for another wedding, and another honeymoon?"

Mother stared at us. She is not the type who would ever remarry a man whom she divorced. "Very well," she said, after a moment, "I suppose there is nothing that we can do about it. I shall even try to be cheerful when they come to us for another divorce."

THE END

Catalog of
Rue Morgue Press titles

The Man from Tibet
by Clyde B. Clason

The only witnesses to the murder
were the masks of Tibetan gods

Locked inside the Tibetan Room of his Chicago luxury apartment, the rich antiquarian was overheard repeating a forbidden occult chant under the watchful eyes of Buddhist gods. When the doors were opened it appeared that he had succumbed to a heart attack. But the elderly Roman historian and sometimes amateur sleuth Theocritus Lucius Westborough is convinced that Adam Merriweather's death was anything but natural and that the weapon was an eighth century Tibetan manuscript.

If it's murder, who could have done it, and how? Suspects abound. There's Tsongpun Bonbo, the gentle Tibetan lama from whom the manuscript was originally stolen; Chang, Merriweather's scholarly Tibetan secretary who had fled a Himalayan monastery; Merriwether's son Vincent, who disliked his father and stood to inherit a fortune; Dr. Jed Merriweather, the dead man's brother, who came to Chicago to beg for funds to continue his archaeological digs in Asia; Dr. Walters, the dead man's physician, who guarded a secret; and Janice Shelton, his young ward, who found herself being pushed by Merriweather into marrying his son. How the murder was accomplished has earned praise from such impossible crimes connoisseurs as Robert C.S. Adey who cited Clason's "highly original and practical looked-room murder method."

But *The Man from Tibet* is more than a classic fair play detective novel. Clason carefully researched his subject and in between the planting of clues he presents a vivid, in-depth portrait of forbidden Tibet and its religion, one of the earliest examinations to be found in popular fiction. Clason's work was also remarkably free of the xenophobia that marred so many Golden Age mysteries. At a time when anti-Japanese sentiment was at its height, Westborough offers up some deft social commentary and gently rebukes his associates for their racist attitudes.

ISBN 0-915230-17-8   **$14.00**

Murder, Chop Chop

by James Norman

A classic late Golden Age novel of
detection and adventure set in China
in 1938 during the Sino-Japanese War.

*"The book has the butter-wouldn't-melt-in-his-mouth cool of Rick
in* Casablanca."—Jane Dickinson, *The Rocky Mountain
News*

Fans of Golden Age mysteries set in exotic lands with eccentric characters
will love this long out-of-print masterpiece that many critics said should
have been included in the Haycraft-Queen list of cornerstone mysteries,
written by a man who fought in the Spanish Civil War and was a victim of
the Hollywood Blacklist.

In these pages you will meet Gimiendo Hernandez Quinto, a gigantic
Mexican who once rode with Pancho Villa and who now trains *guerrilleros*
for the Nationalist Chinese government when he isn't solving murders. At
his side is a beautiful Eurasian known as Mountain of Virtue, a woman as
dangerous to men as she is irresistible, and a superb card player as well—
so long as she's dealing. Then there's Mildred Woodford, a hard-drinking
British journalist; John Tate, a portly American calligrapher who wasn't
made for adventure; Lt. Chi, a young Hunanese patriot weighted down
with the woes of China and the Brooklyn Dodgers; Nevada, a young cow-
boy who is as deadly with a six-gun as he inept at love; and a host of others,
anyone of whom may have killed Abe Harrow, an ambulance driver who
appears to have died at three different times.

There's also a cipher or two to crack, a train with a mind of its own,
and Chiang Kai-shek's false teeth, which have gone mysteriously missing.

ISBN 0-915230-16-X   **$13.00**

The Mirror

by Marlys Millhiser

How could you not be intrigued, as one reviewer pointed out, by a novel in which "you find the main character marrying her own grandfather and giving birth to her own mother?" Such is the situation in Marlys Millhiser's classic novel (a Mystery Guild selection originally published by Putnam in 1978) of two women who end up living each other's lives after they look into an antique Chinese mirror.

Twenty-year-old Shay Garrett is not aware that she's pregnant and is having second thoughts about marrying Marek Weir when she's suddenly transported back 78 years in time into the body of Brandy McCabe, her own grandmother, who is unwillingly about to be married off to miner Corbin Strock. Shay's in shock but she still recognizes that the picture of her grandfather that hangs in the family home doesn't resemble her husband-to-be. But marry Corbin she does and off she goes to the high mining town of Nederland, where this thoroughly modern young woman has to learn to cope with such things as wood cooking stoves and—to her—old-fashioned attitudes about sex. Shay's ability to see into the future has her mother-in-law thinking she's a witch and others calling her a psychic but Shay was an indifferent student at best and not all of her predictions hit the mark: remember that "day of infamy" when the Japanese attacked Pearl Harbor—Dec. *11*, 1941?

In the meantime, Brandy McCabe is finding it even harder to cope with life in the Boulder, Colorado of 1978. After all, her wedding is about to be postponed due to her own death—at least the death of her former body—at the age of 98. And, in spite of the fact she's a virgin, she's about to give birth. And *this* young woman does have some very old-fashioned ideas about sex, which leaves her husband-to-be—and father of her child—very puzzled. *The Mirror* is even more of a treat for today's readers, given that it is now a double trip back in time. Not only can readers look back on life at the turn of the century, they can also revisit the days of disco and the sexual revolution of the 1970's.

So how does one categorize *The Mirror*? Is it science fiction? Fantasy? Supernatural? Mystery? Romance? Historical fiction? You'll find elements of each but in the end it's a book driven by that most magical of all literary devices: imagine if...

ISBN0-915230-15-1   **$14.95**

Cook Up a Crime

by Charlotte Murray Russell

Meet Jane Amanda Edwards, a self-styled "full-fashioned" spinster who complains she hasn't looked at herself in a full-length mirror since Helen Hokinson started drawing cartoons for *The New Yorker*. But you can always count on Jane to look into other people's affairs, especially when there's a juicy murder case to investigate. This one starts when Jane's friend, Detective Captain George Hammond, puts the idea of publishing a cookbook in her mind. That leads her to visit Jessie Nye, an irritating woman who unfortunately is the safekeeper of her family's famous recipes. Jesse thinks a cookbook a marvelous idea but immediately announces that she is far better suited to put it together than Jane. So when Jessie turns up dead, Jane decides to look for clues—and recipes—among the murdered woman's effects.

In the meantime, Jane's hapless brother Arthur—a true lily of the field—gets a valentine from a secret admirer and goes courting, only to find himself accused of the murder. Sister Annie warns Jane to stay put and goes off to watch female wrestling on television. Through it all, Theresa, their long-suffering cook and general housekeeper, keeps one and all well fed with tempting treats from her kitchen (the recipes for these and other dishes are included between chapters).

First published in 1951 and set in a fictionalized version of the author's hometown of Rock Island, Ill., *Cook Up a Crime* is what you might get if Joan Hess or Charlotte MacLeod wrote the culinary mysteries of Diane Mott Davidson.

ISBN 0-915230-18-6

$13.00

Murder is a Collector's Item
by Elizabeth Dean

Twenty-six-year-old Emma Marsh isn't much at spelling or geography and perhaps she butchers the odd literary quotation or two, but she's a keen judge of character and more than able to hold her own when it comes to selling antiques or solving murders. When she stumbles upon the body of a rich collector on the floor of the Boston antiques shop where she works, suspicion quickly falls upon her missing boss. Emma knows Jeff Graham is no murderer, but veteran homicide cop Jerry Donovan doesn't share her conviction.

With a little help from Hank Fairbanks, her wealthy boyfriend and would-be criminologist, Emma turns sleuth and cracks the case, but not before a host of cops, reporters and customers drift through the shop on Charles Street, trading insults and sipping scotch as they talk clues, prompting a *New York Times* reviewer to remark that Emma "drinks far more than a nice girl should."

Emma does a lot of things that women didn't do in detective novels of the 1930s. In an age of menopausal spinsters, deadly sirens, admiring wives and air-headed girlfriends, pretty, big-footed Emma Marsh stands out. She's a precursor of the independent women sleuths that finally came into their own in the last two decades of this century.

Originally published in 1939, *Murder is a Collector's Item* was the first of three books featuring Emma. Smoothly written and sparkling with dry, sophisticated humor, it combines an intriguing puzzle with an entertaining portrait of a self-possessed young woman on her own in Boston toward the end of the Great Depression. Author Dean, who worked in a Boston antiques shop, offers up an insider's view of what that an easily impressed *Times* reviewer called the "goofy" world of antiques. Lovejoy, the rogue antiques dealer in Jonathan Gash's mysteries, would have loved Emma.

ISBN 0-915230-19-4 $14.00

The Rue Morgue Press
*reprinting the kind of books that made
people start reading mysteries in the first place*

The Rue Morgue Press was founded in 1997 by Tom & Enid Schantz with the intent of bringing back in print some of the books they have enjoyed calling to the attention of their customers during the nearly 30 years they have operated their mystery bookstore, The Rue Morgue (which opened in 1970 as The Aspen Bookhouse).

The books chosen for publication by the press (with the exception of *The Mirror*) aren't necessarily immortal classics but rather are the books that mystery bookstore owners might have pushed into the hands of their customers back in the 1930s, 1940s or 1950s had such stores existed then, explaining: "This just came in. We think you'll get a kick out of it."

At the same time, the editors hope to draw the attention of contemporary readers to the many little-known gems in the field that have long been undeservedly out of print. In this endeavor, they are inspired by the words of George Norlin found above the entrance to the main library on the campus of the University of Colorado in Boulder: "Who knows only his own generation remains always a child."

Since The Rue Morgue Press was conceived with readers in mind rather than collectors, we are always interested in hearing from people who read our books. If you would like to send us comments—which may be used in promotional catalogs or just to guide us in our selections—please do so.

For more information on The Rue Morgue Press and future titles write:

The Rue Morgue Press
P. O. Box 4119
Boulder, CO 80306